Donegal Tears

by

Paddy Mc Kinney

Published by Swordpoint® Intercontinental, Limited
Malin Head, Co Donegal, Ireland

Cataloguing in Publication Data is
Available from the British Library

ISBN 978-0-9544530-9-1

Cover art by Aelorae Qahlwyn

Typeset in Adobe Garamond
by Swordpoint® Intercontinental Limited

Published in Ireland by
Swordpoint® Intercontinental Limited
"Solas Tobann"
Ballyhillion
Malin Head
Co Donegal
Ireland

Telephone (353) (0)74 93 70278
Facsimile (353) (0)1 6849930

www.swordpoint.com
jgreenleaf@swordpoint.com

Paddy Mc Kinney

Paddy Mc Kinney Paddy lived through the times he writes about in *Donegal Tears* and tells the reader of his clear vision of the life and times of post-war Ireland in general and Donegal in particular.

A native Irish speaker, Paddy calls up the ghosts of long ago—the school masters and mistresses, the parish priests, farmers and farm wives to tell an engaging story of real life, real people and genuine Donegal tears, shed by many. This is Paddy's first book. He lives with his wife in Co Donegal, Ireland.

chapter one

Peter was the second son of Tom and Ciss McGinn who lived comfortably on a forty-five acre farm on the side of a hill called Cruckban, near the tiny village of Dooras in Donegal. His older brother was named John, and Kitty was their little sister. It could be said that their parents protected them over-restrictively. They were not allowed to mix freely with the children of the district, especially those from the village of Dooras, which was almost three miles from the main village of Ballintober.

The McGinns were seen as decent country folks. Being small farmers their social status did not permit them access to the higher reaches of society, but they were endeavouring to advance. They took pride in the fact that they kept a servant man, who ploughed the land with two well-fed and neatly groomed horses. He was an angry, aggressive little man named Dinny, who the children learned to accept had considerable authority over them. Except for one six-month period when he left after a disagreement with the Boss, he lived and worked with the family for many years. He occupied a small attic room in the house, which was his exclusive sanctuary and which housed his worldly possessions. He was treated like a member of the family and he ate, sat and talked with them in the white-washed kitchen in the evenings. His consuming passion in life was war, and he listened attentively to the news bulletins on the old battery-operated radio. The war had ended several years before, but Dinny remained an ardent admirer of Hitler and his cause, and he lamented the downfall of the Third Reich bitterly. However, he was confident that very soon, the Reich would rise again; meanwhile the Russians would fill the void and bring about another glorious conflict, with the eventual triumph of the aggressor. He became furiously enraged at the nickname "Hess", a title he earned through his deference towards the German dictator. Clever at hiding his poor literacy and keen to be seen perusing the newspaper which Tom McGinn bought every

Saturday, he even laid claim to being versed in the works of the man he called 'Burns The Poem'. However, the many years he spent with the McGinn household were a tribute to his artisanship. He was snugly content in his work and circumstances, but what the hell was holding back this bloody war?

From an early age, the oldest boy, John, was considered the material for a higher calling. Unlike his younger brother Peter, he was diligent and scholarly. At least that's what both boys would hear their parents say. It appeared that these conclusions were based upon observing how the two boys were coping with the school regime. Perhaps there were other considerations as well; in any case, Tom McGinn had a particular liking for his eldest son. Even the illiterate Hess had a say in such matters, thus adding weight to the parental conclusion as to what was practical and sensible. As Kitty, the youngest, had not yet started school, discussion on her destiny could wait until another day.

Peter developed a consuming fear of going to school, even before it started for him at the age of six. He was not protected from the horrific stories about what went on there from grown-ups, not even his own parents. However, go there he must, as his brother had done two years earlier.

Peter started school on the first Monday in March. That morning he walked beside John and the other children from the Dooras area along a track that ran up the meadow beside the Mondeel River and alongside the railway track. The track was worn by the feet of many generations of fearful children on their way to and from the schoolhouse. On arrival, the infamous Miss Maguire, or Gusher as she was better known, greeted him. It was a strange and frightening environment for a six-year-old coming from the safety of a cosy hillside home where freedom was given in plenty.

With muted apprehension, he watched the process unfold. The green sally rod was taken from a drawer as his brother's class assembled around the blackboard for sums. Soon Gusher commenced action, with these bigger boys and girls being beaten heavily on the backs of their bare legs with the well-seasoned weapon whenever a wrong answer was given. The new crop gathered in a vacant corner of the room to be introduced to a large cardboard chart, which contained the letters of the alphabet. A Miss Helen O'Doherty, the daughter of a prominent businessman, supervised this exercise. She was a favoured pupil and a bully from a higher class, and she was almost ready to progress into the Master's room.

Little Peter's mind and attention were on things other than learning the alphabet, however, and he cried aloud as he watched the sally rod being applied to his only protection, brother John. Promptly the reprimand came his way as Gusher placed the heavy rod tightly against his trembling shoulder, with a stern warning that such blubbering would not be tolerated — her valuable time must not be wasted as she had a moral duty to teach the ways of the real world.

What a reality this world had in store for Peter, as well as the dear people with whom he would eventually find himself so much involved. Indeed, it was a reality more than worthy of the worst fears any child could be born to experience. It would continue for another eight agonising years for those who had the stamina to withstand the drill. Still, for most there was one ongoing escape. Even in the most humble abode, we do feel a sense of wellbeing and safety simply because it is our home. It is true to say that home is the bastion of security, the final rescue of the tired and oppressed, the impregnable fortress from where even "they" cannot get to us. For Peter it was all of that and more, it was a place for relaxing the mind and the dreaming of dreams. At night, he and John would lie back on the old iron bed they shared in a tiny loft room under the thatch and talk themselves to sleep. Peter dreamt of a life on the land, while John, like many boys at that time, dreamt of a life in the priesthood.

By the time Peter was ten it became apparent that he was only suitable for life on the land. For him this was an accolade with which he was elated to have been conferred. This meant he would probably only have to endure another two or three years at school. From there on, he talked or thought about little else but the day when he would be walking out to the fields of his dreams with those two shiny horses walking briskly before the plough that turned over the brown sod of Cruckban. Equally, he was happy for John, who continued to excel at school. Peter could see him one day coming back to say his first mass in the old chapel. He knew how happy this would make his parents, as he often heard his mother say that every sacrifice would have to be made if such a blessing should be bestowed upon the family.

In those early years at school, Peter observed the arrival of many new and bewildered faces. The year after he started, there arrived the bright-eyed Maggie Dunne, followed one year later by little Jimmy Dunne, looking so gaunt and afraid. They lived with their poverty-stricken parents in a tiny cotter's cottage about a mile from the McGinn residence and nearer to the village of Dooras. The McGinn children seldom associated or played with them. The reason for their being kept apart was never explained or alluded to; perhaps it had something to do with class and respectability. This gradational arrangement was very much part of the school ethos. Indeed the McGinn boys had discovered that their place in the pecking order was not sufficiently high for them to enjoy the favours of their teachers. There were, on the other hand, people like Helen O'Doherty, who could do no wrong. Mr O'Doherty provided free fuel for the school fires, which was a great comfort to the teachers who stood with their backs to the warm glow on winter mornings. The O'Doherty's was a household frequently visited by prominent people, including the parish priest, Fr Gillen, and of course the teachers of the parish.

In spite of her relative smartness, Maggie Dunne was never spared the wrath of the Maguire method. At the same time, she did manage to live with it and did her best at bringing her weepy brother along with her. How disturbing it must have been for her to hear his cries for mercy while being beaten so cruelly.

It was autumn when the new Master arrived from another county; most of the pupils were back after the potato gathering had ended. Peter had been kept from progressing into the Master's room as the old retiring Master and Miss Maguire judged him not to be ready. This meant that Maggie Dunne would now have caught up with him, something that did not bother him all that much. In any case, it would be some comfort and reassurance to his little sister Kitty to know that he was near at hand. He was not at all like his brother John, who had moved on two years earlier.

Before the new Master's arrival, a timely warning was issued to all pupils not to be expecting any mercy. It was said that Master Tom Herron was a great teacher but he was not a man to take any kind of nonsense. Stay in line or else, they were told. When he finally came in to inspect the junior classroom, everyone rose to greet him with "Good morning Master Herron." After resuming their seats, a palpable silence descended upon the place. He was a sturdy, dour-looking individual with very blond hair combed back sleek, held in place by soapy water. His neck seemed very short with a thickness that went round from under each ear.

He just looked around and took stock of what was happening, talked for a short while to Miss Maguire and then left the room. Very little sound came from his quarters for the first week as he spent the time tidying and rearranging things into order. From where the juniors were, it appeared that things were not too bad behind the flimsy partition separating the two compartments of the old school.

But, alas, this was soon to change. It began one Monday morning after roll call. Master Herron's loud, irate voice echoed through the entire building with a frightening tone. Then came the strange-sounding lashes accompanied by plaintiff wailing of pain and agony. For once Peter was glad to have been held back in Maguire's room. These odd-sounding lashes, his brother John later told him, were coming from a large hard leather strap being applied to the backsides of young children with ferocious intent. Thus, the education system of the village school began a new chapter.

For the remainder of that year all that could be heard coming from behind the partition was the constant screaming of hurting children as Herron flogged relentlessly. What a prospect for those who would be moving in there the following year. The last months of Peter's stay with Gusher remained bearably unpleasant. Perhaps there is a level of tolerance that can be attained whereby the sufferer may be able to sublimate excess energy into some form of pain absorption. However, in the circumstances where could this excess be coming from? If such energies existed, they would certainly be needed more than ever in the years that loomed in front of him.

Still, one member of this class showed no signs of fear or apprehension about moving into the Master's room. Miss Carmel O'Doherty, like her sister Helen, knew the ways of the world, and how her family status would make everything right between her and the Master. She was overheard one evening as she brushed Miss Maguire's hair beside the fire, saying that while she would be sorry leaving her caring role model, things would still be good with Master Herron. She would miss doing the little things of privilege, like teaching the little ones their ABC's and emptying the large jam jar which Gusher used as a urinal out on the school porch (perhaps that was how she first got the unsavoury title). Only the chosen few would be trusted with such intimate chores. This appeared to be how things were and nothing was likely to change them; everyone gets their just deserts in a near perfect world.

In keeping with local tradition, the new Master was given a manly title: the Bull Herron. He was in his late twenties and still single, fairly athletic in posture, and he soon made his way onto the local Gaelic football team. By no means a skilful player, he relied mainly on strength and robustness. From the corner back position he would run out to meet the oncoming attack, to the cheers of the children hoping to win for themselves some favours on Monday morning. He was considered by Fr Gillen to be a most valuable asset to the parish. Apart from being one of the best teachers in the land, he actively engaged himself with the elite parish committee as well as the society of St Vincent DePaul. On special occasions, such as First Communion and Confirmation, Fr Gillen reminded the children, as well as the wider congregation, of their good fortune and asked them to be ever thankful and to pray sincerely for such good and caring people. No one ventured to disagree with these pious sentiments.

Finally, as summer approached, it came to the dreaded day when Peter and his classmates would be taken into the Bull's room for assessment. This lasted for a half day as each was individually tested in arithmetic or sums. The Bull seemed to get particular pleasure from beating the little ones, as he did so in a laughing manner. It was great fun getting them into shape and a means of showing them a taste of what was to come. This, he would tell the boys, would make men of them, and remember, "No crying; only babies cry." This man of valour would be their new role model, teaching them how to be real men in a disciplined and Godly world.

For better or for worse Peter and the entire group passed on into senior level, thus beginning the final phase of their formation. With only a few weeks remaining before the summer holidays, the Bull devoted all his time and energy to the newcomers. Now they could both visually and physically experience what they had become accustomed to hearing from the other side of that partition. It was painfully disturbing for John McGinn to watch his younger brother being made to lie over a table to be beaten senseless for lack of comprehension in the art of long division.

Amazingly, a few, but only a few, did manage under these conditions to come to terms with the system, but not young Peter McGinn. He counted the days, even the hours, until the start of the long summer break. As it happened, he fell quite ill just one week before that. His delicate body was simply not able to withstand the intensity of the abuse, and for that reason, his holiday began that much earlier.

chapter two

With the freedom of summer, all anxieties eased away and Peter was soon out and about playi,ung and roaming around the fields of Cruckban. With the encouragement of his parents, he began to take an interest in the affairs of the family farm. This would have been about the time when Mr and Mrs McGinn began mapping out a future for their two boys. Happy and thriving again, Peter engaged himself usefully, helping in the fields and farmyard. He always felt reassured by the least words of affirmation from a father who he sensed was more favourably disposed towards the older boy. However, at the same time, Tom was glad to see a happier boy emerge and becoming useful as well.

Hess the workman was not quite so ready to see any merit in Peter's contribution to the enterprise and was determined not to let the young pup anywhere near the horses. He knew how much the boy wanted to do the harrowing, as it only involved walking behind the well-trained steeds, or to sit on the harvest reaper with the reins in his hands, but the War Wizard was not having any of it.

It was a good summer with ideal weather conditions from the end of spring right up to the beginning of harvest. Ciss McGinn was happy making wholesome food for the men and boys who were out in the fields working hard at attending the crops. The potatoes were hoed, the turnips were thinned and even the flax and hay crops were looking good. Kitty was beginning to help her mother with the kitchen chores; she loved to be feeding the hens and collecting the eggs. With excitement, she would come running to Mammy saying she had found another nest of eggs hidden in the hedgerow, or better still a clutch of newly hatched chicks hidden in the shrubs. It was a time of contentment and fulfilment for everyone in Cruckban; there was a place and a role for all of them and the feeling was good.

For the boys, nothing could equal the excitement of going to the bog to cut turf on a sunny summer day. The work was hard but it bothered them little. Every so often work would cease and the black kettle would be boiled over a blazing fire made from dried peat and wood for the making of sweet strong tea, to be consumed with currant bread and boiled eggs. It was John who prepared the food, while Peter prided himself at being considered nearly as good as his brother at spreading and footing the turf.

In the long summer evenings, Peter liked to walk the mile down the road to his old bachelor uncle's house. Uncle Henry lived alone on a small fifteen-acre holding called the Blue Rock; it connected the narrow Cruckban road with the one leading to the village of Dooras. His small thatched cottage was almost ready to fall down, but it was situated on an attractive spot beside a little wood with a gentle stream flowing past. The land was divided into three adjoining fields, two of which were considered good fertile land and accounted for almost ten acres. The remaining portion was quite barren with a massive granite rock occupying almost half of it. The fertile section was situated at the bottom end, running close to the little house where the Dunne family lived — these were called the middle and hollow fields.

Even though this land was situated a good mile away, the McGinn children never thought of it as anything other than their own property. Tom McGinn had been renting it for grazing and tillage at a modest price for as long as they could remember. Henry received other payments in kind, like potatoes, milk, eggs and country butter, a cosy little arrangement.

The old man liked relating to Peter the adventures of his younger days — how he had ploughed as much as one and a half acres per day for some of the biggest farmers in east Donegal and how he had won the county championships for cross-country running over four consecutive seasons. The medals of proof were still somewhere in the house but seemed always hard to find.

For the boy, it was an ear upon which he could rely for a friendly reception. He discussed his ambitions and fears at length, always getting the reassurance he needed. His dreams of being the next farmer McGinn were what kept him going; nothing else really mattered. It was the only thing he had, without it, he could never be anything. In this, his uncle was so much more sensitive than his parents were.

Henry was not Peter's full uncle but was related to his mother Ciss on her own mother's side. She seemed reluctant to get very close to her uncle; there was something or other holding her back. There seemed an unwillingness to talk openly with her children about his relationship to her people. However, it was best to maintain ongoing contact through the children. After all, the fifteen acres would one day turn the family farm into a substantial holding and that would confer additional status on the family as well.

Ciss McGinn's obsession was about keeping up a respectable front through hard work and having money in the bank, to be as highly thought of as the larger farmers in the neighbourhood. No wrongdoing or deed of misconduct should ever bring disgrace upon the family name, and there would be no place for the one who dared to breach this moral code. Preserving decency could best be served by associating with the right kind of people: "Show me your company and I will tell you who you are," she often said.

No doubt, part of her obsession was well meant and perhaps driven by a fear of a return to the hard times that she had experienced while growing up. She was one of a large family, most of whom had gone to America. She was from a remote area nearly twenty miles from Cruckban, but with roots in the Dooras area, and she was secure in the knowledge that she had married better than any of her siblings who had stayed in Ireland. As for the young, now was the time to instil in them a noble sense of values; they would one day be grateful for it.

As harvest time grew near, the weather took a noticeable turn for the worst. However, the corn would not be fully ripe for another two weeks, by which time it was hoped the sunny days would have returned. There would be a useful role for the two boys in the reaping as well as gathering in the harvest, and Peter was preparing to give this one his best shot. The golden colours of ripening cornfields spread across the countryside without any improvement in the weather. As the days and weeks passed an air of gloom crept over the land. Not only was it bad for the farmers but also for the many women who came out to the fields to tie the sheaves of corn and earn the much-needed shillings to buy a few essentials for winter. Surely, the Good Lord would not allow such a plight of deprivation to visit an undeserving people whose only mission in life was to feed and clothe their children. Few, if any, of the small farmers would be able to survive the consequences of this looming disaster.

Fr Gillen initiated prayers at Sunday Mass and urged the faithful to engage in sincere prayer that the Lord in his mercy might send weather for the harvest. It was hard on the McGinn children to watch their mother cry as they all looked out the window at the rain. "What are we to do?" she sobbed. The thought of losing a whole year's work as well as the expense involved was too much for her to bear.

During those dark gloomy days, the boys and even wee Kitty found a new and lucrative pursuit in the picking of blackberries, which grew in abundance around the fields at harvest time. They would gather them in small buckets to be stored in an old creamery churn, which they kept in the turf shed. Every Tuesday morning the McHugh brothers or wee Bob (the blackberry merchants) would arrive at a collection point on the lower road. There, men, women and children would assemble to sell the fruits of their labours. The McGinn boys would transport the churn on an old disused pram that had long outlived its usefulness. A happier Ciss McGinn managed a smile as she put the fifteen shillings the boys brought back into a special purse, which was kept securely out of sight. She assured them that the money would be put to good use in paying for their food and clothing. This they accepted without question but were disappointed at not receiving the least reward for their effort.

On hearing about the fifteen shillings and that other men were also getting into the blackberry business, Hess quickly got to work. He did his gathering later in the evenings and on Sundays if the weather was unsuitable for harvest work. He found himself an old zinc-coated basin, which had been used as a bath, and he too kept his blackberries in the turf shed. After a few days, he managed to gather a quarter full of the basin. Then by good fortune, there was a sudden improvement in the weather, thus calling an abrupt end to his supplementary enterprise.

Over the next few days it was work non-stop with everyone playing their part from early morning until late at night. All around, the air was sweetened by the sound of reapers and a binder or two on the bigger farms down the valley. Sunday morning was no different from the others as the men and hired hands (mostly from the village of Dooras) came out to the cornfields ready and anxious to avail of the weather. Tom McGinn advised that they put in an extra effort that day, as he was sure the good spell was ending. By midday, they had cut down almost two acres. In order to save on time Ciss and Kitty brought the food to the field, where it was consumed with haste and laughter. Ciss had brought a second basket full of buttered and jam-sweetened bread to be used later in the evening, and she stayed to lend a hand at tying the corn. In the process of accommodating the inclusion of Mrs McGinn, Tom concluded that output could be further increased if Hess were to start stooking the massive amount of sheaves that were now lying on the stubbly ground.

Peter felt the pain of rejection as his older brother was given the role of horseman, but on a day like this people have more to contend with than the feelings of an eleven-year-old boy. Now with all systems in place the entire operation was going like clockwork. Everyone was happy, especially young John as he sat in the driver's seat beside his father, who was leaving off the sheaves to be tied.

With tears of uncertainty, Peter stooped down and began lifting another of the sheaves that was left for him to tie. "Tie them properly," his mother called as she watched the boy perform his thankless task. "If it's not done right, you know, it's best you leave it to someone who can."

By nightfall of that Sunday all of four acres was harvested on the McGinn farm; it would be the talk of the parish for many a day to come. That night both boys slept the sleep of the just; John's opiate was the feel-good sense of having been highly commended by his parents, who added that Peter had done his bit too.

The next morning work resumed in the one remaining field further away from the house. Hess was back in charge of the horses, at least until the afternoon. Perhaps, Peter thought, he might get his chance today; he even whispered a silent prayer for that intention. Things were beginning to move nicely when a noticeable darkness came about, and it was obvious the rain was returning.

The two horses were loosened and taken into the stable followed by the hungry workers. It was their intention to resume when all had eaten and a brighter day returned, but the weather was not cooperating and by afternoon most of the hands had gone home. Mary Ward, a near neighbour, was still in the kitchen helping Ciss with the washing up while the boys were out in the turf shed enjoying the exaggerated stories coming from Jimmy "Peen" McDevitt. He was a witty young man who lived with his elderly parents Ned and Bella in a council cottage at the end of the Cruckban road. Peen was always ready and willing to play a prank, especially on those unfortunates who were devoid of a sense of humour. An ardent follower of the English football league and championship, he talked about all the great players as if he knew each of them personally. Again, true to the character of this area, he earned for himself the nickname "Peen", after a popular Scottish footballer.

As the boys passed the time in the shed, Peen noticed the half-filled churn of blackberries, then the smaller quantity in the zinc basin. He asked the boys who their owners were. "So these belong to Hess," he smirked as a thought ran through his mind.

Just then, a voice came from outside the shed door. "Are you ready to go home, Jimmy?" It was Mary Ward taking her leave from the kitchen after obliging the woman of the house. Little Kitty came to the top of the path that led from the kitchen door to the yard, and she called after Mary to enquire if she would be back tomorrow. After receiving an assurance that pleased, she and her brothers stood and watched as the two made their way down the road towards the village.

The boys were reminded that tomorrow was Tuesday, which was blackberry market day and "that old creamery can is hardly half full". Before long, they were both on their way up the barn field with buckets in hand. Time could not be wasted in these days of thrift and need.

A tangible air of hope crept over the countryside that evening as the weather improved. Most of the corn was now cut and with a bit of luck would be gathered in by the end of September. There was little doubt in any of their minds that all of this was an answer to the prayers of the just. Hope is the fuel that propels the spirit of endeavour and it is in perseverance that we overcome adversity. Nowhere would these sentiments be more prevalent than on the mind of Tom McGinn as he and his workman finished stooking the wet and heavy corn. He was more than gratified in the knowledge that he had overcome considerable adversity. However, it was much too soon to be resting on one's laurels; that bottom field still had to be finished before the gathering in could commence.

The large willow pattern plate sat in the centre of the table; it was stacked with fresh homemade bread. A pleasant aroma was coming from the bowls of strong tea that were scenting the evening air outside. The Boss (as Ciss liked to call her husband) sat at the head of the table. At the other end sat Hess, who expressed his discomfort at the juniors being allowed to join them at the sides, he being the custodian of propriety and table manners. After getting back with their buckets filled with berries and the old churn looking the better for it, they both felt that a place at the table was justly earned.

"The crops should be well worth saving this year," exclaimed Hess.

"And why, Dinny, do you think that?" the Boss enquired.

"Well, I really believe it takes a scud of a war to get things moving again, it always brings demand for what you produce, and the Russians are now just about ready to crack the whip."

After tea, the men sat and smoked their pipes while discussing and finding easy remedies for all the ills of the world. Ciss took John to the upper room for a quiet word, while Peter and Kitty were advised to stay in the kitchen and do the tidying up. When Ciss reappeared, she announced that she was taking John into Ballintober on a most important errand.

It was a bright and pleasant evening as the two cycled off on their three-mile mystery journey. Barefooted, Peter ran down the road and over the track to pay a quick visit to Uncle Henry. There was a lot on his young mind that he wanted to offload to his elderly friend, whom he had learned to trust. Puzzled by a strange expression on the old man's face and a lack of real interest at what was being said, the boy enquired how Henry was feeling. Henry left him in no doubt that all was well and asked him to pour out a mug of hot water, as he was feeling a bit tired and would soon go to bed with a hot whiskey. They parted company on a promise from Peter that he would be back before the end of the week, hopefully for a longer stay and more chat.

Running back over the same path with even greater haste, he spotted the figure of Maggie Dunne coming in his direction. She was carrying a small can of blackberries, which she had plucked from around the fields of the Blue Rock Farm. He let her know that she was trespassing on McGinn land, but he did not mind too much, there would probably be enough for all of them. Maggie smiled and reminded him that school would open again the following Monday. This was a reality that greatly disturbed both of them, but they took heart in the knowledge that it would soon be potato-gathering time, and they would be taken out of school to help in the fields. Maggie said she was glad to see that he was well and happy again, remembering the sickness that had caused him to drop out of school a week before the holidays began. "It's not so easy to be happy with a sick person in the house with you," she said. She spoke as if she knew what that was like. Would there be any hope, she asked, of her getting to gather potatoes on the McGinn farm? Maybe, he replied, but she would need to ask the Boss.

For the remainder of his canter back to the house Peter tried hard not to dwell on the thought of going back to school. Anyway, he might be allowed to stay away for a little longer. After all, the gathering-in would take another couple of weeks after the bottom field was cut. There were so many little jobs he could usefully apply himself to — perhaps build the loads of corn onto the cart or lead Bob the quiet old horse to and from the Stack Garden. Then a more confident mindset took hold as he got to thinking that little more than three years would see him free and taking on a man's role.

Alone with his father sitting near the kitchen fire, he broached the subject of how he might help in the work that lay ahead. In truth he was only testing the waters in the hope of finding out if any decision had been made about his fate the following Monday. Tom was neither receptive nor forthcoming in relation to his son's inquisition; things would just have to wait, he was told. At the same time, Peter derived some comfort from the fact that there was no mention of the dreaded word "school".

Tom McGinn was a heavy-built man in his mid-fifties. He liked to drink Irish whiskey and cycled to Ballintober on Saturday evenings to get the provisions for the week ahead. Never a man to over-indulge, he would always be back home at a respectable hour to read the local *People's Press* under the light of the old oil lamp hanging from a nail on the wall. With a reputation for being a wild man, he could be heard throughout the townland when angry or bringing in the cows morning and evening. He was said to be the wake-up call to farmers and workmen; no one slept when Tom McGinn was raised. People knew to tread carefully and to approach only when the time was opportune.

No doubt, it was a reputation he grew to be proud of. It was said that he modelled himself on some old man of his younger acquaintance who was still the subject of many outlandishly funny stories. When in one of his tantrums, this old fellow with volume alone was able to topple the delft of the dresser. Tom was by no means a tyrannical man in the home, or towards the family, but liked to put on an act when an appreciative audience was present. In a so-called rage, he would kick an old bucket or some other object around the yard, calling them all the sweet names one could imagine. He had a naturally strong voice, which family and neighbours came to accept as rather harmless.

As Tom was putting the glass globe over the newly lit wick of the oil lamp, Ciss and John entered the kitchen. Ciss announced that John was to become an altar boy. They had been to see Fr Gillen, who would be recruiting a new team shortly. Their hopes of him going to boarding school in twelve month's time had also been touched upon, but not discussed in depth with the priest. This was a subject best dealt with by the Boss himself.

Kitty was amused at this development and wondered how her brother would look in the white surplice. Peter was not surprised, as this seemed to be the logical first step on the road to a higher calling. Young John was quite pleased about his elevation and talked at length about it with his brother long after they had gone to bed. They could still hear their parents discussing the issue over supper by the kitchen fire. "It should stand him in some stead when he goes to the college," Ciss proclaimed. Tom agreed but did have some anxiety about the cost of embarking upon a five-year tenure in a prestigious boarding school. However, it now looked as if the crops would all be saved and who knows, perhaps the Hess predictions might even happen. With that, the door latch lifted and the little man of the Third Reich stepped inside. Being aware that a serious conversation was in progress, he had to know what was being talked about or how indeed it might affect himself. Without divulging every detail of their chat, Ciss and Tom were pleased to share a broad outline of their intentions toward their son. That Monday concluded with all three kneeling by the fireside for the nightly prayer ritual.

All hands were out early the next morning, attending to the routine chores before moving on to the harvest field. As the hired hands were assembling, a light shower rained gently upon them, which lasted long enough to quell any thoughts about cutting corn until at least after dinner. The two boys were preparing the old pram frame to transport their blackberry freight to the bottom of the road. Hess entered the turf shed to discover that his portion of blackberries had miraculously increased from a quarter to more than three quarters full. How, he thought, could this have happened? Then, joyfully concluding that the boys in their stupidity must have unwittingly emptied their buckets into the wrong container, he decided it was best to say nothing and for once be the winner. "What I have I hold," he mused. "Those two silly gobshites." So pleased was he that the horse and cart was hitched up to transport the two containers as well as the boys to meet the blackberry man. A couple of the harvesters availed of the lift home on the cart; Peen had left a few minutes earlier.

They were a happy little party going on a fruitful errand. Hess was particularly happy, with a conquering smile on his face. By the time they reached the collection point quite a number of others had already gathered. With eager anticipation, they could hear the foot rhythm of the trotting horse drawing the blackberry merchant's rubber-wheeled spring cart nearer to them. Young McHugh was a welcome caller indeed. He set up his weighing bucket and each supplier was taken in turn, but everyone remained until the last transaction was completed. This happened to be the McGinn brothers, followed by their gloating minder. Hess thought it best that they stay up on the cart, as it would be easier to empty the containers into the weighing bucket from the height. This seemed a good suggestion and was agreed to. The young McGinns were more than pleased with the money they received and did not take much notice of what was happening at the back of the cart.

"Ah sweet Jaysus," was heard coming loudly from Hess. With his hands, he had been carefully guiding the flow of blackberries from the old basin into the weighing bucket. The onlookers moved forward to see what had happened.

Young McHugh was holding the weighing bucket directly

under the flow when out came a mixture of turf, a decomposed rat and a considerable amount of human excrement. For once, poor Hess was rendered speechless; not another word came out. He just stood on the cart looking down into the contents of the terrible act of sabotage. An occasional blurt of laughter would break the silence. "It looks like somebody has played a joke on you, Dinny," said the young man as he asked one of the women for clean water to wash out his bucket. Looking visibly shaken but with a fearsome gaze directed at the two boys, Hess turned the cart around and started up the road. As he was moving away from the gathering, one of the others called after him, "Will we see you next Tuesday, Dinny?"

The two boys walked back home while keeping a safe distance away from the cart and its lonesome occupant. They knew that there was going to be an in-depth enquiry into the incident, but their mother would be happy with the eighteen shillings they had earned. By the time they had reached home, Hess had related the story in detail over his ten o'clock tea. The two boys steadfastly denied any knowledge about what had happened to Dinny's blackberries, and they were believed as well.

However, the humiliation was not over for Hess. There was a special house in the village where he and a few other men would assemble in the evenings; it was called the parliament. There, all the problems of the country and the world would be discussed in detail and sometimes with an irate passion. With the conviction of informed statesmen, they would eventually agree to differ before adjournment until the next session.

There was, however, one protagonist called the Hawk McArt. He and Hess had a mutual dislike for each other, with the former being more literate and articulate. It was a certainty that he would not let such an important episode pass without comment. Going to parliament would not now be an option for at least a couple of weeks. Hopefully the heat would have gone out of the story by that time. Although not witness to the incident, the Hawk learned later that day how Peen McDevitt had sat concealed behind the thick hawthorn hedge watching the events of the blackberry market unfold. It also emerged through an accomplice that Peen had hatched the idea in the turf shed the evening before while taking shelter with the two young McGinns.

Before parting company with Mary Ward that evening,

Peen had asked if she would tell her younger brother Mickey that he wished to see him. In the dead of night, the saboteur with his young friend had returned to McGinn's turf shed carrying an old empty bucket. He emptied the contents from the basin, and then filled it up with pieces of turf as well as the other mixture, some of which was produced on site. The job was finally executed by spreading the blackberries evenly over everything to make it look good and non-suspect.

The Hawk McArt stored away this information in readiness for his next encounter with Hess.

chapter three

Fortunately for all, the weather improved sufficiently for harvest work to recommence. This, more than anything else, took the focus away from Hess and the demise of his ego. With the blackberry season ending, he felt that new events and happenings would intrude upon these idle minds. The gathering in of the harvest was a long and tedious process with the wet days being availed of for the cutting of thatch to shelter the corn stacks from the heavy rain.

The following Monday morning saw the dawn of a beautiful harvest day and the departure of John and Kitty with their schoolbags suspended from their shoulders. The little one was weeping while being comforted by a brother who was better able to endure the daily routine and who took succour from the promise that it would one day all be worthwhile.

Peter climbed in over the tailboard of the cart, which was being driven by his father towards the cornfield. His happiness was profound. He had been informed of the good news two nights earlier. It was felt and expressed that being a school dud he might be useful for a number of reasons, not least the bringing of food to the hungry working men. On a busy harvest day, many minor tasks could be attended to by a willing young lad who is afraid to go to school.

Old Ned McDevitt, along with his son Peen, were in the field waiting for the commencement of work. Being the expert, Ned would build the tall and neat cornstacks in the Stack Garden while his son would fork the sheaves up to the men who were loading the carts as they alternated between the field and the Stack Garden. Peter loosened the tying at the top of each stook to facilitate the forker, as this would help to speed up the operation.

The accomplishment of a good day's work is cause for an unbelievable feeling of wellbeing in the farmer. With high spirits, the McGinns all sat down to evening tea and Tom asked

John about his first day back at school. It would be his last year at the old school and it was going to be a tough one. As they had assembled that morning in a joyless classroom, he had noticed that a number of his classmates were absent. The explanation was that they were awaiting the commencement of the potato gathering. Bull Herron had read the note delivered by John explaining that Peter had not fully recovered from the sickness that had beset him in early summer. Bull had just shaken his head and announced that there would be a day of reckoning for all of this.

John started into his homework immediately after tea while Ciss and Kitty started into the dishes. Peter made his way to see Uncle Henry. Entering the kitchen, he noticed that the fire had not been lit. There were few signs that anything much had happened there for some time. In the little outshot room off the kitchen, he could see the sickly features of his good friend peeping out over the old patchwork bed quilt. Henry put out his cold hand in greeting.

"Are you not well, Uncle Henry?" Peter asked with a touch of anxiety.

With a voice little stronger than a whisper Henry admitted to not feeling good for the past couple of days, in fact not since his last visit almost a week ago.

Peter offered to light the fire and make him a hot drink but then decided it would be better to go and get help. He told his uncle that he would go and get Tom. When he got outside Peter saw Mrs Dunne, Maggie's mother, walking towards the house. The woman had become anxious about her elderly neighbour after not seeing him for a few days and, stranger still, no signs of smoke coming from the chimney. Peter told her how he had found his uncle and that he was going home to seek help. He was relieved to see her go into the house to be with the old man.

Sally Dunne was a woman who knew and lived hard times. She worked as a creamery maid in Glenleigh Creamery, which was at the far end of the village. There she earned a meagre wage to support her two children and a very sick husband. Sammy Dunne was in his mid-forties but looked much older; he had been struck down with a stroke about a year earlier. It was thought at the time he would not survive for more than a week, but against all odds, he did begin to improve after a long stay in hospital. However, his recovery would never be complete. Never again would he resume his work as horseman to Captain Morrow, the largest landowner in the district, with whom he had been highly regarded. Nothing better than partial power would ever return to his right leg and arm. In his prime, Sammy was considered a fine-looking man, well built with an athletic appearance. At the same time, a swelling and redness had been noticed around his face and eyes for a period before he was suddenly struck down. He was later to learn that this was the sign of very high blood pressure. What a cruel hand this poor man had been dealt.

Now with a gradual improvement that he hoped would continue and see him back to what he had once been, he spent his days moving with the aid of a crutch around the house and sometimes a short distance outside. His being at home allowed his wife Sally to go back to work, while he could see the two children off in the morning and look after them after school each day. This was some comfort for a woman who struggled to provide the bare essentials, all on her own. Her life with husband Sammy had never been an easy one. Their marriage did not take place until their daughter Maggie was almost one year old and Sally herself not quite eighteen. She had spent a lengthy period in what was called the County Home, a place of incarceration for unmarried mothers.

Because her mother was at work, ten-year-old Maggie was unable to be a child, having to acquire the skills of an adult carer towards her father and brother. Like her mother, she was counsellor and comforter to both of them. This was to be her lot for a lengthy period. Sammy acknowledged her goodness and reassured her that things would improve for all of them, when she and her mother would be justly rewarded. The prescribed medication was having partial effect on his overall condition, allowing him periods of relative ease and peace of mind. Of course, there was also the unquantifiable benefit of devoted care given dutifully and without question. Every little respite was a blessing for Sally, who felt very much alone and at times forgotten. She was still a beautiful woman, in her late twenties, with thick black hair and sharply defined features.

In the evenings after her day's work and attention to the needs of her family, Sally liked to take a leisurely stroll along the old track. It was a pleasant escape for her, where she could spend a half hour or more in pensive solitude and shedding solitary tears, something she would not permit herself in the presence of her family.

After coming across Peter outside Henry Meehan's house that evening, she entered the old cabin, which was no better than her own humble abode. There she assured the ailing man that help was on its way and not to worry, he would not be left alone. The hearth was cold as she knelt down to light a fire. It was difficult to light, but with pieces of dried wood and turf, she soon had it going nicely, and a little pan of water beginning to boil.

By the time Mrs McGinn arrived on the scene Uncle Henry was sitting up in bed. Sally had found an old cushion that she had placed behind his back, and she was feeding him small sips of hot whiskey. Ciss thanked Mrs Dunne for her help and assured her that she would be able to manage on her own. Sally handed the mug of hot punch over to Ciss and bade goodnight to the patient, who managed a faint smile as she departed the company.

Alone with her uncle, Ciss soon got down to the business of practicality, advising him that for the present he should agree to going into Lifford Hospital for care and treatment. Her husband Tom would soon be here with the doctor, so perhaps it might be better to think about making some arrangements about settling his affairs. Henry did not react in any way to these suggestions, but refusing to go into hospital was hardly an option for him.

Dr Martin arrived in his Ford motorcar, one of the few in the area at the time. When Dr Martin observed the situation, he was of little doubt that this was a case for the infirmary. The old man was wrapped in a heavy blanket as the doctor, helped by Tom and Ciss, carried him to the back seat of the car. Ciss went back to her own house and sent Hess with the pony and trap to collect the Boss from the hospital, as he had accompanied Henry in the doctor's car.

On their way back, Tom called in to Fr Gillen to let him know what had happened and where Henry had gone. As Tom and Hess were approaching Cathers' Pub, Blossom the pony instinctively drew into the back yard; it seemed the normal thing to do. After all, these men had more than earned their treat in the harvest field that day. Quickly they consumed a couple of stiff whiskies before settling down to bottled Guinness. The chat was mainly about harvesting as well as the outlook in terms of markets and prices. Tom was of the opinion that yields were going to be high and have an adverse effect on prices.

"Not so," said his faithful workman as he called on Andy the barman to pull another two stouts. He explained how the world was now preparing for this Great War and that would undoubtedly create a demand for farm produce. "If I were a farmer I would be growing more of everything — spuds, wheat, corn, if only I had a bit of land," he lamented.

"Yes," shouted the Hawk McArt, "it would surely be better than the blackberries." This caused a stir of laughter among the customers, all of whom had heard the story of what had happened the Tuesday before. "What the fuck are *you* laughing at?" Hess screeched at Tom, whose only response was to laugh even louder. By now, the beverages were starting to take effect, along with a lessening of control on the part of the victim. Again, that fearsome gaze was being directed at his boss, with a loud warning that he still suspected those two wretched bastards of having something to do with the prank.

By this time the entire bar was in uproar with laughter while Tom tried to divert the focus towards a new topic, that of the all-Ireland football final. The Hawk was non-compliant and to the amusement of the others, kept the pot stirring. He suggested that this could not have been the work of youngsters; on examining the evidence he was certain they had passed through a fully-grown man.

Hess was rapidly feeling the loser and reminded Tom it was time he was buying another drink. Drink and rage are never congenial mates, nor do they rest easily with the vanquished. It was to McArt's advantage that he seldom lost his composure, always cool and cunning yet delivering stinging jabs. Hess knew he was no match for his adversary.

"Let's be on our way, Dinny," said Tom.

"Not until you buy another fucking drink and I sort out that useless bastard that lay in his bed until the bloody house fell in on top of him."]

With that he shot across the bar floor armed with a stout

bottle, raising the weapon above his head, half its contents showered over him. He made a desperate but futile swipe at the Hawk only to land with his face in the coal bucket, thus bringing a speedy end to this particular little war.

Out in the back yard the two men got back into their conveyance, watched by the others who had also been ejected from the premises. As they were leaving, Blossom the pony answering the distant call of another horse that neighed loudly across the valley. Tom, with an almighty roar, shouted, "Shut up you unhappy old hoor," to the laughter of the onlookers. He then drove off content after getting a laugh at final curtain, with only the miserably defeated to keep him company. Little or no words passed between the two on their journey home. The pony neighed a few times more but in the absence of an audience, Tom did not react.

Ciss was relieved to hear the sound of the Blossom Trot coming up the road; she had been worried as to what was keeping them so late. By the time they had all gotten back into the house, Hess was sporting a black eye as well as a nasty cut on his cheekbone that needed her attention. She could smell the strong scent of alcohol from both of them as Tom warmed the pot of stirabout for supper.

In bed, Tom and Ciss got to talk about Uncle Henry's condition. Ciss wondered if he would pull through and be able to come out of hospital. She thought about why the Dunne woman happened to be near the place that evening. Peter had told them how he spotted her coming towards the house.

"Indeed there is nothing unusual about clever women courting the attention of old men with land and money," said Ciss.

Tom protested that her thinking was bordering on the absurd. "That poor woman was only doing what a good neighbour ought; in any case she has trouble in plenty of her own with an invalided man and two children."

Feeling tired and sleepy Tom went silent; it had been a long and eventful day and morning would soon be calling.

At dawn, Tom McGinn was preparing breakfast for the entire household, except for his good wife, who had earlier gone to the hospital. It was a pleasant cycle run on a morning that was fine and bright; she would be home in good time for the ten o'clock tea. At the table, poor Hess looked the worse for wear. The boys were amused at his contorted facial expression; they even observed the way he was struggling to eat his food.

Ciss got back shortly after the harvest workers departed the farmyard. She met John and Kitty just as they were leaving the road to take the track through the fields, with the little one looking anything but happy.

Peter accompanied Hess to the cornfields. The horse and cart drew to a halt between the symmetrical rows of stooks. Hess stood up on the floor of the cart and ordered Peter out and to get moving. Peen winked to the boy as all three got to work. Ten o'clock teatime brought news about Henry's condition — he was comfortable but still very weak. Perhaps a week or two in the infirmary would bring an improvement and see him back to himself again. In the meantime, a close eye would have to be kept on him.

Before dinner, everyone got their warning from the Boss not to be talking about blackberries and more importantly the incident in Cathers' the night before. It was preferable that dinner be enjoyed in an atmosphere of quiet joviality. Just as they began peeling the jackets off the floury potatoes, Peen took out a double woodbine packet from his pocket, passing it across the table, saying, "Dinny, you might be able to eat better with these in your mouth." The package contained an upper set of false teeth, which Hess had spat into the coal bucket as he fell in acrimony the previous night. It was not in the least appetising to see the unwashed dentures being pushed swiftly into his mouth as he looked in the direction of the kitchen window. Peen informed him and the others that none other than the Hawk McArt had delivered the package to his house late the night before.

Bedevilled by this cursed debacle with origins in something as trivial as a few blackberries, the poor man would never be allowed to lay the incident to rest. This did not make for a harmonious atmosphere on the McGinn farm throughout the rest of that day or indeed for the remainder of the harvest. Peter was particularly afraid of his angry state and had been physically bullied by him on more than one occasion. This was something he was prepared to live with, as it was preferable to going back to the Bull Herron. The stories that were coming from John and wee Kitty about what was going on in that department dispelled any lingering doubts he had about what was best. After all, he was Tom McGinn's son and would one day be taking over the reins. With that thought, he continued to do all that was asked of him, sometimes even more, and he remained reasonably contented.

With a struggle, the harvest was eventually gathered in and stacked securely. Old Ned and Peen were paid off; they would not now be needed until the potato gathering had commenced. In the intervening period, the men would be kept busy thatching the corn stacks, while Peter would be the rope twister. It was a device made from strong bull wire with a hooked end and used to twist straw into a strong rope. This was suitable work for an eleven-year-old, walking backwards and turning the twister while Dad fed the straw into the lengthening rope. A quiet accord seemed to emanate from the procedure, although few words passed between them. As the autumn peace softened the air, they were really alone and doing something useful together. Feelings of well-being filled the boy's frail body; he could sense that value was being placed on his contribution. Why, he wondered, could it not always be this way?

chapter four

The dark autumn evenings were taking hold of the countryside, and the noise of cartwheels increased considerably as darkness fell. It produced a strange kind of music, like a plaintive anthem lamenting not only the passing of day but summer as well. This was one of many sounds unique to the land and which only the country ear was able to decipher. The mighty steam engines that powered the threshing mills were all on the move; for them autumn was the beginning of a new season. The threshing mill was the final phase of the farmer's routine; it was a rewarding time when the fruits of good labour would at last be realised. For a while, everyone in the neighbourhood would be busy helping each other, as many hands were needed on threshing day. The McGinns would not be threshing until the potatoes had been dug, perhaps not until after the New Year, as they were people who did not need the money so urgently. This was a sign of respectability and good management and should be seen as such by their neighbours.

It was a festival time for Mr McGinn and his workman, moving from farm to farm, giving Tom the chance to play his wild man act and give performances that would be talked about with amusement throughout the parish. His job was always at the bags; it was a most responsible post, which he shared with the host farmer. Hess would always be found building the stacks of straw, which he was said to do a better job of than anyone else would. Where a young boy could be found he would be given a knife and put on top of the mill to cut the straps that tied the corn sheaves. He also had to position each of them as they were forked from the stacks; it had to be done in a way that pleased the man who fed the mill. This, the tough men would say, is an easy wee job. In fact, it was such an easy job that all of them were afraid of it. The thought of kneeling on that exposed position all of a cold winter's day with a smothering dust rising from the drum pit of the mill frightened the tripe out of all of these hardened men.

By late October, the potatoes were ready. There was a sharp frost on the ground as the team stood on the headland while Tom paced the length of the potato field. By simple division, he was able to allot equal portions of ground for each couple to gather. Peen McDevitt and Mary Ward were given a few steps more than the children, one of whom was Maggie Dunne. Old Ned would be partner to the Boss at the top of the field, with two other boys from the village making up the entire workforce. Hess signalled the horses to move forward as he lowered the digger spade into position. Each pair of gatherers took to the starting point that had been marked out for them. Without his consent, Peter was left to partner Maggie at the bottom of the field. He was not at all happy with either of these allotments but knew it was best to proceed without protest.

As the day progressed, the sun came out to warm the tender cold fingers of the young ones and create an atmosphere more conducive to conversation. Maggie told Peter about the terrible beatings being inflicted by the Bull since the school reopened. She was worried about going back after the potato gathering but hoped he would accept her plea of being absent out of necessity. With so much sickness in the house and only her mother earning, the extra money was badly needed. No one possessed of a human heart could but warmly accept this plea. Her greatest worry had to be for her sickly brother; it was not possible for him to go there alone without the support of his sister, but a day of reckoning loomed in front of all of them. What a pity, she said, that Jimmy was not able to be like other boys and take his place in the potato field. She said how much he would like to and how he would enjoy the food provided by Mrs McGinn as well.

Her melancholy state brought some discomfort to young Peter and he changed the conversation to something livelier. Halloween was less than a week away, and he told her how much he was looking forward to it. This was always a happy time with fruit and a variety of nuts laid out on the floor in front of the hearth. A special evening tea with currant and treacle bread as well as two large sweet apple tarts was something to be looked forward to. In the fine art of baking few, if any, could rival his mother. The three children would play the Halloween games, like taking a bite from an apple suspended from the ceiling or from the bottom of a basin of cold water. With some amusement, the parents would look back from the comfort of a huge turf fire, but who could know what thoughts they might be thinking. All games and play-acting must be ended before the nine o'clock news came over the wireless. Hess would need to know how much closer the world was getting to the Great War.

The Russians were now well equipped with what he called the "atonic bomb". They should never forget the great Hitler and his outstanding team of inventors. These were the people who, through their brilliance, passed on to others the wherewithal of great warfare. This was the secret tenet of a mind that functions in a world of fantasy, perhaps the sublimation of an energy that was circumstantially frustrated and propelled by an aggressive nature. Where would these people be without their dreams, be it about world conflict, or family success and achievement. All of it is pleasure untold for the dreamer. However, this was a night for the children; them that had the means would play their games and feast at will. No school the next day, it being the feast of all saints. Worries and anxieties could be set aside for a little while at least, the party concluding with the promise of a comforting dream.

A livelier thought it certainly was and enthused Peter considerably, but it was obvious that Maggie could not relate comfortably to the scene he was so eager to depict. At the same time she was interested enough to question him further and perhaps get some insight into the goings on around the homes of the supposedly privileged. She was most grateful for getting the work and looked forward to being paid the seven shillings per day. Peter reckoned it would take at least five days to complete the job, and this should give her enough to buy the clothes she was promised. Indeed, there might even be a little treat for Jimmy and herself. For a child she had a selfless desire to see her brother happy; his joys would be her joys just as she could feel the pain of his sorrows. On several occasions, she was seen saving pieces of the tasty treacle bread that had been given to her by Mrs McGinn when tea was brought to the field. She hoped it might bring some joy and put a smile on the little boy's face.

Ciss brought good news from the hospital about Henry's steady improvement, he was eating well and walking freely and unaided. Nevertheless, Ciss was showing signs of anxiety about his impending discharge. It would not look good on her part if he were allowed back into that old shack with the bitter cold of winter rapidly approaching. There was the added danger that others might take advantage of the situation. She had not forgotten how quickly the Dunne woman seemed to appear on the scene that evening. This was clearly an issue that required her urgent attention, and she would need to have a talk with the Boss right away — decision time was nigh. Tom assured her that he would have no problem with her uncle coming to stay with the family. He did, however, allude to the fact that until recently she had never wanted to know much about him or indeed consider him as family. To this, she made no reply. It was out of consideration for the fact that he was getting on in years that Peter was allowed to visit the old man. Of course, there was the undeniable benefit derived from renting the Blue Rock Farm with the prospect of ownership now looming.

Shortly after noon on Saturday, the potato digging ended, and all hands would be paid for five and a half days' work. A wholesome dinner was waiting to be consumed, and everyone was in a joyful mood. "Another mission accomplished," said Tom, as he took his place at the head of the table. Even Hess managed a half smile at one of Peen's jokes; it was one without reference to either blackberries or false teeth. Peter was not as upbeat as the others were, the past few evenings had brought more than just a hint of his returning to school, and the dreaded day was approaching. The same subject was brought to the dinner table when Ciss reminded all the children that they no longer had a reason or an excuse for staying at home. From there the focus shifted to Master Herron and his cruel temper. Ned McDevitt said how much it disturbed him to see weeping children walking along that track with a look of helpless fear on their little faces. Old age brings to the human heart what is so lacking in the collective body that fashions behaviour.

The Boss placed the knife and fork down on his empty plate, using strong language to describe his thoughts about the infamous master. He went on to say that the only thing keeping him from confronting the beast was his fear of not knowing when to stop. "I would more than likely go too far and be sorry afterwards," he said. Old Ned knew different and agreed that this was exactly what the fellow needed. A real man should bring him down to size and it should be done in a public place, where he could be humiliated even more. However, in truth, this would never happen; even the wild man Tom McGinn was simply afraid of the consequences of an angry Fr Gillen. Under the system, parents did not have the right to protect their children; they had no choice but to passively hand them over and into bondage. The ritual of the wild man act was well and truly subdued.

Maggie looked at the two green pound notes that Tom had given her along with the advice to hand it over to her mother. The little girl was pleased beyond words; never before had she handled such an amount of money. At the same time, she expressed sadness that all this had now ended; it had been a pleasant week and a new experience for her. She would like to think that Peter could now be her friend; soon they would be joining each other on the weeping track. As she was leaving, the kitchen Ciss handed her a paper-wrapped parcel, which contained almost half a freshly baked currant scone. This was for her and her brother, she was told. Thanking Mrs McGinn for her goodness, she gave Peter a smile and said goodbye to all in Cruckban.

Chapter Five

As all the names were called out at roll call, each of the returning absentees was summoned to the table. The Bull seemed to enjoy listening to the pitiful stories as to why they had not been to school, but he was not in the least receptive to any of them. Each of the boys and girls were given the weight of the leather in relation to the extent of their default. It was the heavy instrument to the hands or backside in relation to the number of days missed and kept increasing accordingly. Maggie screamed, as she had to endure six heavy lashes to her little hands, hand that were tender and forever ready and willing to soothe the pain and distress of her loved ones. Only her own folks knew of her goodness; the people that mattered were neither aware nor interested as to what went on in the lives of these sorts of people.

Peter's case was heard with amusement. Yes, he had been sick for a time but word had reached the school about him working daily in the harvest and potato fields. He now hoped and prayed that what he feared would not happen. Pleading for mercy and saying he felt very afraid and sick, Peter faced the tyrant, who got up from a cushioned chair and put the boy over it, face downwards. The beating to the backside was severe, painful and humiliating. When the Bull was in a serious rage his hair always seemed to fall from its sleek position and down over his eyes. It was most distressing and frightful for the onlookers, not least brother John. Maggie too was deeply upset but was only about recovering from her own ordeal, little knowing that much worse was about to follow.

From this brutal violation, Peter staggered back to a vacant desk. Through teary eyes, he could see that it was Maggie who was sitting beside him. The ritual of morning prayers was about to begin when suddenly the door of the partition opened. It was Miss Maguire pushing two weeping infants into the room in front of her. She informed the Master that the two had been absent for a long time and felt it was his decision as to how to deal with them. One was a little girl from Ballintober who lived less than half a mile from the school. Maggie felt physically sick in anticipation of what might happen to her poor little brother, who happened to be the other victim. Bull sat down to hear what else Gusher had to tell him, and when she had finished he lifted the leather strap from the windowsill. Maggie screamed as he pulled Jimmy across his knees. With that, the hair again fell over his eyes. He shouted to her to come up while he proceeded to belt the delicate boy without mercy.

To his and his assistant's astonishment Jimmy neither cried nor lamented after the first or second blow, but more alarmingly, did not get up after the punishment had been administered. Quickly Herron lifted the limp body from his lap. The little head fell to one side and the boy rolled to the floor flat on his back. His hysterical sister made to lift him into her arms but was advised by Miss Maguire that it might be best to let him lie for a time and he would probably soon recover. She also enquired if the likes of this had ever happened to him before. As best she could, the trembling child said how Jimmy suffered from a shortness of breath and could get weak during bouts of coughing. "But never," she cried, "anything like this." A handkerchief soaked in cold water was applied to his forehead, but it had little effect. At first Herron turned white and looked frightened, then a flush of sweat enveloped him, and he appealed to Miss Maguire to do something fast. She offered to take the boy back to her own room but immediately decided that enough of the pupils had witnessed the incident. Instead, they both carried him out to the porch.

The entire classroom was in turmoil; order had completely broken down. Through lack of thought or sensitivity towards his sister, someone announced that Jimmy was dead. Maggie ran out to see what was happening, and to her relief Jimmy's eyes were beginning to open a little. Then, coughing out a blockage from his throat, he began to breathe freely again. Like so often before, she put one arm gently around him while rubbing his back with the other. Jimmy gradually came to as the pair of bullies looked on in anxious discomfort. Nothing much was done by way of teaching for the rest of the day. The little girl from the village escaped what was intended for her, but from what she had witnessed by way of fear and violence there had been no escape.

Bull spent most of that day with his assistant in the other room; their thoughts were mainly about how to minimise the impact of the horrible incident that had taken place. They both felt safe in the assurance that Fr Gillen would stand by them. Hopefully, he might never get to hear about it, as parents were most reluctant (simply afraid) to interfere in the important business of schooling. Sending the boy and his sister home early was not an option as it would be likely to attract unfavourable attention. Questions might be asked as to why. For the pupils of Ballintober school it was a day unlike any other. The worst and the best had been experienced: no lessons, no beatings, not even a scrap of homework was given. Jimmy was given a cup of sweet tea and a biscuit but showed little interest in it. In the unsupervised room, Peter and Maggie sat together in a state of bewilderment. They talked a little, mainly about Jimmy — how he was and how he might make it home. Maggie was grateful for Peter's offer to help with her brother on the homeward journey.

Herron re-entered the classroom at the hour of three; it was only to dismiss his class for the day. He was indeed a greatly subdued man; a grave look of sombre anxiety had taken hold of him. Would the incident harm his reputation in the locality, he wondered? Standing at the door of the school, he watched in trepidation the departing trio. Jimmy was walking between his two minders with Peter carrying his schoolbag, and most of the others walked in sympathy with them. Everyone wanted to help his or her little friend who had been so cruelly violated.

"Thank God for that," Herron said to Miss Maguire. "Hopefully all will be well again by tomorrow." In hoping for a better tomorrow, the Bull's concerns were more about his own discomfort than anything else was.

News of what had happened soon spread throughout the district, and people talked in anger, saying that something would have to be done. However, like so often before, it was only talk. There would be no initiators of reproachful action; these people were the law, let the common people be in deference to them.

Back in their humble dwelling, Sammy and Sally Dunne sat beside the bed where their traumatised son lay. He was coughing a lot and fighting for his breath. Sammy was angry and close to tears, he had been keeping reasonably well of late but this sort of thing disturbed him greatly. Sally begged him not to get excited and raise his blood pressure. Maggie and she would look after the boy, but first she would put the hot water jar in the bed to warm her husband's cold feet.

It was to the Bull's advantage that these suffering people were so deprived; they possessed neither the means nor the energy to take him to task. As the evening progressed too late, he grew confident that the matter had not been brought to the attention of the parish priest. The boy was probably all right again. It was obvious that he had had these kinds of attacks before; it was something his people were used to. With these reassuring thoughts a good night's sleep was in the offing and hopefully, the wretched boy would be back again tomorrow.

Jimmy did not join the others the next day, nor was it likely he would ever be walking the track again. It was later in the week before Maggie started back. She reported that Jimmy was confined to bed with a bad cold; he was coughing and sweating badly and she was the only one to attend him. Herron was somewhat circumspect in broaching the subject with her and only did so in the presence of Miss Maguire. They were obviously going to face this one together; their guilt was equal, hence they would have to stand in unison. This time morning prayers were said without interruption. The Master stood in front of his class with joined hands pointed in a heavenly direction. He prayed for all present as well as for those who were absent, especially those that were absent through sickness. Then a mindful reflection on the love and mercy of a caring God and how fortunate were those who understood and accepted it.

Everything ran smoothly throughout the day, and lessons were conducted in a much quieter setting. Perhaps it was a strategy designed to facilitate a calming period, so that there would be no complaints from either children or parents. Shortly after lunchbreak, Fr Gillen came into the room. After acknowledging the customary greeting "Good Morning Father" from the pupils, he glanced quickly around the place but did not attempt to address or question any of them. Instead, he talked quietly and at length with the Master. They then went out to the porch to continue their discussion. After a while, the Bull came back and took the strap out with him. It was obvious the instrument was being examined; it was also clear that the priest had heard what had happened to the boy Jimmy Dunne.

When Herron returned he looked more relaxed and

immediately went in to see the Gusher. It looked as if they both had the reassurances they sought, and the dreaded weapon had received the seal of approval.

chapter six

It was about the beginning of November when Uncle Henry came to live with his niece in Cruckban. He was to share the boys' attic room over the kitchen, as it was considered warmer and more comfortable than the one occupied by the servant man. His sojourn in the infirmary had brought him back to a state of reasonable mobility. He liked to move around the place and see the daily happenings. The boys noticed strangeness about his appearance, most noticeably that his hair had gone completely white. "Yes," their mother laughed, "it's amazing what a little soap and water can do."

For the family it was a new situation, and they would have to get used to a few necessary adjustments. Room would have to be made for their guest at the fireside and at the table. This might encroach upon Hess and the few privileges he enjoyed. Equally so the two boys would need to show more restraint. Out of consideration for the old man, noisy bedroom pranks would have to cease; it could even mean an earlier bedtime.

It being John's month as altar boy for eight o'clock morning Mass, it meant there would be no dispute about early bedtimes. He would be leaving home more than an hour before the others. The mornings were dark, so Tom always accompanied him on the start of the journey. Peter too got interested in becoming an altar boy, and both parents agreed to it if John could teach him the responses of the Latin Mass. To everyone's surprise, he had mastered it well within a couple of weeks, so next time John would have company for the early morning shift.

Henry took it upon himself to wake the boys up; he would be up from an early hour to light a candle for their convenience. Reclining comfortably in his bed with his hands behind his head he liked to chat with them as they began their day. "It's good for you, Uncle Henry," said Peter. The old man smiled to himself and said nothing. Like old Ned McDevitt, he too understood and felt for the boy's fears.

The twelfth of November was hiring fair day in Strabane, and it was considered a holiday in farming circles. This day and the twelfth of May were the only days of the year that Hess claimed as his own and free. In the morning before leaving the house, he would agree a new contract with Tom McGinn for the following six months. As he was such a reliable and skilful workman, the Boss was most keen to retain his services. It would be at least another three or four years before young Peter would be able to take on such responsibility, and according to Hess, there was a serious doubt as to whether he would ever be suitable for such duties. He never attempted to disguise his dislike of the boy; perhaps this had something to do with Peter's consuming interest in learning the craft of horsemanship. In this, Hess could influence the thinking of the parents, as his opinion was sought and valued greatly by them.

The town was a hive of activity; people were moving round the various places of interest. Men and women would visit the second-hand clothes shops where children's wear could be got at a price they could afford. The working men were usually attired by the likes of Timoney the street trader; it would be first call of the day for Hess and his fellow hirelings before making their way to Hanna's bar. He had a fetish for army wear, breeches that laced tightly below the knees with an over-supply of material around the backside, certainly more ballroom than he needed! On a day like this Timoney had little time for niceties or bargaining. With customers in abundance, he could afford to be rude and insulting towards them. When Hess found the item he was looking for, the price demanded was six shillings. As he was putting his hand into his pocket, he got a gentle tap on the shoulder. It was Peen McDevitt, who whispered, "Dinny, he is selling these breeches for four shillings, offer him that and no more." Hess complied and was verbally ravished by Timoney in the presence of many men and women. "Go home you miserable hoor, your effin tool will never stand in them." This was the funny story of that particular hiring fair; it was told with laughter throughout the land and at every gathering, save the pulpit.

Allowances would have to be made for a workman not quite himself the day after the holiday. Everyone knew to keep a safe distance away from the wee man in the wide-arsed breeches. He kept himself occupied at preparing the old wheel plough and other implements for the commencement of the ploughing season. This was the conjunctive season; it was the link between the old and the new farming cycle. The year that had passed was neither the worst nor the best that Tom and Ciss would experience by way of return from their holding. Tom was able to make a fairly accurate assessment of what to expect in payment for his produce. It was one of those rare occasions when they found themselves sitting alone in the kitchen; Henry and the children had gone to bed, while Hess had not yet returned from the parliament. "It's going to take a lot of money but I think we should be able to manage it." This was Tom's considered judgment in relation to John's pending move to college.

Overhead John and Peter listened quietly to what was being said, and they sensed that this was an issue of grave importance to their parents. Yet they could not understand their deep concern about cost and money. True, they did operate on a tight budget, and every penny had to be accounted for. Nevertheless, at the same time there never seemed to be any shortage in that department. It is only they that work the land and depend solely on its bounty that harbour such uneasiness. Ciss could not forget what things were like in her growing up years; both she and her husband would need the security of knowing that there was money set aside for the rainy day. Now there was a real danger that this venture would leave them more vulnerable to the harshness of life on a mountainy farm. This was a reality beyond the comprehension of the young and carefree. However, she was certain that through hard work and prayer they would succeed in their noble endeavour.

It was the subject of hard work that digressed their conversation towards Peter and the hope that he would get strong enough to take over from Dinny. The benefits that would accrue from this development were enormous. The savings on not having to pay out a weekly wage would more than compensate for the money spent on education. This was their plan for the future, though they did not intend to share it with Hess, whose footsteps they could hear approaching the front door. All of this was music to Peter's ears; it was exactly what he wanted to hear. He could now go to sleep reassured and re-enthused. John and Uncle Henry were already in the land of nod.

chapter seven

Word came from the school that wee Jimmy Dunne had been taken by ambulance to the sanatorium forty miles away in Carndonagh. Concern grew for the boy after a couple of weeks with no noticeable signs of his condition improving. Dr Martin had little doubt as to what the condition was, and he made the necessary arrangements, which was standard procedure in a situation of this kind. First the patient had to be removed, the house fumigated and all its occupants tested for signs of the deadly disease. It was the good doctor himself who transported the rest of the family to Letterkenny for these tests. A gentle and caring man with a deep concern for the welfare of his patients, he was delighted a week later to bring the news that all of them appeared to be free of tuberculosis. It was an anxious and distressing time for a family so distant from the joys of life. Sally Dunne continued to work out of necessity, and Maggie returned to school and sat beside Peter McGinn.

Master Herron and his pupils continued with the daily routine, which began with the usual prayers of thanksgiving and invocation. Miss Maguire was more specific and mentioned Jimmy by name. She did not appear to suffer the same degree of discomfort as her superior in relation to this serious development. They were both satisfied that the poor boy's condition was nothing of their doing. What had happened to him that morning was only a symptom of something more serious. In any case that unfortunate incident was now well and truly in the past and hopefully forgotten. Consoling each other in this fact, they once again got down to the business of running the village school, where things gradually returned to normal.

Maggie told Peter that her brother had gone to be cured; soon he would return and bring happiness back again to their home. She was looking forward to the next Sunday, as Captain Morrow had called and offered to take them in his car to see Jimmy at the sanatorium. This would be their first visit since he had been taken there three weeks earlier. For her it was going to be a happy excursion, travelling by car through undiscovered countryside, maybe having a treat along the way. The joy of seeing the brother she was so fond of, after three weeks that felt like as many years, kept her spirits up. In prayer, she was begging the Good Lord that Jimmy would be coming home with them. To the wishful mind of a child, this was more than just a hope. It is said that sincere prayer will never go astray; good will derive in some form. However, from the lips of an innocent child it comes with a sincerity and conviction that the heavens cannot deny.

Captain Morrow was a well-to-do farmer with a military background. He owned 150 acres of prime land and Sammy Dunne had spent many years working for him before his illness. Apart from his regimental appearance, the Captain was of a kind, benevolent disposition. Maggie heard him arriving early that Sunday morning in his shiny black Vauxhall car. Christmas was in the air as the little party made their way through the quiet Inishowen countryside. The Captain drove at a speed that made the journey pleasant and comfortable.

"Many a tough game I played in this town and it was here that I won my first county title for cross-country running," Sammy reminisced.

"Yes Sammy," said the Captain. "No doubt there are many in Buncrana who can still remember you on the sports field."

"Thank you sir, but sure what does it matter now."

"But Sammy, these are happy memories, they are your memories and that certainly does matter."

Mrs Dunne in the back seat was quick to concur with these generous sentiments, knowing how her husband needed even the least affirmation.

Drawing to a halt at the entrance to the hospital, the Captain announced that he would go a bit further and pay a visit to an old friend who lived outside the town. Before leaving, he placed a five-pound note in Sally's hand, saying he would be back in a couple of hours and that all of them would stop for tea on the way home.

For the present Sally thought it best not to say anything about the money, she knew her husband was a proud man who would not want to be considered a charity case. Indeed no one understood this better than the Captain himself did. He had a lot of respect for Sammy Dunne but also knew his sensitivities. However, these were times of extenuating circumstances, and no blame or stigma should attach itself to what are the afflictions of nature.

Jimmy was weepy at first, but so glad to see his protectors once again. He was not well enough to be allowed out of bed. This was a disappointment for all of them, as they would have liked to take him out for a little pampering and to simply be alone with him for a little while. Ominously it was a sign that things were not at all well with the boy. It was a most chilling experience for people who had never before been inside such a place. The ward was dull in appearance, with little signs of hope or promise. An arrangement of beaded holly surrounded two large holy pictures that hung on the wall opposite Jimmy's bed. It was a narrow room with a single row of beds occupied by patients of varying ages. The children were kept by themselves at the upper end. The ravages of this disease were potently displayed before the visitors' eyes. An old man coughed in agony, holding fleshless fingers to his chest; another boy was fighting furiously for a breath of air.

There was a look of total despair on the faces of visiting relatives, all of whom endeavoured to be the comforter in the face of the grim reaper. How well Maggie played the role of her natural self, laughing with Jimmy just as she would back home when helping him to do his homework. He responded in kind but it was clear he had neither the strength nor the will to engage her fully. To lift his ebbing spirit she talked about what they might do when he returned — spring was not all that far away, and brighter days were on the horizon.

A senior nurse beckoned Sammy and Sally to the desk near the bottom of the ward. In the doctor's absence, she was allowed to tell them that their son had active tuberculosis but they had succeeded in reducing his temperature. She also assured them that there was no immediate danger and that Jimmy was eating a little better. However, at the same time no promises were given.

As they looked up at the large wall clock, a feeling of awe took hold of the visitors; it was telling them that visiting time was ending. Soon they would all be saying their goodbyes; alas, for some it would be the final farewell. Sammy Dunne leaning heavily on his crutch, he was feeling tired and low. Physically and emotionally drained, he looked around and took in the hopelessness of what was all around him. How far removed from the world of his glory days, he mused. However, it was his world; his here and now, there was nothing apparent that would make it better. The visitors' bell suddenly brought him back to himself and the others. It was time to go.

Sammy felt awkward putting his functional arm around his son at the time of parting, and Maggie and her mother made for the door as the scene was too disturbing for them to watch. On their way out, they met the Captain coming up the corridor. He thought it best to turn back with them and let the boy settle down after the distress of separation. He was visibly moved by what he was seeing — sorrow and grief surrounded him as he looked on at a flood of tears flowing from the broken-hearted. Nothing in his experience, which was varied and colourful, could have prepared him for what was taking place before his very eyes, and he certainly had not seen the worst. There was a palpable feeling of oneness amongst all the folks as they stood and chatted a little before heading back to their pitiful homes and people.

The subdued family had travelled a few miles before the silence was broken; it was Sally who commented on how fast the evenings were falling. "Yes," said the Captain, "it will be another four or five weeks at least before there is any noticeable change and hopefully all things will have improved by that time." This was a most sincere wish and one certainly shared by all present. Maggie and her mother, their tears not fully spent, were trying to comfort each other in the back of the car. In spite of adamant protests, the Captain stopped at the hotel outside Buncrana. This was something he wanted to do and nothing was going to stop him. The Dunnes felt somewhat out of place to be sitting down in the company of one so highly esteemed, a man of class and substance. However, thanks to the generosity of their host, they all came out feeling the better of their experience. He possessed a sympathetic expression and was able to communicate in a manner that reassured. The setting too was reassuring and heartsome, in stark contrast to what they had witnessed earlier in the day. The place was warm and brightly decorated for the season's festival, and a glistening sheen radiated from a Christmas tree that occupied the corner of the lounge. Sammy was feeling much the better of the brandy he consumed before and after his meal. Sally thought a little about its effect on his blood pressure but then again this was a once-only occurrence. "May it heighten his spirits," she prayed to herself.

It was an emotional thank you they imparted to their benefactor when leaving the car to walk down the lane towards their little house. First, they would fix a fire of turf and wood. It was important that Sammy be made warm and comfortable before going to bed for the night. There was no need for supper as they had already eaten extra well, just a warm drink before retiring for the night.

Sally would always be last to go to bed; there were so many chores to be attended to in her demanding schedule of work, school and an ailing husband. However, more than that, this was a time she had to herself. Now she could allow her tender feelings to be fully expressed without causing grief to the others. She pined for her wee Jimmy and yearned for the days and nights she and Maggie had spent easing his suffering. How, she wondered, is he coping this night? He had us for a little while but then we had to leave him again, she thought. Oh God, is this what you call fair?

The fairness of the situation was again the subject of her conversation the next day with Aggie McCrory. Aggie was her very good friend who ran a small grocer's shop beside the creamery in the village. Each day at lunchtime, they would have a lengthy chat. It was good for Sally to have a listening confidante like her, a person to whom she could turn and trust through stressful times. On more than one occasion, Aggie's generosity took the family through times of desperate want. She and husband Dan lived comfortably on their earnings; he was a bread deliveryman employed by the local bakery. Their teenage son Barry had started serving his time as a builder with Lafferty the contractor. It could be said that they were the fortunate people, enjoying good health and the means to live in modest comfort. Through their work Aggie and Dan were both in touch with the under-privileged and the hardships they had to endure, and never were they found wanting in the face of suffering.

Little mention was made of Jimmy Dunne either at school or on the way to and from. The exception of course being Peter McGinn who listened with interest to what Maggie was telling him about their Sunday visits to the hospital. There was a developing affinity between the two; it had begun at potato-gathering time and was reinforced by the events of their first day back at school. He told her all about his Uncle Henry coming to live with them and that there was talk of his old house being renovated for his return there in the spring. His parents had been talking to the old man about this possibility for some time and it was a suggestion that did appeal to him. Ciss would not mind investing in this if she could be certain that the property would pass on to her or her family. On this issue Henry kept his thinking very much to himself. He had a few pounds put away and it might as well be put into this project. In so doing, he would still be in control of his own affairs. He was reasonably contented where he was, but still harboured the notion of returning to his home.

It was an uneventful winter around Cruckban and its immediate neighbourhood. In the absence of war, Hess progressed contentedly with ploughing the land. Tom diligently tended the livestock; he fed and bedded them with care night and morning. It was a sign of a good farmer that he looked after his stock in a way that had them looking better and cleaner than those of his neighbour. The five two-year-old bullocks would get special attention so that they could later thrive on the early spring grass. Fetching a handsome price at the May fair of Raphoe was the prize he was aiming for.

Rabbit hunting was a popular activity amongst the menfolk of the area, and men carrying ferret boxes and iron hunting bars were a common sight on the hill. In the afternoon, they would set wire snares on the rabbit pads, and these were checked again in the early morning for results. Peter and Henry formed a kind of partnership for this winter enterprise, the old man's experience combining well with the boy's agility and enthusiasm. They enjoyed limited success, but Ciss was pleased that the younger boy was showing promising signs of usefulness and contributing a little towards his keep.

At the behest of Aggie, Dan McCrory arranged to transport Sally and Maggie Dunne on their Christmas visit to see wee Jimmy; it was the Sunday before that holy and special day. The journey in the old bread van was not as comfortable as in the Captain's car, and for that and other reasons it was thought that Sammy would be better remaining at home. No complaints, however, they were more than grateful to the McCrorys for their kindness. At the hospital, things were much the same as before. Jimmy was neither better nor worse; a fact confirmed this time by the house doctor. The emotional trauma was still the same, nonetheless; and he asked to be taken home for Christmas. Bad as things were, there he had managed to preserve comforting memories of how that time had been with his Mum, Dad and sister. Much as she would have liked to, it was not in Sally's power to accede to this pitiful request. With love and sorrow, they placed a little Christmas gift beside his bed, and Dan added to it with one from Aggie and himself. The present from Santa would be brought as soon as they could after Christmas.

A retired hen was always taken from the roost on the morning of Christmas Eve. Hess, who liked the job of decapitating the bird, executed the task. John in his brightness would inform Peter about the reality or folly of Father Christmas. Both agreed, however, not to disillusion wee Kitty and play along to their own advantage. The Christmas stockings never contained anything elaborate but enough to bring joy and laughter to children of modest expectations. Celebrating the true significance of the day was the priority in the McGinn household. All but Uncle Henry would attend early morning mass in Ballintober chapel. The parish was in a festive mood; greetings were exchanged in a spirit of community and faith. From the pony trap, the headlights of an occasional motor vehicle enabled the children to see their school friends walking the road home. They could see the Hawk McArt walking with Maggie Dunne and her mother.

Like any other winter morning, the farmyard chores must be attended to. Hess would be helping Tom on this special day when even the animals would be treated to an extra sheaf of corn. Ciss had the pot of tasty beef broth prepared from the night before; it was a nourishing and savoury start to the day of Yule. Before dinner, the men would be treated to mugs of hot punch, and perhaps a little sherry for the woman of the house. After dinner, a bright fire would be burning in the parlour, and the family would withdraw there for a while before commencing the evening chores. Outside the dog and cats disputed violently over what was left of the old hen.

This was always a special night in parliament; its members

never bothered about Christmas recess. As night fell, Hess put on a heavy and deep-pocketed overcoat, and then walked down the road fortified with a half pint of whiskey and a few bottles of stout. It was understood that the others would be doing the same.

After tea it was back again to the parlour. Tom revisited the bottle of Paddy for a time or two and was feeling the better of it. Uncle Henry preferred to remain in the kitchen; he and Peter were amusing themselves putting together a jigsaw puzzle that came from the Christmas stocking. John discussed with his father the contents of a book he had just received from the same source. The little one was blissfully happy with it all; she engaged her mother's attention to what she was doing with a dainty little sewing kit. She also enquired as to why it was that Santa did not call to every house; she knew from talking to others that this was the case for many. This discomforting subject was not one that could be taken on board at such a time; the ills of the world had to be tackled by other people. However, the high spirits did survive when talk shifted to the precious subject of John going to college.

The next day was a leisurely one; nothing much was done beyond the routine and it would be another day or two before life returned to normal.

With the dawn of another year came talk of lengthening days and preparation for spring. The corn would be thrashed and taken to Swilly Valley Mills, while John James McDonald, the potato merchant, had an order for the Kerr Pinks before the middle of February. Predictions made by Tom in relation to returns seemed to have been accurately assessed. Peter was counting the weeks, even the days, for the time of sowing and planting. In this he would be able to spend a couple of weeks with his father doing what he liked best and safely away from the one he feared most. The old ways had fully returned there. Even worse, as the school inspector was on his way in April. Preparation for this as well as the ecclesiastical inspector was always intense and brutal, and Peter begged his parents to allow him to miss it all.

chapter eight

It was a late spring, and the sowing and planting was progressing at a slower than usual pace. The McGinns were also later than usual but by no means worse off than their neighbours. Around the middle of May, Tom and his workman began the refurbishment of Henry's old house. When what remained of the thatched roof was stripped off, only the crumbling walls remained. Both men laid claim to proficiency in the area of construction work, hence the decision was made to undertake the work by themselves, thus saving on the cost of employing a tradesman. Henry insisted on buying the materials and was hoping for the job to be finished in a couple of weeks.

The immediate task was to get the asbestos roof on while the weather was still good, in that way the few items of furniture would not be damaged. A sense of partnership was much to the fore during the early stages of the operation. The old wall heads were evenly shuttered and levelled off with concrete, and upon this would rest the firm wall plate and roof.

It was at the cutting of the roofing timber that the first signs of discord began to show. Hess claimed to have had some experience of this when he worked in Scotland as a young man and he convinced the Boss enough to let him at it. He began by measuring the distance from the ridge to the wall plate on both sides. Allowing for a slight variation in length between each side, there should have been no serious difficulty about cutting the rafters accordingly. Having assessed the situation to his satisfaction, he filled his pipe with Crowbar tobacco and puffed the smoke of self-assurance, then got down to work with a newly sharpened handsaw. Tom had taken the horse and cart to the village to do his daily milk delivery to the creamery. At this time of year, the five cows were almost able to fill two ten-gallon creamery cans every day.

At dinner, Dinny proudly announced that his work on the roofing should be finished by evening and ready for nailing down next morning. This was good news for old Henry, who was hoping to take a dander down there in the afternoon.

Dinny did not get to the site the next morning. He had to go to the creamery instead, as the Boss and his wife were going to Strabane. They both had errands there, and of course, a good part of the money from the sale of the heavy bullocks needed to be lodged in the Hibernian Bank. They were also going to visit a prominent individual from the world of academia called John Gallagher, now retired and living there. He was a distant relation to Tom, and he would be able to advise them and their son on the ways of college life.

This subject had now taken on a life of its own. Not a day would pass without mention of it and more often a journey somewhere in relation to it. The parish priest was seeing more than enough of both of them — his quarterly pastoral visit to Uncle Henry was not nearly enough. They had to be talking with people in the know, as their newfound interest was a bit foreign to the ordinary people around Cruckban.

Later that afternoon a terrible commotion broke out at Henry's house, and the loudness of Tom's irate voice echoed over the entire countryside. Workmen in the fields, women in their homes as well as people on the roads all stopped and listened. Henry looked on in total dismay as Dinny brandished a claw hammer in front of his foaming employer and threatening to knock his effin' head off. What the wee man lacked in volume was more than compensated for in aggression. The fracas broke out as soon as the two began putting the newly cut rafters into place. Before nailing them down it was discovered that half of them had been cut nine inches too short. With poor literacy and numerical skills, the bold Dinny either misread or miscalculated his measurements. Unaware of this, he completed the work of cutting without testing any of them for accuracy. Apart from the destruction of expensive timber, Henry was also worried that this dispute might put paid to the entire operation.

On this particular occasion, Tom McGinn was not playing to an audience — his temper was really and truly out of control. So much so that he made the mistake of calling his adversary by his famous nickname — that was how the claw hammer came to be introduced. "Hess, you blood-sucking fucking bastard, why did I ever let you anywhere near the expensive timber? A stupid hoor, that couldn't tell his tool from his foot only that you don't put a shoe on it!"

This was the kind of sound that filled the valley that otherwise peaceful May evening. In this state, Tom's ultimate release was to kick some object with a final roar, and running towards an old bucket, he let go with mighty force. His roar was indeed loud and seemingly painful — the old bucket was full of hardened concrete that had been left over and forgotten about. The wounded man lay groaning on the ground, his anger now giving way to lamentation. He called on Henry to remove his shoe and fetch a bucket of water.

"I think that lunatic of a man has broken his big toe," Hess shouted to Ciss as he came into the yard. He had come for the pony and trap to bring the casualty back home. She asked few questions as to what had happened but did say she could hear that unearthly roar. Even at that distance, she knew something had to be wrong. She was told less than half the story, but enough to figure out how the Boss came off the loser.

With the aid of an improvised crutch, Tom made his way from the trap to the kitchen. Ciss looked at the injury — there was some blood oozing from under his big toenail and considerable swelling at the ankle as well. Under no circumstances would he allow the doctor to be sent for — the fewer that knew about this the better. Whatever about the injury, a man's pride must not be violated. Here was a man who felt like the loser, but in that particular contest, there were no winners.

This put an end to a glorious but short-lived partnership in construction, but like so often before Hess the survivor remained on as horseman at the farm. Work on the old house ceased for a while; it was not a subject anyone dared to mention until well after the cooling off period. Eventually Henry got through to Ciss that something should be done before the weather broke and that they should think about employing a handyman. The suggestion was not well received by Tom, who was against spending money on the project. He wondered if the spoiled timber could still be used, if only he could find somebody knowledgeable in this field to advise him. It would be easy enough to explain how the timber came to be ruined in the first place. He could do this at his workman's expense, but the question of him using a crutch was another matter.

"Did you have a mishap Tom?" came a man's voice from over the privet hedge in front of the house. It was Dan McCrory, the bread man, on his weekly round. Awkwardly Tom said something about wrenching his ankle while working at Henry's house and went on to relate his problem about the rafters being cut too short. Timber, he said, was an expensive item and he would like to find some way of using what he had. Dan replied that his son Barry, even in his short experience as an apprentice, might have come across a similar problem. Tom considered this. The boy's employers were thorough in their workmanship, they would not tolerate substandard work to be done in their name, but Henry's was an old house where mistakes could easily be hidden. However, Tom was taking full responsibility; nobody but himself and one other would be castigated for bad workmanship. So by all means, let the young lad go up there as soon as possible. "This evening," said Dan. "I will tell him to meet you there before seven o'clock."

In view of what had happened, faithful Dinny volunteered to help out, but it would have to be at a lesser level. They would both go down to Henry's on the pony trap. Young McCrory advised that the only thing was to cut up one or two of the lengths into pieces and nail them to the end of the short rafters. With Tom's blessing, he got to work. First, he accurately measured the distance and gradient of the roof and in a short time had things under control. It pleased Tom immensely to see the first two rafters fit neatly into place, and everyone worked in harmony. Even with his dented pride at the young whippersnapper knowing the source of the problem, Hess managed to operate in a tone of civility. By the time darkness had fallen, there was an impressive amount of work done and an agreement that Barry would return the next evening.

There was congeniality in the kitchen that night as Tom and Ciss sat down to supper; Henry and the children had gone to bed. Ciss was told about how clever a young man was the son of Dan and Aggie McCrory. Another evening or two would see them ready to nail down the asbestos sheets. The cost of paying the lad would not be too serious, three evenings at the most. Dinny should be able to nail down the roof under supervision from the Boss. Tom did not go so far as to say that in the presence of his subordinate. It was better not to re-ignite a smouldering fire. In the loft above, Peter was listening. He was hoping that they would not be doing the roof before Saturday. Homework and early bedtime was what was keeping him from seeing Barry McCrory at work. He had to make do with looking in on what had been done as he travelled to and from school.

It was early summer, just before the school holidays, and Maggie Dunne had not been to school for almost a week. Little notice was taken of her absence, and few enquiries were made about her. Although unable to show or say it, Peter missed sitting beside her. On many occasions, her quick prompting saved him from the wrath of Bull Herron. After school on Friday evening, his freedom took him in the direction of Henry's. He wanted to make a thorough inspection of the new roof, which had just been completed. As he was passing the point nearest to where Maggie lived, he eyed her standing at the door and looking in his direction. Wanting to ask why she had not been at school, he stopped and beckoned her to meet him at the fence. She looked frail and tired; her pretty eyes were red from sobbing. In distress she said her mother had been at the sanatorium since Sunday, Jimmy was gravely ill and little information was coming through to them at home.

It was now more than six months since Jimmy had been taken away. Like others so afflicted, the passage of time had him almost forgotten. When first we are confronted with the ravages of disease and suffering the effect is profound. Our pity is heartfelt, expressed with tears and a desire to help. However, all too soon, our feelings give way to other interests and concerns; what is uncomfortable will succumb to the impulses of a more ecstatic nature. Yet man cannot function by the ecstatic impulse alone, hence a more benevolent creature should be in control. "Should be," are the operative words, for in too many cases benevolence is usurped by an ugly and more sadistic component of nature. Nevertheless, for Jimmy that was all in the past, he was now surrounded by love and affection, the nursing staff were the epitome of goodness. Sally never left his bedside. On his last night, as she held him motherly in her arms, she could sense a peacefulness come over him. There was nothing else that could be done for his feeble body; medical intervention had nothing more to offer.

Jimmy's body was brought from the hospital to the parish church in Ballintober. Fr Gillen came later to the Dunnes' house and spent some time with the grief-stricken family. He talked and prayed with them in as reassuring a way as he could. At the burial service, the next morning he reminded them and others present that these prayers were for the bereaved only.

Jimmy Dunne was no longer in need of prayer: "He is the blessed one, now singing and playing happily with the angels in heaven." Both schoolteachers sat with the children, occupying the pews immediately behind the family. Their presence may have caused some to wonder what thoughts were going through their minds as the congregation wept in anguish for a precious little soul. Sally, who had stayed and held him tenderly until he slipped away from her, was now enwrapped in a peacefulness that was blissful. Jimmy had taken her grief with him, and now she was free to be there for them that needed her most.

The two of them would put Sally's strength and resilience severely to the test. Physically and mentally, Sammy was sinking, and Maggie's reaction to Jimmy's death was somewhat peculiar. She talked about her deceased brother as if he was still alive and with them. Every day she would spend time attending to the few remaining items that belonged to Jimmy, washing his clothes and polishing his shoes with meticulous devotion. Even his old schoolbag and books were cared for and arranged as if he would need them tomorrow. Denial was her way of grieving; she needed time and space to do so. Her mother's love and understanding were constant, but all too soon the poor woman had to return to work. This increased the melancholy of their lonely days, and there was nothing apparent that was going to make life any better. Again, Maggie would do her best for her Daddy but this time without the spirit that made her special.

chapter nine

As spring passed into the longer days of a new summer, attention shifted from the tedium of darkness to activities of a livelier sort. The fertile lushness of the countryside was refreshing and conducive to feelings of hope and promise. The white flowers of the hawthorn brightened up the laneways and the heather brought colour to the hills. The longer evenings invigorated the youth who were doing the things they were best at, playing games at the crossroads and devilish pranks on their detractors. Courting couples walked the byroads, not to be seen by Fr Gillen. No greater sin than to walk deliberately in the way of temptation: "Remember, there is no such thing as a venial sin of impurity." That was the theme of the annual parish mission, which reminded married couples that procreation was the sacred and sole reason for their union. Many promising relationships came to an abrupt end at mission time, just as there would be a sharp increase in the birth rate nine months later. The scruples of a deprived community were fairground for the doctrine of retribution. It usually took a couple of weeks for the fervour of virtue to subside sufficiently to allow nature to reassert itself. Fortunately for many, this did happen when the call of sensual love and romance was heeded. That was how things had to be; anything less would have been to the detriment of humankind.

This wanting was manifestly in evidence around the area; the likes of Uncle Henry, Dinny (Hess) and the Hawk McArt were object examples of this deprivation. They were not the authors of their earthly inheritance but their lot did not permit them the means to change it, and they were sadly set apart for the solitary state. Their sensual deficit was as pitiful as the material ills of people like the Dunnes. In their dreams, they fantasized how things might be, but the voice of virtue called a halt. Such things were not ordained for them, and unholy flesh had to be subdued. Life had brought them to a barren plateau beyond which there was no advance and where expectations fell in line. They lived on the fringes, far removed from the depth of human experience.

By late summer, Henry had not yet returned to his own house, even though work on the new roof had been completed for some time. The few remaining pieces were set aside until after the hay and flax had been secured. In farming practice, time always poses a problem. As one job is completed, another beckons, and soon it would be harvest time. The old man was ill at ease with the delay, but other things were more important.

Young Peter was happy to still have Henry living with the family. They were able to relate to each other at a time when Tom and Ciss barely noticed their presence because they were in the throes of preparing for greater things. Soon the new school term would begin and John would be leaving home to begin five years at boarding school, which they hoped would lead him towards greater things. They wondered how it would all turn out. Would their son achieve as they prayed he would, or were they really reaching beyond themselves? In any case, they had to try and hope for the means to see it through.

In bed at night, Peter and John were aware that these were the last days they would spend together as boys. John would be eighteen when he was finished at boarding school. They talked about how this change would affect them both and what direction their lives might take. No doubt, Peter was going to miss his brother, just as John would pine for home and family.

Peter thought about how different things might be at home with his rival sibling gone from the scene. It was a vain hope that he might replace John in the order of things. In the meantime, life had to go on in the usual manner. Just as before, the two boys would make themselves as useful as possible, gathering the blackberries and helping in the harvest field. At the same time, there was a feeling of change about the place; they were beginning to grow up and perhaps apart. From there on, they would be working in different fields; Peter's were the hilly ones of Cruckban, while John's were in the dreams of hope.

In such a climate it is nigh impossible to take on or even think about the demands of an old man who should be grateful for what he had. Uncle Henry's dream of moving back would just have to wait, perhaps until after the spuds were dug in October. Hess was the one to bring him the disappointing news: "At a time like this we have more to think about than the likes of you and your old shack," he snarled at the old man. Like the children, Henry's frailty and dependence made him forever vulnerable to the aggressor. Conquest is sweet; it invigorates the victor, elevating him to a state that becomes addictive, like soothing balm that is craved. Hess was always able to put in a strong performance on the home turf and probably had to use it as a means of compensating for his lack of immediacy in dealing with the likes of Hawk McArt or Timoney the street trader. Henry paused for a moment and smiled at Peter. "Aye you are right, Dinny, it is only an old shack, but after all it is my own," and that was how this brief encounter ended.

On the morning of John's departure Tom McGinn got the pony and trap ready while his wife packed the newly purchased suitcase. All the family were present, as it was a special day. An air of sadness beset the place, and not a word was spoken. Ciss broke the silence by telling John to get a move on, it was almost time for him to leave and catch the train. The goodbyes were an awkward affair but painful nonetheless; it was a totally new experience for all of them. Outside Tom disguised his pain by shouting his displeasure at a crowing rooster; he did not come into the house. Ciss' tears infected the others, most of all the boy who was leaving home. Her kissing him on the cheek was something that had never before been seen by any of them. Tom came in to collect the suitcase; it was parting time. John's gaze was focused straight ahead behind his father, as he faced the road ahead with a little nausea in his stomach. Uncle Henry slipped a green note into his trembling hand.

They were well down the road and out of sight before the others moved back into the house. Ciss was wet-eyed and praying silently without a listening ear to console her. Life progresses in stages, and for her this was a milestone; her firstborn and dearest had just gone away from her. Peter and Kitty were nervously quiet and unable to relate to their mother's distress. They just hoped for the day to brighten.

It would not be a speedy recovery, and the days and nights that followed were short on merriment, with Mr and Mrs McGinn having only one thing to talk about. Things did not improve much until after the first letter arrived. It was short and simple as they expected but enough to assure them that things were all right. John wrote that the place was a bit strange but that he was settling down. In truth, he was traumatised and afraid, though as a dutiful son he was not going to disappoint his proud parents. However, in such a place, life was tough and regimented, and the country boy had much to learn.

Tom visited his son almost four weeks later, and they were glad to see each other. John did his best at hiding much unhappiness and longing for home. He was very relieved to be taken out from the place that had imprisoned him for a period that seemed like a year. As they sat in a café having tea and buns, Tom related to him the entire goings on around Cruckban. The spuds were dug and Peter was back at school, not that it was going to do him much good, but they thought it best he accompany Kitty for another winter at least. They talked of his obsession about taking over as horseman, though according to Dinny that was unlikely to ever happen. He was not the type that could easily be taught any of the basic skills. Unlike his brother, he was lacking in all respects. At the same time, who could tell what way things would turn out? If Peter's dream should happen, Tom and Ciss would be pleased immensely, as the saving on wages was a prize to aim for.

Not having the confidence of his parents was something that Peter was well aware of. On many occasions, he overheard them discussing these very issues. This undermining of confidence can, in some cases, extract from the individual the highest endeavour. However, more often, its effects are destructive, and it can kill initiative to a point where one becomes afraid even to try. The understanding of this was surely beyond the comprehension of those so engrossed in the business of being successful and respectable. It fell to Uncle Henry to do the reassuring and he did so with good effect. Every night he and his young friend would talk themselves to sleep about better days ahead.

Henry brought up the subject of Peter to his hosts once when he found himself alone with them in the kitchen. This was not at all unusual as Ciss often planned such encounters to remind her guest about the good care and attention he was receiving from her. Such care and attention does not come cheap, but all she wanted was that he settled his affairs.

Henry stated that Peter was not getting as much attention as his absent brother, and that his future and welfare should be just as important as John's. He also reminded them that they had a very good wee girl there as well. Henry's intervention was not at all well received by the two; they were good and devoted parents who worked hard to provide for their children's needs. Peter wanted for nothing, he was fed, clothed and sent to school just the same as John had been; it was hardly their fault that the poor child happened to be dense. Henry did not like their choice of words but decided it was best to desist from further comment. Instead, he filled his pipe and went out for his evening dander. He hoped at least that the discussion might give cause for reflection and not be too discomforting for Tom and Ciss.

In the kitchen, Tom sat down heavily by the fire. There was an air of tension about both of them and they remained silent for a while. Then Tom composed his thoughts. "It would be better if we did not disturb him too much right now," he said to Ciss. "We know how much he has always taken to Peter."

"Indeed," said Ciss. "At least it shows that our Peter has some taking qualities after all."

"Yes, and do you not notice the old man growing feeble again? He may not be very much longer with us altogether."

Not long afterwards, Henry accompanied Tom and Ciss into town in the pony trap. He looked frail wrapped up in heavy warm clothing for the outing. They were going to see the solicitor about the making of Henry's last will and testament. The pony was stabled in Hanna's yard and all three went into the bar, hot whiskey on their minds. It's only in keeping with the ethics of delicate family business that we drink to the success of what we are about to execute. After fortifying themselves at Hanna's, Tom and Ciss accompanied Henry to the solicitor's waiting room but were debarred from the table of execution. This arrangement suited the testator; he was not one who took kindly to being told what he should do. The entire transaction took no longer than twenty minutes, the solicitor and one of his staff members acted as witness, hence giving it legal and binding status. Ciss suggested they go back to Hanna's for another drink and perhaps a cup of tea, as she was most anxious to get some indication as to what the old boy had done. However, despite her best efforts, Henry was not giving much away.

As the days and weeks passed, she grew more anxious and agitated. Why, she wondered, was he so secretive about this matter? Could he have played them all for fools? She suspected he had paid the funeral expenses of the wee Dunne boy who died during the summer. She could not be sure about this, but Fr Gillen was overheard praising him for his very commendable gesture at around that time. For some reason or other, she showed uneasiness about this impoverished family. The Dunne woman, as she usually called her, seemed to be over-attentive towards the old man, especially at a time when she had more than enough trouble of her own. Tom tried hard to ease her anxiety by reasoning that the poor woman was of a kind disposition and had no interest in Henry's possessions. "In any case the man is appreciative of what you have done for him and he has a deep loyalty to family." With these reassurances, Ciss relaxed a little; it was best to simply wait and see.

The wait would not be very long, for within a few weeks Henry was found lying by the roadside near the entrance to the track that led to his old home. Peen McDevitt was on the road going rabbit hunting on the hill; it was the dog that drew his attention to the man who was barely conscious. Recognising it to be old Henry Meehan, he bent down and tried talking to him. The old man's speech was so hard to follow that Peen gave up and ran towards the house. He found Tom and Ciss and helped them to bring the patient home on an improvised stretcher made from heavy corn sacks. Henry made no response to their comforting words of reassurance; his eyes were closed and he breathed heavily. This time the ambulance was brought to take him to the infirmary, as there was no way that Dr Martin could get him into his car. The doctor told Ciss that her uncle was gravely ill and was unlikely to ever recover. Peter and Kitty had not yet returned from school, and their parents were pleased that they had not had to witness this unpleasant scene.

At the hospital it was noted how clean and tidy Henry looked compared to the last time. This was due to the good care he was getting from his niece. What money he had amounted to nearly two hundred pounds, and it was in the inside pocket of the coat he was wearing. Ciss took possession and put it safely away; she said it would be needed to pay the hospital expenses in the event of him having a prolonged stay there. It seemed unlikely that he had additional assets or deposits other than the little Blue Rock Farm. However, the question of why he was carrying all this money bewildered her; he had never done anything like that before. As for the will he had made a few weeks earlier, there was little likelihood he would ever be able to revoke it, it was just a matter of waiting it out.

The children arrived home from school to find Ciss sitting quietly in the kitchen. They could tell something was wrong. She gave them their dinner and then told them the sad news about Henry. She would write to John later. Peter was noticeably upset and wanted to know more about what had taken place. He talked about the old house and how much Henry wanted to go back and live there again. It looked like he was attempting to go down that way but failed to make it.

In rural Ireland, this has been referred to as walking the land and seen as an omen for imminent death. Something instinctive and unique to the people of the land, its call must be answered before the final bugle. This folklorist phenomenon explained most of what had taken place with Henry, but why he had taken the money with him remained a mystery.

Except for Peter, his departure would not be the cause of pathetic grief among those remaining. The ritual of tears and pious platitude would be fully enacted before getting down to the real business. For the first couple of days Ciss spent a lot of time at her uncle's bedside. She wondered was he aware of her presence or indeed if he appreciated it. It was easier for her to sit with him now, as she did not have to communicate with him in words. This had always been difficult for her; there was something regressive about her attitude towards him. However, right now Ciss McGinn had a duty to perform. As family, she could not be seen wanting in relation to doing what was right and honourable.

Hess was not at all happy about the woman of the house being away so much. Tom was not the best in the kitchen and mealtimes were not occasions to look forward to. These were days when Peter and wee Kitty knew to keep well clear of the workingman. The tea and bread they brought him to the field was never right. "Why does that woman have to spend so much time with an old hoor that will soon be coming back in the boards, and that pretence dinner is enough to give a fuckin' horse the bound ups?" He went on to tell them that if things did not improve, the Boss would have to make do with a lesser man.

His employers took on board the message, and Ciss and

Tom began to make do with alternate evening visits to the hospital. They could not afford to lose such a fine workman through neglect; it must not be allowed to happen. They had not forgotten the last time Dinny had left them in the lurch several years ago. It would have been a disaster had they not found the young man from the Glensmoyle side of the hill. His name was Artie, and he was always full of joy and laughter. He liked to play games with John and Peter, who were small children at the time. Their memories of him would always be of fondness; those six months with Artie was a time of playful innocence. Peter's earliest memory was of being carried on Artie's back to the summit of the Foyde. From the ring fort at the top, they were able to see the entire Lagan Valley as well as both cathedral spires in the city of Derry. For the boys that happy time was all too short as Hess soon re-established himself and was again calling the tune.

This meant that the old man's needs must not be allowed disrupt the Hess rhythm. In any case, nobody knew how long old Henry would last, so it might be better to save their energies for a more needy time. Under this arrangement things returned to near normal and everyone was almost happy again.

Ciss valued her reputation for feeding the workers the best of fare; in fact, Hess was more than a little spoiled by its quality and presentation. He talked disparagingly about a few places in the neighbourhood where he had worked and where the dogs were always overfed. As a way of stressing his expectations to Ciss, he would relate to her the stories about life with a particular farmer from the other side of the hill called Monty. He was an aging bachelor who kept two workmen and a servant maid (come cook) on his hundred-acre farm. Hess was of little doubt that the poor man eventually died from hunger or through the consumption of something raw and indigestible. The cook of this establishment was called Biddy The Rum and she was considered the worst in the country. She was as black as the metal pots she used for cooking on the open fire. The food was always cold and undercooked, and the milk was sour and curdled with a heavy, sickening smell emitting from what was called the kitchen. Some wondered was it even safe to eat the potatoes that this woman had dug, not to mention the bread she baked, but old Monty seemed pleased enough.

She was unquestionably the law around that place; nobody

dared to criticise or slight the Rum. Her tongue was like a hacksaw blade, sharp and rough. She usually saved her fire until she had her prey in a public place. This was most likely when she had consumed a quantity of black Jamaica Rum, and in her inebriated state Biddy settled many a score to the grief of her victims. For that reason, the workingmen suffered in silence and longed for the end of their six-month contract. However, Biddy outlasted all of them, remaining faithful until the demise of her employer. Her liking for the wee drop kept her close to Monty for as long as he felt that way, a feeling that ended sooner than it should have. After his death, she married the quiet yardman named Dim Corr. The Hawk McArt thought him aptly named 'Dim', totally devoid of either life or humour, but who could be other, living with Biddy The Rum? Nevertheless, he was still around and working for the Captain, and they were still living in an old shack near the Dunnes, not far from the village. Biddy now filled her idle days exchanging whatever gossip she could glean about those around her.

chapter ten

When John returned for the Christmas holidays, his parents became concerned about his physical condition. He looked a bit pale and gaunt, and he was having difficulty with the severity of the institutional regime. The boy was obviously distressed and unhappy about all of it, and once again, the quality and quantity of the food was very much an issue. On this occasion, there was little that could be done. Parents had little control beyond taking their child from the place; it was a case of take or leave it. No concession could be entertained there. This was going to make Christmas an anxious time for all the family.

The holiday period would be short, and Tom and Ciss knew a firm decision needed to be taken and taken soon. Their son's happiness and peace of mind was important to both of them, but equally important was his education and the privileged status that went with it. Every night John was taken to the parlour and sat down to a warm fire, where they talked at length and reassuringly to him. None of the others was permitted.

Both Tom and Ciss expected a good return from their investment in terms of their son's success and were alarmed that John's unhappiness might put it all in jeopardy. What if he failed to achieve what they envisaged for him? It was a discomforting thought indeed, and they prayed it would not happen. The priesthood was still very much on the mind of proud Ciss McGinn.

They were reluctant to seek the advice of Fr Gillen, as they felt that such a disclosure about their son would be a big letdown. Would the priest think their boy did not possess the necessary qualities or suitability for academic success? They had enjoyed a curious admiration from the common folk of the parish; young John McGinn was no longer an ordinary boy from Cruckban.

They need not have worried. The good man of the cloth was friendly and receptive, and he told them a little about his own experience and doubts many years ago, which were not at all dissimilar to John's situation. In spite of the fact that he had a priest uncle teaching there, things were by no means easy. After all, this boy had only been there for a short while, soon he would form friendships and interests, and there would be numerous activities for him to engage in. As for the food, he agreed that some things are slow to change. "We just had to make do and rely on what came from home and I was often hungry," he told them.

Regardless of what John felt or hoped for, the priest's advice did have an effect on Tom and Ciss, and they persuaded John to give it another try, at least for the remainder of the year. Who knows, by that time maybe he would develop a liking for the place. In the meantime, they would have to intensify their praying. Ciss had little doubt it was through prayer that John came to be in college in the first place. Now they would have to continue more than ever. "We will have to be making more frequent visits to John with a constant supply of homemade bread."

John passively assented to his parents' wishes; he was always most anxious to do what was pleasing to them. In any case, the comfort of home life could well turn out to be a doubtful blessing if it was to the disillusionment of his parents, who had invested so much of themselves in this programme. With this decision taken, an air of normality returned to the house of McGinn, and the daily routine was smoothly on track once again.

As a school boarder, John was permitted an occasional visit to the cinema along with other students. Peter listened with keen interest as his brother recounted the exploits of John Wayne and Roy Rogers. That was as near as poor Peter would get to experiencing such ventures for himself. Going to the pictures was a popular recreation for the young people of the area, but according to Mr and Mrs McGinn, it was neither a good nor a virtuous practice for a boy to engage in. In their opinion, only those who knew no better, the commonest of people devoid of intellect or ambition, pursued it. Money was too hard to come by to be wasted on such devilish things. It was very different in John's case. The wise men that ran the college knew what was good and educational, and this was simply part of his training. Whatever about the educational merits of John Wayne and Roy Rogers, Peter was not expected to understand the value of sound advice; he was not endowed with such discernment. At the same time, he did wonder about not being able to do like others of his age. Was it really a privilege to be as he was?

Because of John's problems it was not the happiest Christmas in Cruckban, but the religious and feasting routine were followed through fastidiously as usual. On the day before John was due to go back, word came from the hospital that it was close to the end for Uncle Henry. In fact, he slipped away just before Ciss and Tom had time to get there. They knew from their last visit that the end was nearing but were somewhat surprised that it happened so soon. With haste, all arrangements were put in place regarding the funeral. Dixie Quinn, the undertaker, would bring the remains to Cruckban before dark and Dan McCrory would bring the supplies for the two nights of wake, including tea, sugar, bread, butter and plenty of red jam. A quantity of cigarettes would also be needed for the customary handing round.

Peter was afraid to go into the parlour where Uncle Henry was laid out in an open casket that rested on two sturdy wooden stools. It was the first time the children were confronted with the reality of death, though they may have heard adults talking about the subject from time to time. They could remember the tragedy of their young friend Jimmy Dunne and still got upset about him, but this time it was right before their eyes and in their own home. Every effort was made to protect wee Kitty from the sight of that dismal casket. Peter knew he had lost his true friend. He had gotten used to Henry being away from the place, but this time his leaving would be final. As for John, this meant an extra few days at home.

It was the novelty of seeing the constant stream of people coming and going that took their young minds away from what had taken place. Men and women from the surrounding area came to the house and shook their parents' hands, saying "Sorry for your trouble", while neighbour women came to help with the tea. On the second night, the numbers increased considerably and continued until the early hours of the morning. The entire household, including Hess, stayed on duty throughout; a couple of hours sleep may have been snatched during the day. Sally Dunne appeared on the second evening, shortly after dark, with daughter Maggie accompanying her. They were given a cup of tea by one of the neighbour women and they left again after extending sympathy to the bereaved. Tom was his usual affable self, and he thanked her sincerely and enquired about her husband. Ciss was more circumspect and appeared to be busy on other matters.

Peter and Maggie exchanged brief words out in the yard as Sally had stopped with two other visitors on their way in. He talked to her about the strangeness of seeing his dead uncle and why it was that people had to die. Maggie could identify with his turbulent thoughts; her own grief had not subsided. She wiped the tears from her eyes and smiled a little, then taking her mother's arm moved off down the narrow road. Peter remained standing and holding the two cigarettes he had managed to retrieve from one of the plates that were provided according to custom. It was his intention to explore the mystery of the manly habit; he had also hoped that Maggie Dunne would willingly be his accomplice. The brevity of her visit put paid to his cunning scheme, and instead he decided to try it alone. Armed with two Sweet Aftons and a box of matches he slipped quietly behind the turnip shed. He coughed at first from the burning sensation of the smoke hitting the tender palate, but soon found relaxation beneath a bright moonlit sky, listening to drifts of conversation coming his way from the wake house.

Waves of sensation gradually took hold of the bold adventurer and before he reached the halfway mark, the moon had given birth to a thousand stars. Unable to rise from his sitting position and the shifting earth moving away from him, a nauseate numbness weighed heavily upon him. He languished silently for a while on the frosty ground, but by the time he regained composure the figure of a man was standing over him. "What have you been up to?" spoke the voice he recognised to be that of the workman. Hess was holding the half-spent cigarette and matches in his hand, and he sounded just like he had pulled off a major coup. "By Jaysus I have you this time," he laughed to himself. "Come on till I see your old boy." Nothing would have pleased him more than to see Peter being smacked and humiliated in the presence of the visitors.

Peter was dragged into the parlour to face the assembled group. Tom and the others present received Dinny's account of Peter's transgression with amusement. The setting was not conducive to chastisement, but some form of reprimand might come later. Relieved that it had all ended so well, Peter left the room, pleased but unlikely to forget his first nicotine fix.

Three days after Henry had been laid to rest, Tom McGinn received a letter from the solicitor informing him that he and his wife were the executors to Henry's will. As requested, they went immediately to the office. The encounter was brief but detailed, the terms were simple and easy to execute. They were somewhat surprised to learn that there was still one hundred and fifty pounds remaining in deposit with the Hibernian Bank, some of it to be used by them to cover funeral and other expenses (though it remained a mystery what Uncle Henry had intended to do with the other two hundred pounds he had with him the day he collapsed). "The holding known as the Blue Rock Farm plus one hundred pounds shall come to the ownership of Peter McGinn, the second son of the executors, when he reaches the age of twenty-one years. In the intervening period, the said property is to be used and maintained by the executors." This was by no means disappointing news for Tom and Ciss. They had already come to a decision regarding their two sons. Peter was for the land and this was indeed good news. Hopefully, he might improve and acquire enough usefulness to be one day worthy of his inheritance.

In jovial mood they took leave of their legal mentor and headed for the nearest licensed establishment. There they sat at a glowing fire and talked with some emotion about their good fortune. Now with sixty acres of holding they could be described as substantial farmers. It mattered little who was the registered owner; the McGinn farm would be a thriving family enterprise. Their feeling was that the boy beneficiary had a right to be told of what was bequeathed to him. It might even give him the impetus to smarten up.

The following morning, while Tom and Hess were out in the fields, Peter was helping Ciss with the milking of the cows. She said, "Peter, do you know that Uncle Henry has left you his farm and some money as well?"

This news was a bit frightening for the boy who had never before been taken seriously. Turning away from his milking, he looked at his mother and asked, "Mammy, won't I be getting this home farm as well when I grow up?"

Ciss gave him a questioning glance and replied, "Yes, if

you can prove yourself suitable for such responsibility."

For Peter this was already part of his dream come true. He was overwhelmed and had difficulty comprehending what all of this meant. In spite of Henry's liking for Peter, at no time did he ever signal his intentions to him or to any member of the family. Now all that had to be done was wait for the growing up. At thirteen, that day seemed tediously slow in drawing nearer, but perhaps in another couple of years he would assume greater responsibility for the running of the home farm in Cruckban. Uncle Henry's generosity had certainly boosted his confidence in that direction. He worked hard and with enthusiasm throughout that spring and summer.

chapter eleven

John went back to college and successfully completed his first year. His results were considered reasonably good and were proudly extolled by his doting parents. It now looked like he would be returning there in the autumn. By no means happy, he nevertheless made up his mind to weather it out. By now, Uncle Henry and his bequest had long been forgotten, though there was the occasional derisory comment from Hess about Peter and his Blue Rock. Peter remained small in stature, perhaps underdeveloped for his thirteen years. Nevertheless, his determination was strong, with a willingness to do the work of a man. One night in his lonely loft room, he heard Tom say to Ciss, "He might be more useful at home, and God knows, he is doing his best to be useful."

Believing he would not be going back to school after the potato gathering, he said as much to Maggie Dunne. He went on to tell her that the field in which they were now working was actually his property and he would no longer be walking with the other children on that morbid track. Sister Kitty was now well able to manage on her own.

At Mass the following Sunday Fr Gillen was uncompromisingly cross. He laid down the law with a stern warning to those parents who were abusing the potato gathering concession. He would not hesitate in bringing them to the attention of the Guards; too many children were roaming around under the pretext of earning this supposedly needed money. "Mind you, very little of it ever makes its way to the stipend collection." He rounded off with a promise to visit the homes of every defaulting family and said there had better be a good explanation. Many in the congregation became uneasy and felt as if he was talking directly to them. Sitting in the front pews, which were always reserved for the children, Peter wondered about his parents and how they were receiving the priestly warning. There was little to question on that one; no respectable parent would turn a deaf ear to a sacred pronouncement from the pulpit. To do so would be a breach of sacred trust, not in keeping with what was expected from the parents of a promising student.

The next morning Peter was walking the track to school crestfallen and dejected. This humiliation in front of Maggie was more than he could bear. However, much worse was the fact that he had to face the Bull for another time, and he was in the grip of a terrible fear of the violence that awaited him. He was not alone in his plight. The warning from the pulpit had taken effect, and it would be another morning of retribution for those who had missed the beginning of the school term. Knowing the futility of offering any kind of excuse or pleading for mercy, Peter passively awaited his lot. His tortured mind was totally blank. Fear and confusion beset him. For him life and consciousness was anything but a blessing. Like many such mornings his only wish was to fall into one of the deep holes of the Mondeel River, but such an option was denied. The doctrine of retribution frightened him even more; the wrath of an angry God and the flames of eternal hell awaited such souls with vengeance.

The lashes to the buttocks that Peter received were lengthy and severe, and he screamed lamentably long after he resumed his seat. When justice had finally been executed, the books were opened and work began. Peter, feeling nauseous and sore, requested permission to go out to the lavatory, but he had another plan in mind. It might have worked but for the mistake he made of taking his schoolbag with him. Bull observed this and quickly moved to the front window. Looking out he could see the boy running out the gate and across the field towards the bridge. Like a flash, he left the room in pursuit, shouting furiously and threateningly. The children scrambled to stand on top of the desks to get a good look out the windows at the chase from the classroom. All except Kitty McGinn, who sat in terrified fear, Peter tried hard to reach the steps at the far side of the bridge that would have taken him to the track down the long meadow and safety. However, before he got that far the strong manly grip seized him by the collar of his jacket. It was a painful grip, where he could feel the sensations of choking while being dragged back in haste. The villagers stood in awe at the spectacle of such manly conquest over a delicate thirteen-year-old.

What followed once the Bull had dragged Peter back to the classroom was a scene never to be forgotten, much more violent than the one involving Jimmy Dunne. Peter fell helplessly to the floor, weak from exhaustion and asphyxia. Bull screeched and yelled with uncontrolled rage, and he lashed with all the power of his being at what was sprawling feebly on the floor beneath him. When the arms got tired from using the strap, he would throw in the occasional kick for good measure. A good five minutes had passed before Peter's ordeal came to an end, by which time he was barely able to get up from where he crouched. His respite was only for a short while; several times that day he was recalled to the table, each time for a different offence. For defiance of authority, for disrupting the class, but worst of all for exposing the Master to public humiliation. Each of these occasions was almost as horrific as the first, and the entire class sat spellbound. Maggie Dunne clasped his aching hands each time he came back to the seat beside her. She wept for him and the memories it invoked of her dead brother. Outside there were people listening to the commotion; they were concerned people, but lacked the courage to take any kind of action.

chapter twelve

There was only one person capable of doing something about bddringing this disdainful savage to heel, but unfortunately, this man was afraid of going too far. There was a real danger of Tom McGinn doing something that would have serious consequences for school and parish — some hope. Both he and his wife were deeply disturbed about their traumatised son; they were tenderly attentive towards him all that evening and night. Wee Kitty was also in need of attention; after all, it was she who had had to endure watching the violation of her brother.

After lengthy deliberation well into the night, it was decided not to make too much fuss about the incident. They would keep Peter at home for a while and with a bit of luck his absence might be overlooked for the remainder of the year. Not having Uncle Henry to turn to for reassurance was a loss deeply felt by Peter that shivering night. It was not good for him to be left alone after what had happened, but nobody seemed to be taking this into account.

After a sleepless night, Peter was found in a deep state of anxiety. He was still in bed but not responding to the morning call. He was unresponsive to any form of stimulus, with little or no interest in his surroundings. Dr Martin was called and, on hearing the story, administered a sedative and advised that the boy be kept under close observation for a few days. However, how does one measure recovery from an ordeal such as this? True, the welts and bruises to the flesh will fade away, but not so easily the damage done to the inner person. These torturous recalls would forever intrude upon the consciousness of Peter McGinn, nor would what was done to him ever be forgotten by those that witnessed it.

This was to be the cost of Peter's deliverance from the education system; it was a brutal ending to a lengthy incarceration. The doctor certified him not to be well enough to withstand the demands of a stressful routine. Fr Gillen got to hear about the incident through another source, but he scarcely ever mentioned it to either Tom or his wife. At the same time, he was appreciative of their acting responsibly and refraining from the sort of action that might hinder the good work of the school. As respectable and responsible people, there was no need to remind them that the system was put in place for the good of the child. Everything that happened there was executed with good intent. Tom and Ciss were falling increasingly under the spell of this doctrine. With a son in college and showing signs of promise, they could not succumb to common behaviour. There was perhaps more to be gained from being respectable than from doing what was right.

Nonetheless, the days and weeks that followed saw them do what was right by Peter, which was to reassure him that no matter what, never again would he enter the door of Ballintober National School. Soon a much happier boy began to emerge. It was finally over. He remained indoors for most of that winter but longed for the days of spring and work in the fields. His dreams about the future had not diminished.

A slight and welcome diversion took place that winter with the arrival of a consignment of books that Tom had purchased for a few shillings at a clearance sale in one of the oldest residences in the area. They occupied most of the floor and sitting space of the pony trap that ferried them to Cruckban. "These will look well on the bookshelf in the parlour," commented Ciss.

"Yes," Tom replied, "and they could be of much benefit to John as well."

Perhaps there was even something among them that the Boss himself might find interesting. There was also the added value of status at an affordable price. After all, books are indicative of substance.

Their greatest value was in the fact that they were varied; they could have catered for a plethora of tastes as well as intellectual strengths. Strange to say, it was Peter who first began searching through the pile of literature. He found something that seemed interesting and with a simple storyline. Reading slowly as his lexicon would only permit; he spent his days following the story about a boy and his dog. By the time he reached the happy ending, the joy of reading had taken hold;

soon he was in search of another read. In this way, his period of recuperation became a happy time, and it would be fair to say that by the end of winter Peter had read substantially more than he ever did during his entire schooldays. Through this source, his reading skills vastly improved, as did the quality of the material he was choosing. Books were no longer his enemy; he could see them in a light so different to what was contained in that old schoolbag.

There was an irony about Peter's rescue through the power of literature. Along with his passionate desire to be a farmer, it occupied a sizeable portion of his interest and thinking. A rescue it well turned out to be, because right through the spring and summer he worked hard and joyfully in the fields. There were other changes coming over him as well; his physique and disposition were developing positively and fast. The healing power that comes from contentment and peace of mind was all evident about him. He was now able to assess the value of his own contribution, and not afraid to say so to them that once belittled him. By November, and him almost fourteen, he informed Tom that he felt ready to take over from Dinny as ploughman. His goodness and willingness were highly commended, but declined because he was a bit young and did not have the practical experience. Peter accepted this reasoning but pointed out the difficulty of acquiring the necessary skills while that man was still around. He could also sense that there was reluctance on the part of his parents about letting the wee man go.

It was laudable that an employer should have such loyalty as to show concerns about the future of a faithful servant man. At the same time, this man laid claims to being the best in the land, and that every substantial farmer in the Moneen Valley was actively seeking his service. However, Peter's own concerns were real. How could he ever be seen as a person of worth? Was he going to remain the errand boy forever? By assuming the manly role, his status would increase tenfold; he would earn pocket money, which would enable him to be like other boys of his age.

He was starting to realise that there was a world beyond the values he had internalised and it was not all bad. As yet, this was not his world; he had neither permission nor the means to be part of it. However, a second-hand bicycle was bought for him at Christmas. It was considered to be something a boy of his age would need. They could see nothing wrong about a fourteen-year-old boy taking a bike run through the countryside of a Sunday evening when the days got longer.

Peter accepted the gesture for what it was, though it did not represent freedom for him to be what he felt he was. He would have much preferred to read his books on the afternoon of the Sabbath and then be free to go with his friends to play football later in the evening. Although not yet equipped to express his feelings, he did have serious doubts about the merits of his introverted socialisation. Brother John, now moving into the senior ranks of college life, was anything but helpful. To the pleasure of his parents, he derided the value of practices such as going to the cinema or even playing football. He had experienced all of these things and was able to make a mature judgment about them. It was much to John's advantage that he took this stand; he knew it was what his parents wanted him to say, especially in front of Peter. They also saw it as the rich fruits of what they had laboured for. This was the advice of one who was educated and knew what he was talking about, not at all like the ones Peter was aspiring to be like.

Peter began using his bike to go to Mass on Sundays, he had outgrown the pony and trap and the parental control it represented. In this way, he could at least be like his peers rather than the lifeless zombie he was afraid of being perceived to be. His tentative steps towards independence were less than welcome at home. Why, they wondered, could he not keep faith with the family principle of exclusiveness?

In recognition of John's faithfulness, he was rewarded with a blue gabardine coat and skullcap that was emblazoned with a suitable emblem. Wearing it was a heavy price for a young teenager to pay for his eagerness to please. In truth, he had no desire to be aloof from normal society nor did his rhetoric represent how he really felt. Like any other adolescent boy, he liked to do all the things he so conveniently disparaged, but in the interest of peace and a comfortable home life, it was better to play along with the illusion.

It was a source of amusement for Peter, then, the day that John came home from First Friday Mass without his skullcap. The fracas that followed was loud and inflamed, and the inquisition was intense. He was not sure if he had left it behind in the church or lost it on his way home. In any case, Tom said it was a case of sheer carelessness, ill becoming a person in his position. Without success John retraced his steps all the way back to the gallery of Ballintober Chapel, where he had sat for morning Mass. The gallery was upstairs and out of view of the priest, and was frequented by the more common type of people. The precious skullcap had vanished it simply was no more. "What the hell took you to the gallery?" was Tom's final say on the matter. It was not considered the proper place for a promising young man to be seated in church. The story of what happened to the cap has never been revealed. Was it really lost or simply discarded by the self-conscious young lad who was condemned to wear it? There was a reported sighting of it floating down the Mondeel under Tylefort Bridge.

chapter thirteen

Peter worked hard throughout that summer and harvest, and by now, he was beginning to acquire many of the skills that were considered to be the exclusive remit of self-assured men. He even managed an occasional turn with the horses when Hess was otherwise engaged. By November, Peter had grown to be almost as big as his brother was. However, he was still without practical experience in horsemanship, an area of expertise Hess was determined to keep to himself. A few nights before the hiring fair Tom suggested to Peter that he should consider going for a while to work on a larger farm. A period of apprenticeship would teach him new and more progressive ways and at fifteen, he should be entitled to a few shillings of payment as well. This, he was assured, should leave him well ready to take over the reins next year.

Tom had a farmer cousin to whom he was favourably disposed, and in farming circles he was considered extensive and thorough. The place was ten miles further down the Lagan country. Maurice Farrell and his wife Susan were friendly and welcoming people, and it should be easy to feel at home with them. Ciss liked the idea of Peter going to be with respectable people who also happened to be related, and a period of six months apprenticeship was arranged.

A little sorry on the Sunday evening, Peter cycled the ten miles to the Lagan, but he was comforted by the fact that he would be returning at the weekends. Maurice and Susan Farrell greeted him warmly and fed him a wholesome meal. From the start, he got a very good feeling about this place.

The Farrells had one son, Paddy, who was in his early twenties. Their eldest child was daughter Antoinette who lived and worked as a teacher in Derry. Paddy was ploughman and good at his work. They also kept a young man from the neighbourhood called Norman, who was about three years older than Peter. He was tall with a robust physique, friendly at first, and willingly showed the young apprentice the ways of the place. It was a vastly different scene to what he was used to in Cruckban, and everything was greater in size. Paddy was in charge of two mighty Clydesdale horses that tilled the flat fertile fields overlooking Lough Swilly. Another Clydesdale was kept as spare and for heavy cultivating in the spring. Norman used an old quiet carthorse for bringing the produce in from the fields.

Peter soon found his niche there and worked with enthusiasm both in the farmyard and out in the fields. He particularly liked trimming the hedges in the fields where Paddy was ploughing. There he was allowed to take an occasional turn with the horses, and it was then that he was at his happiest, knowing Paddy was his friend.

As the farm was mainly tillage and drystock enterprise, Peter was allowed to go home for most of the weekends. He rode the bike home to Cruckban on a Saturday evening and did not return until Sunday evening or Monday morning. His parents were pleased to see him and to know that he was happy with his relations.

By the second week, Peter noticed that Norman was becoming bossier and less friendly. He would give sharp orders to Peter and always addressed him as "Young Buck" instead of by his proper name. This, he soon learned, was the mark of a true bully who liked to belittle and put fear into the timid. He was preoccupied with his genitalia and the greatness of his sexual virility. On this, Peter was no match for him. Owing to his sheltered upbringing his knowledge in this field was somewhat stinted. At the same time, through his reading he had managed to acquire more than the basics about human sexuality as well as its conflict with morality. However, his refusal to engage in this fellow's sickly obsession brought him further belittlement and made him the victim of taunts and ridicule. Peter was no different from any other fifteen-year-old boy; he was aware of the sensual nature of his own body and wondered about the mystery of the female form. However, he was ill equipped to take on board the aggressive crudeness of what came from the mouth of this beastly individual.

Peter liked going with Paddy to the village shop in the evenings after work, as it was a popular gathering place for a variety of country folk. The younger ones usually congregated on the road outside the shop door; there they could spend a couple of hours engaged in youthful chat and devilish pranks. Paddy Farrell's cousin got a friendly welcome from the boys and girls; it was a sign of Paddy's own popularity. To Peter this represented freedom. Here he could be an ordinary teenage lad, free from the shackles of respectability. He was comfortable in the company of these people and was able to acknowledge the attention of the girls without embarrassment. What went on there was no different to what it was in his own village of Dooras, which he only knew through fleeting visits. Nevertheless, this little place was his heaven; he enjoyed the lively company that made him feel he was one of them.

That was until the evening Norman appeared on the scene. His presence immediately provoked uneasiness in Peter, and somehow he knew that things would never be the same again. In the crudest possible expression, Peter was exposed as "the young buck fresh from the tit and not knowing what his thing was for". Spoken in the only vocabulary Norman was capable of, it sounded funny to the others and was received with some laughter. The young people were not concurring with Norman but they lacked the sensitivity to understand how damaging such exposure and humiliation can be to a self-conscious young person. There is nothing more debasing than to be the centre of ridicule to the amusement of others, especially when the others happen to be your friends. Even Paddy gave a thoughtless laugh and dismissed it as only a bit of local craic. On their way back home, he sensed Peter's unease and assured him that big Norman meant no harm; that was just the kind he was, "just a bit of craic".'

Good as Paddy was, he failed to understand that this was bullying of the worst kind and that his workman was by no means harmless. Even though Paddy was more than able to bring this fellow down to size, too often he stood and listened to him castigating his young friend in a most vile manner. That was until the night he had to intervene when things began to go too far. It was again outside the village shop. Norman thought it would be a good idea to take the trousers off Peter and expose him to the others. He almost succeeded but for Paddy coming to the rescue on seeing the distress it was causing to his young friend. Norman quickly backed off from the advance of a better man, and the others stood in anticipation of a fight that never happened. Peter was lying on the ground trying to regain his breath from severe hurt to his private parts; this had been inflicted before his ordeal was brought to an end. The pain was excruciating, but the confrontation between the other two took the focus away from his moaning. He recovered and composed himself enough to make it appear that all was well again. It was now time for Paddy and him to leave, only this time he would not be returning.

His injuries were such that he had to keep silent about them, they were much too personal and private. A bit frightened by the sight of the bruising caused by the abuser's hand, he was sore and uncomfortable and it would take time for him to heal. Over the next couple of weeks, he did manage with difficulty to carry on working. As for Norman, he chose to ignore Peter in the days that followed and his relationship with Paddy was far less easy than it used to be. By the end of the second week, he was gone from the place but certainly not forgotten. This was a tremendous relief for young Peter; now he was able do his work in peace and enjoy the goodness of the people he was with.

It was a laborious journey home that weekend on the old bike, but he still kept his injuries to himself. In truth, he told all of them that he liked the place and was happy to be there. He would now be in charge of the old carthorse and it was something he very much looked forward to. He spoke praising words about all the Farrells, especially his friend Paddy who was teaching him well.

He would have very much liked to go back to the village with Paddy, but knowing that his bullying adversary was still frequenting the place, he went back to his books instead. Maurice Farrell was a keen rod fisherman who spent most of his spare time fishing the rivers and lakes of Donegal and far beyond. He was also an expert at tying colourful fly hooks, an art that fascinated Peter. It was that, along with his reading, that compensated for the loss he felt at not being able to join his friends in the village. In recognition of his interest, Maurice promised to take him one day to the river when the days lengthened. The idea very much appealed to Peter — it would be something new and interesting, and this was a promise that Maurice would not be allowed forget.

Susan was a kind and motherly type of person who epitomised contentment; her mission in life was to see that everything and everybody was well. Her only other interest was the

Irish language. Coming from an area close to the Gaeltach, she worked hard to preserve the mother tongue and pass it on to others. Not surprising then that daughter Antoinette happened to be an Irish language teacher. However, the menfolk could never manage more than a couple of words, like *"Na abair smid"* when asking others to show restraint. All of these things made it a blissfully happy time for the young lad from Cruckban. He was learning to do the things that he loved and now other things as well.

The date of the Lagan ploughing competition was ringed on the calendar that hung on the kitchen wall; it was to take place on the twenty-first of January. This was an event that enthused the entire family and commanded their full attention for weeks beforehand. Not only because it was a local event, but Paddy would be defending his title there as well.

Little work beyond the necessities was carried out for the three days preceding the event and the two horses were clipped and groomed to excellence. The leather harness had to be meticulously oiled and blackened with shoe polish and the brass buckles polished to a shine. Even the old plough and chains were painted like new. On the night before, Susan offered a prayer that the Good Lord would bless the event and that Paddy would give of his best.

It was a fine dry morning as the two cousins left the yard in search of glory. Maurice and Susan looked with pride at the impressive turnout; they would drive over later in the old Ford Prefect and bring refreshments for the boys. The competition for presentation and appearance was always judged at the start, and their entry was registered in the name of Maurice Farrell. Paddy would compete for himself later as champion ploughman.

Peter was given the honour of driving the entry around the arena for inspection by the judges, and this made him the proudest young man at the gathering. This part of the competition attracted a lot of interest; these majestic animals with their ornamental tassels and plaited manes were quite appealing to the aesthetic eye. The results would not be announced until after the ploughing had finished, which was usually around four in the afternoon. There was much speculation and debate among the local people as to what the result would be; it would be a hard decision, as all of them looked equally excellent.

Small work was made of the picnic basket that Susan brought to the two young men, while Maurice attended to the horses with a supply of quality hay. Paddy had begun ploughing the plot of land allotted to him, and Peter was of the opinion that Paddy's work was much superior to all the others. He took Maurice around the field on a tour of inspection. "I support your judgment, young man," said Maurice. "I think he is going to do it another time, but we must wait for the judges' verdict."

They wandered around, checking the work of Paddy's rivals. There was cordiality in the air as all the farmers exchanged greetings and shared ideas about the state of things. It is the kind of exchange unique to the people of the land; not only do they share a common interest but a shared commitment to the values of their noble tradition. They are proud of their role in the sustenance of mankind, and in solidarity never loath to flaunt this truth to their detractors. This was their own special day, a manifestation of who they were and what they were; rest assured the farmer will always be.

As they made their way back to check out Paddy's progress, Peter was momentarily taken aback, for who was coming in their direction but the one who had bullied him and made his life miserable. It was now six weeks since Norman had parted company with the Farrells. His absence was not at all noticed, as Peter more than adequately took his place. With a man like Maurice Farrell by his side, there was nothing to fear or be timid about. Nevertheless, at the same time, Norman's presence did affect him by inducing feelings of unease or perhaps an emerging anger. On seeing them, the big fellow veered in another direction. He may have feared that his reputation had suffered something of a setback with these people and it might be better to keep a distance. It was on his account that the young relative of the Farrells had stopped going to the village and he suspected they all knew the reason why. However, this was a day for enjoyment and nothing would be allowed to get in its way.

Paddy had reached a crucial stage in his work. For those who are versed in the craft of ploughmanship this is called "lifting the hint". It is where the final sod of green is turned over, leaving nothing to be seen but the straight furrows of brown earth. How this is done in terms of accuracy and precision is what will count when the judges assess the quality of the work.

All three, as well as Susan, were satisfied that Paddy had done a good job. They were also encouraged by the reassuring comments that were coming from those who stopped to admire his work. With his plot completed Paddy handed the horses over to Peter's charge. It was time for him to take a look at the work of his rivals. By this time, the judges were making a final assessment, and soon the results of their deliberation would be announced. This was an anxious time of waiting for all competitors. Paddy's nerves were beginning to show, and his mother thought a silent prayer.

First, the results of the presentation competition were announced. The rosette of victory was not awarded to Maurice Farrell but to a near neighbour who had a splendid entry. Nevertheless, they were happy to come home with commendation for a good second place. This competition was simply for style and appearance and was nothing more than a novelty item designed to augment and add glamour to the occasion. The ploughing contest was what really mattered. Tension was brought to the spectators by the manner in which the spokesman for the judges announced the results: it was given in reverse order from three to one. Paddy Farrell was nervous and scarcely able to acknowledge the applause from the crowd as he was once again proclaimed champion ploughman. His parents and friends were in a state of enthrallment. This was a wonderful day. Maurice invited everyone to the canteen bar where the drinks would be on him.

This successful day was not the end of things; the actual prize giving would take place at the annual ploughing presentation dance, which was coming up in the Church of Ireland parish hall in less than two weeks time. Apart from giving out the prizes, it was a great social event, and all the farming and business people from the area would be there. Peter had heard about such things but had no thoughts about what went on at them. The only connection he could make with the word "dance" was when a lady came to the school to teach the girls a combination of steps to the sound of fiddle music on the gramophone. No matter, this was something he was certainly not going to miss; its association with the happiest day of his life was what made it a must for him.

However, he would have to bring his Sunday clothes back with him next weekend, and this could create a slight problem back home. Neither Tom nor Ciss were favourably disposed towards the idea of any of their children engaging in a practice of questionable moral repute. However, they did listen with some interest to Peter's account of the ploughing match, and more importantly about his own role in it. It pleased them to know that their son was serving his apprenticeship with a champion ploughman. Hess refused to engage with him in any discussion relating to what he perceived as a challenge. His dull perception failed to fully alert him to the fact that here was a developing young man who was on the verge of autonomy.

But, Peter was still lacking in social integration; his parents could not see it as a vital component of emotional maturity. Ciss was strong on the merits of family exclusiveness and would advise her offspring to stay together always. That piece of advice was intended for the particular benefit of Peter and Kitty. What future had this proud mother imagined for her son and daughter, or what was the end for it all? They were not yet ready to know the measure of these things, but time would bring them wisdom to weigh the cost or gain of every choice.

Nonetheless, the move to the Lagan set Peter well on his way to social maturity; even the negative encounter with Norman was a learning experience for him. He could begin to see what it was that nurtured the bullying instinct, or the need to seek a laugh at the expense of others, and why this was tolerated at every level of society. At every level there is uneasy interaction between the passive and the controller, and it operates in an unequal arena. But there is also the in-between group, which blindly accepts that this is how things happen to be, and of course, it is external to them. It is so convenient to turn away and say, "this has got nothing to do with me". To thwart the games of Norman and his likes requires little more than what Paddy Farrell did that night in the village. It is a different matter when it comes to those who claim to be our guardians or even our conscience. Being exposed to bullying is destructive of the person, be it at the crossroads, in the classroom or congregation. However, the value of socialisation is in learning to benefit from the goodness of others as well as how to cope with their opposites. Peter was beginning to know he had a place in a world that went beyond the one he knew, and it was a world he was not afraid to be part of.

There were a number of couples on the dance floor by the

time Peter got there with Paddy, who had the use of the family car for the occasion. Maurice and Susan would be coming later with a neighbour couple; they had to be there for the presenting of prizes. It was the strangest thing to see men and women of all ages holding each other as they ambled around the floor to the rhythm of the music. Yes, some of them as old as his parents. Unthinkable, he thought, that Tom and Ciss could ever be party to such degrading nonsense.

There was an atmosphere of merriment all over the place and Peter felt good about all of it. Many of the friends he had made during the time of his visits to the village were there and would be his company for the night. How he wished to be like cousin Paddy as he watched him take to the floor with one of the prettiest girls at the gathering. This was the other world that he had been warned against and now he wondered what was so wrong about it.

The dance movements seemed simple enough from his observation point, and some of the girls from his group of friends were keen for him to try. Although comfortable in their company, he did not feel ready for such adventure, but the thought of going around that floor with one of them in his arms did appeal to him.

The dancing was interrupted for supper followed by the usual speeches and prize giving. The food was delicious; the women of the Lagan can be relied upon to come up with the best. Speeches were prolonged and a bit repetitive; one person could easily have said it all. The prize-winners were each applauded as they collected their trophies, and with a final word from the chairman, it was time for another helping of music and dance. Maurice and Susan took the floor in a slow waltz, and their mood suggested they had been to the Pipe Bar on their way over. They had gotten round a few times when Susan spotted Peter standing with the others. She came over to him. "Peter," she called, "*ar mhaith leat a beidh ag damhsa?*" He understood enough of the Irish to know it was an invitation to the floor. "You are not leaving tonight without giving your Auntie Susan a dance," and without having time to think about it he was in the midst of it all. It was the kind of dance that suited the beginner, and the large crowd rendered the footwork unimportant, but for Peter it was a new departure; he was at last coming out.

This gave him the courage to invite one of his friends when the next slow air was played. She would have been a year or two older than him, and a more experienced dancer. She was a pleasant and friendly type who would not make him feel awkward or inadequate. The warm sensation that emitted from her body excited him to the core as they moved tentatively to the lure of the soft music. Their conversation was also tentative but not so that it did not maintain. She asked why he had stopped coming to the village and if he was thinking about coming back. He knew she was present on the night he had suffered that violent humiliation, but both were careful not to mention it. Hopefully, this was now forgotten and no longer something people talked about. This was not a night for dwelling upon what makes us cower, but rather the things that make us glad to be alive. Still aware of each other when the music stopped, their encounter was brief but pleasant.

At the end of the night Peter and his friends watched the couples as they left holding hands or with their arms around each other. Each of these couples headed away to their places of aloneness. Paddy sat in his car embracing one who was simply beautiful — Heather was his main prize of the evening. He beckoned Peter to be seated in the back, and then they were off.

On their way back from seeing Heather safely home, Peter talked to Paddy about how great the night had been and how wonderful were all the people. His greatest wish was for freedom to do this occasionally in the future, but at home, things were vastly different. Paddy was sympathetic and understood that some farming parents were like that. He talked about how good his own experience had been in this regard. "This car is available to me at least one night a week, because my parents can still remember what it's like to be young."

He reminded Peter that in taking over the important role of ploughman he had a right to be more assertive and independent. Oh, if only Tom and Ciss could hear their son being so indoctrinated into the vices of a defective world. The protective goodness of some parents is often overplayed; it underestimates one's ability to develop autonomously and is seldom to the benefit of anyone.

"At the same time," Paddy said, "not many fifteen-year-olds are going to the dance halls, that's one benefit of you being away from home." Peter agreed, but nothing was going to stop him from pursuing his dream about working on his own land. He was going to be Peter McGinn the farmer from Cruckban.

It was to be a long time before such an experience would be Peter's again; there would be no such other events for the remainder of his stay with the Farrells. Paddy went dancing every weekend, but that was at a time when Peter would be at home in Cruckban. Yet, it was an experience he would not want to forget, nor think it belonged only to the past. In the meantime, there were other things to be tried out before the end of his time in the Lagan.

He had been sent there for a purpose, to learn new and more progressive methods of farming, and in this, he was succeeding. In addition to that, a more integrated and mature young man was emerging, one who was learning to think and speak for himself.

The long-promised fishing trip with Maurice arrived at last. It was the day after St Patrick's Day and the weather was cold but bright for the start of the spring fishing season. In preparation, Maurice and Peter had to dig deep into the cold ground for the worms that, according to Maurice, were the kind of bait best suited to the weather and the deep spot of water they intended to fish. The dawn chorus was coming sweetly from the trees around the farmyard, and Maurice and Peter were out at daybreak. "Don't leave without the lunch basket and flasks," Susan called from the bedroom window just as they were getting into the car with a variety of fishing gear and bait. "It's best to be going to the river early in the morning before the place gets crowded, and I always seem to do better at that time." This was nothing more than a repetition of what Maurice had been saying the night before when calling for an early bedtime. Paddy agreed to facilitate their day off by taking responsibility for all the morning chores around the farmyard. This kind of cooperation was to the advantage of everyone. By working in unison, nothing was left unattended, nor did anyone feel a prisoner to his or her own allotment. A happy workforce is an efficient one.

There was nothing but a lone heron standing still on one foot observing their arrival from a safe distance. Being first there, they had the advantage of claiming a spot considered best for fishing. Peter had a good teacher in Maurice: how to apply the bait and which one to use according to season and weather;

he was back at school and enjoying it thoroughly.

As Maurice set himself up, Peter looked up and down the passing flow of the Foyle, not knowing what to expect from this new experience. The only thing he could be sure about was the peacefulness that surrounded him and the company of a man he liked and respected. The place was pretty much their own for a good part of the day; the few that did join them were well known to Maurice. A feeling of comradeship was very noticeable amongst these people through their shared interest. Apart from one small spring salmon and a few trout it was not the most successful of days in terms of catch. However, there are other lures as well as hooking salmon and trout. For the true fisherman there is nothing more enticing than the ripple of the river or the stillness of a lake; it is simply enough to be there. In addition, in Maurice, Peter could see a thrilling excitement from the moment that small fish took the bait. The taut draws on the line were pulling the tip of the rod to almost touching the water, and then back to slack again. His skilful hands gripped the handle of the fishing rod and reel, then spinned to allow backward and forward play. Yes, it was so easy to get hooked and Peter could feel the pull, it was something he would like to do again, but the call of spring had first to be answered.

The work was hard but not tedious, and the routine was organised to a method for the spring sowing and planting. Everything was on a much grander scale to what Peter was used to at home; a lot of ground was covered each day. The fields were much larger and less rocky, and there was little doubt they would each yield a rich bounty. It was a heartsome place to be working, where at the end of each day a sense of achievement inspired a feeling of wellbeing. All of this was valuable education to the young apprentice who was willing and capable of learning.

There were many things he felt that needed to be done to the Cruckban enterprise, things requiring a more radical approach than was likely to happen under Tom McGinn or his faithful servant man. Peter knew that change was unlikely to happen quickly or easily. He was still a long way from assuming that kind of authority. His judgment was mature enough to know that it would never be possible to transform Cruckban into a Lagan type holding. Nevertheless, he was determined not to let his valuable experience be wasted or forgotten. Now with his apprenticeship ending, he could change many things for the better when the time came.

He said an emotional farewell to his dear friends the Farrells that Saturday morning in May. Paddy hoped it would not be too long before they could meet up again. The pair was now solid friends and hoped to always remain so. Maurice and Susan both assured him of his potential to succeed because he possessed the one quality that was essential to success, that of being a good worker. With that, they said their final goodbyes and Peter stepped on the old bike to leave the Lagan for good.

chapter fourteen

It was the day after the May hiring fair and Dinny was recovering from the effects of the holiday. It seemed everything had gone off smoothly for a change. Ciss informed Peter that his father had just made a new agreement to retain Dinny for another six months. This meant that things were to remain the same as they were. There would be plenty of work for Peter to do but it would be of a subservient nature. Once again, Hess would be calling the shots and allowed to do so.

Now well on his way to becoming sixteen, this was not what Peter had expected to be returning to after his time of training. At the same time, his developing confidence would enable him to contend better with this peculiar arrangement, and he would not be afraid to say what he thought, regardless of the reaction. The fifty pounds Peter had received from Maurice Farrell the day he left the Lagan was lodged to his bank account along with the hundred willed to him by Uncle Henry. It was not considered safe or right that such an amount should be in the hands of one so young or perhaps not fully responsible. Some things can never change.

For Kitty, the countdown had begun. The number of days it would be until summer holidays was what constantly occupied her mind. She was able to tell Peter that Maggie Dunne had left school and had started working in the shirt factory in Ballintober. She was cycling there with others from the Dooras area to an eight o'clock start each morning. He had not talked to her for well over six months now, although he did see her at church on a few occasions. Now fourteen, her appearance seemed to be changing fast, with an attractiveness that was agreeable to his eyes. It was obvious that from the little she was earning she was able to attire herself in clothing that complimented her stage of maturity. Now he could see her as a young woman who was bright and interesting, and he would have liked an opportunity to talk to her again. However, this was now less likely to happen. Never again would they walk together on the old school track, nor would their paths ever cross in the course of their working days. As for the evenings, there was little chance. Peter had still to make that breakthrough, and at fourteen Maggie was much too young.

That summer Tom McGinn started seeing his son in a different light. More and more they were engaging each other on matters pertaining to the running of their farms. Peter was not in the least reluctant to call the Blue Rock "his farm", especially when Hess happened to be present. It was during one of their conversations that Peter suggested they might consider buying a third horse. He was well able to articulate his thinking, which was obviously influenced by his experience with the Farrells. How much more effective was the system there, simply by dividing responsibilities. Increased output could be achieved by renting extra land, which was widely available in the area. There were at least three large holdings nearby that were being leased annually, as their owners either were retired or had other occupations.

Tom listened with great interest, but was non-committal; in any case, he had the rest of the summer to think about it. Nevertheless, think about it he would. This was a different Peter from the less than useful weakling, often discounted as lacking in either hands or brain.

His persistence was impressive, so much so that he took the case to his mother, not knowing that the Boss had already told her about their over-enthusiastic son and his ambitious plans. Ciss rather liked the idea of anything that could be seen as advancement and capable of adding status to the family name. This was one family deliberation that did not require the participation of an imposing workman whose dislike of Peter had not subsided. There was reluctance on everyone's part to bring grief to the one who was now running out of patience with the Russians, who lacked the aggressive immediacy of Hitler. Apart from that, there was an air of contentment about the way Dinny went about his work. Peter was happy to converse with John, now almost a man and home for the summer. Peter was careful not to intrude at this stage nor did he wish to undermine this individual's sense of security. After all, Dinny had served the family well for many years and would find it hard to settle easily with other people.

John's perception of life was also changing. No longer was

he willing to blindly concur with the sacred tenet of respectability. This introverted vision had inhibited his personal development even more than it had done to his brother. In seeing this, the two became close friends and allies; they readily shared their feelings about how they saw themselves in the future. They were both keen to take their place on the local football team that Peen McDevitt was forming to play in a summer competition down in the village. Parental permission had been denied them the previous year. In fact, a new leather football was bought in an effort to keep them away from external influences. John was an experienced player who had made it on to the college senior team, while Peter had never performed outside the old school playground, where they had used a bundle of rags for a ball.

"What time would this be over at?" was Tom's first response to their joint request. Both he and Ciss thought there were many better things they could be doing of a summer evening. The request was finally granted on the strict condition that the pair return home immediately after the game ended. Under no circumstances were they to linger around the village or along the road.

It was estimated the weekly games should be finished shortly after nine o'clock, allowing them time to be back well before ten. John commented that they were probably the only lads of their age who had to endure such smothering regimentation, which exposed them to a lot of embarrassment. His comments were not at all well received. Tom, who had the answer for everything, asked how he came to form such an impertinent opinion and how much he knew about the ways of the world. "Not a lot," John replied, "and for obvious reasons too." However, in such exchanges Tom could always get the upper hand by simply applying the growl. Peter observed with uneasy interest this unequal contest. With nervous anticipation, he prayed it would not endanger the small concession they had just won. However, the encounter ended with Ciss reminding everyone how much money had been spent on that fellow's education, and they had a right to expect becoming behaviour. Without a hint of threat, this minor challenge was a timely warning that these boys were fast becoming men and things would have to change.

The first game was against a team from Ballintober. Being a much bigger village, it would be fielding a second team in the competition. Peen and all of Dooras were delighted with the fine performance of young John McGinn from up the hill. His fitness and skill mesmerised all of them; it was a classiness that was the mark of a college boy. Their 2–0 victory was sweet, but even sweeter because it was against the boys from the bigger and rival town. It was new to Peter and made him slightly nervous at first, but many assured him that he was by no means the worst player on the local side.

They hated not being able to stay around for a bit longer and chat with the others after the game. That was usually in Aggie's shop where their thirsts were quenched with lemonade. Nevertheless, the rules of the house had to be observed in the interest of avoiding further embarrassment by Tom arriving to see what was keeping the boys. Apart from this ridiculous situation, it was a good and enjoyable evening, with the next date being eagerly awaited.

Tom and Ciss showed little interest in the subject that so enthused their sons, but did warm somewhat on hearing that one of the O'Doherty boys as well as the son of another prominent family were playing on the Ballintober team. Peter was astute enough to see the value of passing on such information; he knew it would go some way towards easing his parents' paranoid mistrust of others. With his reputation for being an amusingly wild man, this was not an attribute worthy of Tom McGinn. However, the two young schemers knew exactly which strings to pull; they could see the flaws that were easily exploitable. Unwittingly, Hess too contributed positively to the case for the boys being given more freedom. He talked about the star performance put in by John and how well it was received in the village. Needless to say, he declined to comment on the other boy and it was better that way for Peter. He knew not to expect praise from that quarter. On that score he was little bothered, as it was promising to be an exciting time ahead.

Hopes of John entering the seminary were beginning to fade; he was becoming much too interested in the unholy attractions of the secular world. It would take nothing less than divine intervention to inject momentum into that cause. With only another year of study to do, he let it be known that his preference was to immediately find suitable employment. First, he would sit the Leaving Certificate examination, and with favourable results, his chances on the job market would be so much the better. In the meantime word came through the college that the Munster and Leinster Bank were about to hold recruitment examinations in Dublin. John applied, and once again, there were scenes akin to what went on the time he was preparing to go to boarding school. New clothing and footwear were purchased; respectable attire was all-important as a means of impressing the assessors. Then there was the worry of letting him go so far on his own — would he be able to make his way in the big city?

This concern took Tom back to Strabane and his retired academic friend John Gallagher. He had a brother Joe who was a publican in the capital. In fact, he was the one best known to Tom when they were both young, but they had lost contact with the passage of time. After being furnished with an address, little time was wasted on getting the letter dispatched to Dublin. They had little doubt that the reply would be prompt and positive; it would take a heavy load off their anxious minds. There, he would be safely looked after for the few days, and no doubt, it would be free as well.

The reply was indeed prompt and generous beyond what they were asking for. Not only was their son welcome, but Joe invited both of them to come and stay as well. The thought of a couple of days in the city very much appealed to Ciss, as neither she nor her husband had ever been there before. This was the last thing that John wanted; he was at an age where he needed to be allowed do these things in his own way. That said, he was aware of Ciss' euphoria and that Tom was thinking hard about it.

As expected, this was too good an opportunity to turn down, and Tom and Ciss announced that they would be accompanying John to Dublin on the train. As a means of payment for their friend's generosity, they would have to take something up with them. A quantity of fresh eggs and country butter were packed securely in a sturdy cardboard box. John thought about the embarrassment of having to accompany this monstrosity throughout the journey. It was going to be left in his care because Ciss had to look after the personal belongings. However, there was worse yet to come. Tom thought that the treat of all treats for city dwellers would have to be a half bag of Donegal potatoes. Hess brought all three with their belongings to Strabane railway station to catch the Great Northern Derry to

Dublin train. Tom hoisted the sack of spuds on his back, just the way he would up in Cruckban with only the hens and ducks observing the spectacle. With self-assurance, they boldly stepped on to the train, oblivious to their son's discomfort.

Peter and Kitty were left in the care of no-nonsense Dinny. He would see to it that they stayed put and did not take advantage of their parents' absence. There was one major problem, however, and it was going to impinge upon Hess as much as Peter. That was what to do about the football game the following evening. Both were more than anxious to be there, but what were they to do about the little one? It would have been a serious breach of trust for Hess to impose a ban on Peter and have him stay in with his sister; after all, he had been given temporary custody over both of them. Another important factor was how much Peter had improved on the playing field after the first couple of games. No longer was there any doubt about his worthiness of a place on the team.

Hess knew how highly Tom and Ciss McGinn regarded old Ned and Bella McDevitt. In fact, it was the one house in the neighbourhood that their children were allowed to visit, and a run down to Ned's corner was always permitted. The two old people would be on their own that evening as their son Peen would be fully occupied motivating his team, which was now surprising everyone by its advance in the competition.

Peter delivered Kitty to a very welcoming Bella, who was sure to have something nice for the little one. Peter said he would collect her after the game and take her straight back to the house. Hess had to be staying a while longer to talk the game over with a few other experts. A quick call into parliament was also on his mind.

Peter was in no hurry about going back for his little sister, who he knew would be very happy in the company of the two kindly old souls. The football tournament had become a popular recreational venue for young people of both genders. It was there that they could engage freely in what Patrick Kavanagh referred to as "the wink and elbow language of delight". He rather enjoyed the attention he was receiving from the girls on the sideline. When in possession of the ball their excitable flightiness helped his game. With John "the star" missing from the squad it was up to Peter to give of his best, and what better place than in the midst of charming attraction.

Coming off the field, he knew that he had played a big part in bringing his team to yet another victory, and this added to his confidence in many ways. With the boots hanging from their laces around his neck, he headed for Aggie's with the others. He had to be quick, however, as Hess usually went that way as well.

After drinking a bottle of lemonade and savouring the accolades for a good performance, Peter was indeed quick at heading back up the road. He was not alone though; a number of his old school friends, including Maggie Dunne, were waiting to go part of the road with him. They talked and laughed in a manner that was carefree and filled with delight. The group gradually decreased as one by one they reached their homes along the way. Maggie would be with him until they parted company at Ned's cottage. It was their first meeting since that memorable day he had left school, and how much both of them had changed since then. They had a lot to talk about as they walked together, shoulders touching occasionally. Her dad's condition had changed little, so, like Peter, she had to be home early to help with the bedtime routine. Sammy seemed to be more accepting of his disability and was glad to be able to go out when the weather was good. Most days he would go to the wooded area behind the house and cut firewood with a handsaw. This was what the doctor considered therapeutic so long as he did not overdo it, but her mother worried nonetheless.

But this was not an occasion for morbid malaise. Here were two teenagers feeling good about themselves, and especially good about being in each other's company. "I heard you had a great time down the Lagan with your relations," said Maggie.

"That I had," replied Peter, "and you know it's not too bad here either."

Maggie smiled a little. "Do you not miss your girlfriend though?"

"What girlfriend? I don't have a girlfriend, why do you say that?"

Nudging his arm with her elbow, she calmly uttered, "I just know you have, and she is the lucky one too."

By the time they arrived at Ned's corner and place of parting, they were holding hands and nervously giddy. He talked about John and his parents being in Dublin, and said that he was now going to take Kitty home from her minders. Then time to part, they let go of each other's hands, standing silently and close to each other with fast-beating hearts; it was the sweetest of awakenings. The fragrant perfume she was wearing drew him even closer to her and then they were cheek to cheek with arms around each other. It was their first kiss and would remain a special memory for both of them.

They did not arrange to meet again as Peter's freedom was measured stingily. However, such a beautiful happening could not be allowed to fade into memory as if it mattered little or counted for nothing. They would have to find some way of being alone again with each other. That was how both of them felt as they pensively walked their separate ways at the close of a special day.

Their joy would also be their secret. In no way could it be allowed into the public domain. It would surely result in a family crisis in the McGinn household, and for Peter this did not bear thinking about. As for Maggie, she would be considered much too young, though she was trusted enough to be allowed out with her friends in the evenings. After all, she was now working full time and earning much needed money as well.

It was the following Saturday when the party arrived back from Dublin; they were relieved to find the house still standing with everything seemingly in order. The question of what everyone had been up to was dealt with but not in detail. Tom and Ciss were both in high spirits after their big time in the city. How lucky they considered themselves to have found such wonderful friends in Joe and Eileen Gallagher, and it was a friendship they were determined not to let lapse.

John was not quite so taken by it all; it was hard for him to form an opinion as to how he had performed in the assessments, which ran over two days. He had met two of his schoolmates at the interview centre on the first morning, but unlike them, his dad accompanied him. This was a severe blow to his sense of manhood, not to be judged capable of making his own way in life, and for this to happen in front of his peers. All this and more he related to Peter, who listened attentively and with some amusement.

Peter had a story of a different kind to tell, though his was a secret. However, was it one he could keep from brother John? His mind was seldom free of thoughts about the beautiful Maggie and a longing to see her again. By next week, things would be back to what they were before — John and himself would play their game and then come home together; their time would be measured in a way that did not allow for delay. What, Peter wondered, would be the outcome if his parents ever found out he had been paying attention to the likes of Maggie Dunne? How long could he hold his secret, or would sharing it with his brother make the situation any better?

He also had to watch out for Hess. Peter knew that if this man should hear about his precious friendship with Maggie he would not be slow to turn the information into good account. Hess was becoming suspicious about how much time the Boss was spending in discussions with Peter. It seemed obvious that the young fellow was becoming more assertive and was being listened to as well. His days of mastery was now ending; here was a young man not in the least afraid to tell him where to go. Nevertheless, it was still a real worry for Peter, for there was no way he could be sure that this would remain a secret in the village. Such things by their very nature have a way of getting noted in a small community, and it is always to the likes of Hess that they are first revealed. Peter was now on the horns of a dilemma, or so it appeared to him, and he felt he would have to talk to his best friend, brother John. He would leave it until after they had gone to bed, as that always seemed the best time and place to talk and deliberate on matters of the heart.

Peter's revelations rendered John speechless for a while; he could not believe what he was hearing from his less articulate brother. Soon they got round to a near normal brotherly kind of sharing. John's curiosity had him anxiously seeking as many intimate details about the encounter as possible. He also lamented his own so-called life of privilege, and how it excluded him from these kinds of experiences. If things turned out as he hoped they should, all this would change, with him having the space to savour the fruits of a bigger world. For Peter this was not an option; his world had to be in Cruckban and its immediate environs. However, why, he asked, did it have to be so restrictive and stifling of joy? This they both agreed was the price of the thing called respectability; it is something deeply rooted in the land and has a near relative in poverty. John's advice almost echoed what his cousin Paddy Farrell had said to him the night of the ploughing dance: "Not many sixteen-year-olds are courting fifteen-year-old girls."

This advice was not meant to be a criticism, but merely to point out that on this issue he was no worse off than anyone else. Peter agreed, but this was not going to make his predicament any easier. He had next week's game to think about, only this time it was not about his place on the team, or indeed how he would perform. What would she think of him walking off the field along with his brother and not even stopping to say hello or give her a smile?

"There is no law against giving the girl a smile," said John. He also reasoned that she would probably know how the situation had changed with Mum and Dad being at home again. He was sorry for not being able to see a way around Peter's problems. With a quiet laugh he said, "I am not as good at solving your problems as Uncle Henry used to be."

The mention of Henry's name put a scheming thought into Peter's head. "Yes, that's what I will do, tomorrow is Sunday so I will take a walk to see how things are at the old house and who knows what I might see on the way." This thought was his opiate for the night, and he manoeuvred himself into a position of ease and then all was silence. Down in the kitchen Tom and Ciss were busy recounting their trip to and travels through the capital. They were overwhelmed by the friendship and generosity of the people, especially the patrons of Gallagher's pub. Some of them intended holidaying in Donegal later in the year and would perhaps be paying them a courtesy visit. Ciss had also formed a friendship with one of the Strabane Gallaghers. She was Johnny's daughter, and happened to be in Dublin at the same time. Her married name was Olive Devine, a schoolteacher by profession who lived with her husband Robert and two schoolgoing daughters on the Derry road outside Strabane. Whether Hess was interested or not, Ciss had to be telling him that the Boss and herself would be going there to visit in a couple of week's time. Now the Gallaghers of Strabane and Dublin had progressed and impressed enough to be called "our cousins".

The next day Peter made his way to Uncle Henry's old house as planned. A faint trickle of smoke was rising from the chimney of the Dunnes' wee house; it was early afternoon so

Maggie should still be in there. Peter called loudly to a few cattle that were grazing in the field nearest to where she could hear his calling; the sound of his voice should attract her attention. With no apparent success he continued over the old track towards the place they now called Henry's. After all, it was there and only there he was supposed to be going. The old mortise lock was stiff through lack of usage; force had to be applied to the key before the door opened. Both inside and out, the place had a derelict look about it. A bag full of turf rested against the hob-stone of the open fireplace; it would have been the last one the old man fetched from the shed before he fell sick. Peter had in his pocket ten Woodbines and a box of matches; at least he could enjoy a quiet smoke. This was yet another manly habit he had acquired in the Lagan. Before lighting up he went out again to find a few pieces of wood that were cracking dry under the summer sunshine. The damp chimney emitted a dense cloud of smoke that climbed gradually towards the sky. Sitting comfortably in front of the fire after his cigarette, he fell into a kind of stupor, imagining strange formations in the burning matter. He watched as each image faded into the embers to be replaced by another, just like he and John used to do around the kitchen fire when they were children.

His flight was interrupted by the sound of footsteps behind him. Looking up, he saw Sally Dunne looking down on him. Peter was startled at first and thought that she might be about to admonish him for his frolicking with her daughter. He rose quickly to his feet and greeted her. Her reply was brief: "Sorry Peter, but I thought the place was on fire, it was the thick smoke, you see." He thanked her for her concern and said he had just come to check how things were, then decided to light a fire; it was the damp chimney that caused the thick smoke. He was satisfied she knew nothing about him and Maggie. In fact, Maggie was not too far away as they spoke. Leaving Sally to the door and thanking her again, he could see the pretty one coming towards them. "Mum, I told you it was nothing. Peter, my mother is so alarmist, she was convinced that Henry's was on fire and ran over here in a panic." All three laughed at this. "Better be sure than sorry though. Come on Maggie, let's go back." With that, Sally started back over the lane.

The two looked after her until she disappeared round the corner and out of sight. "She won't mind for a while," said Maggie as she put both her arms around his neck. All was now well for another time, and they would be able to share tender moments together and alone. It would be a precious time for both of them.

Back at home, he would be able to say how many things needed attending to at the old house, with weeds growing on the window ledges and around the door. He was prepared to go there in the evenings to tidy the place up, even whitewash the walls that had gone green from the dampness. This was nobody's house but his; he had a duty and a right to look after it. The suggestion was well enough received at headquarters and could be acted upon almost immediately. Maggie's reaction was predictably welcoming; this arrangement allowed them the joy of being together every evening for some time to come. She could understand that their seeing each other had to be in secret, at least for the present.

"Does it have to be a secret forever?" she asked. It was one evening when she could see that work on Henry's was nearing completion. She could also feel a sense of rejection at him not paying her the attention she wanted at the weekly game, or on the road to and from it. Hurt was also felt the previous Sunday when he went with John and two others to a Gaelic match in Letterkenny. The thought of him choosing to go there, rather than being with her, gave pain to her tender feelings. Little reassurance was in the offing as Peter had his own worries about the entire arrangement. Sooner or later, they were going to be found out. They walked arm in arm the short distance from Henry's with a strange uneasiness on their minds and then parted with a promise for tomorrow evening.

After their parting, Peter looked back. He could see Maggie running swiftly towards the little house with her mother in conversation with a woman carrying a bundle of firewood. He thought it looked like Biddy The Rum; she frequently came there to collect that sort of fuel, which was free and plentiful.

The next day Hess and the two boys left the dinner table together, they were all heading to work in the hayfield. Almost immediately, Peter was called back into the house. Unsuspecting, he re-entered the kitchen where Ciss was preparing the scraps that Kitty would feed to the fowl. Soon he was alone with two angry parents. "Is this what we have reared you for? What you are up to is a case for Fr Gillen and that is exactly where we are for taking you." Most of the reprimand came from Ciss, who had no wish to hide her anger and feeling of betrayal. The Boss just stood there in support of his angry spouse. Neither was in the mood for hearing what their wayward son had to say. In truth, there was little he could offer to make his sin look any better. This was simply beyond their belief, a deliberate occasion for sin and a betrayal of family values.

"What kind of parent would allow a fifteen-year-old hussy out without knowing what she was up to? These are the kind of dangers that too often threaten the wellbeing of decent people."

This was by far the most serious crisis to ever beset the household of this proud peasant family. Vigilance was what was needed and it would have to be applied immediately and effectively. First, they had to be grateful to Dinny for informing them of this serious matter; they could always rely on him at such times. Ciss would find an opportunity to have a firm talk with the Dunne woman about that brazen lassie of hers. Little did she know that poor Maggie was also in big trouble from both her parents. It was Biddy The Rum who had spotted the pair kissing the evening before and went straight to tell Sally, then on to Hess, who she knew would be in the village. The rest need not be told, suffice to say this young and harmless infatuation suffered a sudden but predictable demise.

John received a negative reply from the directors of the bank; they were not in a position to employ him at that time. This meant he would be going back to college again in September for his final year. Again, his mother resorted to prayer, still clinging to a vague hope that he might yet decide in favour of the religious life.

As for Peter, much atonement had to be undertaken so that his farming dream might be at last fulfilled. First of all, trust had to be re-established, and this required him to stay well away from Maggie Dunne for the foreseeable future. His work and commitment should speak for itself; he had little doubt about his worth as a worker. So with pining in his heart, he set about the business of being a dutiful farmer's son. As expected, the incident passed without the involvement of Fr Gillen, although Ciss did have that encounter with the gentle Sally Dunne. Surprisingly enough, Peter was allowed back to the football, albeit under stringent conditions.

chapter fifteen

A most welcome diversion of focus away from an errant son came in the form of family relations from Canada. It was Ciss' Aunt Rose, now in her late seventies and widowed, home for the first time in forty-eight years. Their stay in Donegal was for four weeks, during which time they would be staying at a guesthouse near Ballintober. It was a good four miles from Cruckban but this was not a problem for the Canadians, who had rented a car. They also planned to stay for a few days in a rented seaside cottage in a quiet but picturesque spot near Buncrana. With Aunt Rose were daughter Bett and husband Paul, whose father's people came from County Leitrim and whose mother was French Canadian. Paul and Bett had two sons and a daughter, all attending educational establishments at different levels; all three were left in the care of Bett's sister back in Montreal.

It soon became apparent that here were people of means. Paul worked for a major financial corporation and at a very high level as well. He was a regular contributor to one of Canada and America's most prestigious financial journals. The entire McGinn family was invited out to dinner in the Park Hotel outside Strabane. No expense was spared and their hosts were generous to a fault. Bett controlled the conversation, mainly about education and matters pertaining thereto, declaring herself to be the holder of a master's degree. She questioned her guests at length about how each of them stood in relation to the issue of learning. She was pretty certain that intelligence was a genetic attribute, and that she herself had taken her brightness from her father's side. Ciss refrained from challenging this modest assertion; she was hardly opinionated enough to engage her cousin.

The three young McGinns were thoroughly enjoying themselves, savouring the food, the soft drinks and above all the unique conversation. Aunt Rose began to reminisce about the Ireland she knew long ago, and they found her to be compulsive listening, recalling her childhood in a remote part of Donegal as well as her early experiences in a strange new land. The changes to the countryside, she noted, were all for the better, but even with the passage of forty-eight years, too many remnants of the old order still remained. At the same time, Ireland was on the move; big changes were happening with the inception of rural electrification and mechanised farming methods.

Paul was totally captivated by the natural beauty of the Irish countryside and said how much he would like to rent or own a little cottage in this particularly nice area. It was a suggestion that immediately won the approval of Bett and Aunt Rose, who liked the romantic notion of a little cottage back in the old country. With heightened spirits from the consumption of Jameson whiskey and a genuine liking for his wife's relations, Tom mentioned the little house called Henry's.

The party in the hotel ended all too quickly but everyone enjoyed it thoroughly. For the young ones it was magic and it helped to take Peter's mind off Maggie Dunne. The following day Ciss would be cooking Sunday dinner as usual, only this time it was going to be special, as she had returned the invitation to her generous relations.

These interesting people were an immediate hit with Andy Cathers and his customers. It was drinks on the house on the occasion of their first visit there; Paul and his mother-in-law were equally lavish. Then it was off to the ball game to watch John and Peter McGinn perform on the pitch. Everything about this place appealed to the Canadians greatly.

"What was it you said about a little cottage, Tom?" It was Rose addressing the Boss who sat at the head of the table with his guests. This special dinner was being served in the parlour; Ciss was using her best tableware and white cloth for the occasion.

"It's hardly the sort of thing you would be looking for," Tom replied. He went on to explain everything about the condition of the old house, how it and the fifteen acres of land were coming to Peter in five years' time. By all means, they could have the use of it for that period at least and perhaps much longer. It was highly unlikely that the new owner would ever pose a problem. On a pleasant evening as it was, what could be nicer than a leisurely stroll down there to have a look at the place, but first they would all relax for a while after dinner.

The cottage was looking much the better of what Peter

had done to it. The whitewashed walls and the freshly painted outer doors created a homely atmosphere and the structure was well preserved by the famous new roof that had been put on for Henry a few years earlier. Yes, they liked it; it had potential to be what they were looking for. Turning to Peter, Paul said how lucky he was to own such valuable property, and assured him that he did not intend to tread on his rights. The man's sensitivity touched the young teenager a lot more than the others knew; in turn, he indicated his pleasure at what they were planning to do. Tom's offer still stood, Henry's would be theirs for at least five years, if they wished to invest in its refurbishment. Only a nominal rent would be charged, and that was as a simple precaution to protect the next generation. He wanted to make sure that no action on his part should ever pose problems for his son. Being a knowledgeable man, Paul agreed that everything should be done properly with all interested parties being fully briefed.

Paul's enthusiasm about getting to work was amusingly childlike. This was understandable when considering the quality of his existence in the world of high finance and living in a large city. Instead of going to Buncrana with the women, he would rather stay and have this important business sorted out, then get to work forthwith. Bett and Rose did not object, after all this was his vacation; if this was what he wanted to do they would not deny it to him.

Rose was quick to suggest that perhaps Ciss and Kitty might come in his place, as there would be ample room in the seaside cottage for all of them. This made Paul the happiest man around, but by no means the happiest person — that surely had to be Ciss McGinn and her precious daughter.

They made their way back to the house, a little tired and ready for tea, and soon it was time for the visitors to leave again. Tom suggested that Paul should call out to Cathers' pub later in the evening. It being Sunday night there would be people there he wanted him to meet.

The place was alive with laughter and chat by the time Paul arrived. Tom was already in conversation with Willy Clinton, the local handyman. He was a carpenter by trade, but equally competent in other areas of construction. The Canadian was in high spirits, and he showed his glee by buying drinks for all in the house. Tom gave Willie a detailed outline of what had to be done in order to make Henry's cottage habitable. Paul was overjoyed to learn that work could begin as early as Tuesday morning, so all materials had to be on site by then. That should not be a problem — at the bottom of the bar stood Eamon McGrane who ran a thriving business as a construction supplies merchant. Eamon took note of what was required; including a black Stanley range, and gave an assurance that all would be delivered the next day. Very soon, the atmosphere became conducive for the singing of a song. Clinton obliged with his rendition of "Fr Murphy". Eamon quickly followed this with "The Moon Behind the Hill". Then it was silence as Barney the fiddler played that sweetest of Irish airs, "An Coulainn", especially for the visitors.

Paul mentioned how much the women would have enjoyed this simply delightful gathering, but not to worry, as it now seemed they were going to have many such sessions in the future. With a busy day ahead of them, both men took leave of the company long before the party ended. Tom entered the kitchen to find Ciss and Kitty still at work. Apart from the packing, extra bread had to be baked for the week ahead, enough to carry the men through until Saturday and hopefully a special cake for taking with them to Buncrana. John was appointed to be cook for the week of his mother's absence. This had the approval of everyone, including Hess, who was afraid it might again be Tom.

The week ahead promised to be an interesting one in Cruckban. Peter and his father would be spending it at Henry's cottage along with Paul and Willy. With a coordinated effort, they all hoped to have a pleasant surprise for the ladies on their return.

The four men were on site bright and early Tuesday morning. Mr McGrane was true to his word and the delivery was made the evening before. The team worked well together, and the beautiful weather made everything that much easier. Paul seemed to be around all the time, he would be there and working long before the others arrived and could always find a reason to remain long after they had gone home in the evening. For him this kind of work was relaxation of the highest order.

Sadly, the time passed all too quickly. Within three days Willy Clinton had his work finished, the black Stanley was in place with all the repair work both in and out completed, even an earthen lavatory was installed at the back of the house. Now with only the cleaning up remaining to be done, the biblical pair got busy with paintbrushes. Tom the outdoor man was doing a good job digging and laying a pathway to the front door of the house.

The Canadian was not overly bothered about the cost of his pet project; his main concern was to get the work finished by the weekend. He knew that this was a good deal; here was their dream cottage, practically rent free, and with surety of tenure for at least five years. He was over-generous towards Willy Clinton, whose workmanship impressed him immensely. On Friday, he went shopping in pursuit of household essentials and returned later that afternoon in a furniture delivery van. This man did things in a most elaborate way, certainly not piecemeal. Inside, the little place smelt of fresh paint and disinfectant, as Paul and the two deliverymen got to work. It was well past quitting time when Tom and Peter arrived on the scene. The transformed state of Henry's amazed them both. The entire floor area was covered in bright linoleum of varying patterns and the full complement of furnishings was being put in place.

The black Stanley was red hot from the heat of burning turf in its firebox. An open fire also burned brightly in the lower room. Both of these fires would be rekindled in the morning, as the place needed to dry out over the weekend. In less than one week, they had achieved almost the impossible, and they congratulated each other and said how good it made them feel. Paul produced a bottle of best Irish Paddy and took two glasses from the newly installed kitchen cabinet. "This calls for a drink, Tom. Sorry, nothing for you this time, Peter." They were all in the feel good state and wondered how the women might react when they returned the next day. There was no reason why they could not spend the last two weeks of their vacation in this snug little place, which was as good as their own.

Ciss looked rested and refreshed. It was obvious the sea air and the company had uplifted her a lot. Poor Kitty lamented the fact that it had ended so quickly. That weekend saw a lot of activity between Cruckban and Henry's. Ciss accompanied the visitors on shopping trips for the remaining few items — they would be moving in Monday evening, all being well. Rose could not allow the occasion to pass without a party. It was mainly for the two families, but Paul had a couple of friends he wanted to invite as well. With this in mind, he and the two women headed for Cathers' on Sunday night.

The party was a lively affair, with food and drinks galore. The McGinn family and Dinny the workman were first to arrive. The four invited guests came later; they were Eamon and Ellen McGrane, who transported Barney the fiddler and Willy Clinton in the back of their pickup van. It was a night of merriment and laughter, with songs, music and recitations lasting well into the early hours of Tuesday morning. Everyone had nice things to say about each other. As is the case where there is mutual dependence, feeble flattery runs amok. There was even time for some serious discussion. Hess gladly shared his opinion about the state of the world and the inevitability of serious warfare. "Shut up your effin arse," shouted Willy Clinton, who was getting impatient with the slowdown in the entertainment. The evening was too precious to be wasted on bullshit of that sort. These extraordinary people were bringing a sense of renewal to a family of limited social adventure, people that were impoverished within the confines of modesty.

Tom McGinn sat in a corner with a bottle of whiskey that was more than half consumed; he had an expansive smile on his face. As Barney drew the first bow on the fiddle, the door opened. It was Biddy The Rum, she happened to be passing and just stopped to bid the visitors welcome. Rose thanked her with a strong drink and an invite to stay for a while. She sat down next to Hess. More than an hour passed before the uninvited guest took her leave. She thanked them again and repeated her welcome. The music continued and a few of them got up to dance a Highland. Hess decided it was time to go out for a breath of fresh air and make room for the dancers. Tom with an empty glass searched in vain for the whiskey bottle; he now had a betrayed expression on his face. Paul asked about Dinny and why he had left the company. Tom just looked to the vacant chair beside him and where the missing bottle had been. He was puzzled as to why it had been taken in a house where drink flowed in plenty. However, the answer came the next day. The empty bottle was found on a grassy spot that had been disturbed and not too far away from the cottage. The long grass had been bedded under the heavy weight of double passion. Yes, Biddy still liked the wee drop and "Hess was a man for all that".

Summer partying with the Canadians became an annual event as each year brought new surprises. Other family members, relations and associates began availing of Henry's cottage at various times of the year. Rose, along with a few ladies of her age, would come earlier in the year, and each season saw additional improvements being made to the old house. With the arrival of electricity, many modern gadgets were installed as well as running water and a bathroom. However, these elaborate facilities were only for people of a higher calibre; few if any in the district were ready for such extravagant nonsense. Being without these things never bothered Ciss McGinn — it was simply gratifying to know that the ones who had them were close to her and her family. For Ciss and Tom this was an age of blessed fulfilment, even a little enlightenment as well; could they ever imagine life without their extremely refined friends?

chapter sixteen

It was harvest time once again, and all the visitors had long since said their tearful goodbyes. John had also said goodbye and was now a final year student. It had been a memorable summer for him, with the football tournament and the Canadian visitors. These things were also very special to Peter, but he was having trouble forgetting the stolen but beautiful moments he had shared with his sweetheart. The events of the summer helped in some way to ease his pining, and no doubt, there would be other things to divert his thinking away from sweet Maggie Dunne.

He saw her at the football final with a few of her friends. He played a strong game that evening but not enough to save his side from going down to a stronger team from Ballintober. In spite of his obvious popularity with the young female spectators, Maggie failed to pay him even the least attention. Like her mother, she was deeply offended by the intervention of Mrs McGinn, and there was now an insurmountable barrier between the two. There was nothing the young man could do about this hurtful situation. Only too well did he know what was expected of him in relation to that particular subject. Deep hurt such as it was could lead only to resentment and bitterness, and the once sweethearts were no longer on speaking terms.

Peter could scarcely believe it when on a Friday evening in October John arrived back from college. He told him it was for the football presentation dance in the old school hall. The event had the blessing of the parish priest and had been announced at church the previous Sunday. Fr Gillen had complimented the organisers of the tournament and thanked them for offering the proceeds of the dance to augment the parish fund. "It was a most responsible undertaking by the men from the Dooras end of the parish. These fine people deserve nothing less than the full support of the entire community; other areas of the parish could do well to follow their lead."

Although Peter was present in the congregation, he never

thought for a moment it would affect his parents' thinking regarding the presentation dance. Nor did they show any signs of being so touched in the days that followed. However, the college was contacted on John's behalf and the response was predictably positive; no doubt, the wishes of Fr Gillen were mentioned.

What on earth could have come over Tom and Ciss McGinn, with those two weans off on bicycles to a very common sort of gathering? Not the kind of place that would induce a high degree of responsibility or respectability. However, when it had the authoritative approval of the priest, a more positive view had to be taken. After all, the two boys were highly thought of around the area — their performances on the playing field had earned them that. It was a popularity that they and a couple of other lads had justly earned, and it made their parents proud and for the moment more tractable.

The dance reminded Peter very much of the ploughing dance down in the Lagan. At least this was one advantage he had over his educated brother; he had been to such a thing before. The little hall was packed full of people, and this should make it easy for the footless ones to take the floor. John was hesitant at first, but on seeing his junior take off with seeming ease and confidence, he soon made his way towards an old school friend from Ballintober, Helen O'Doherty. Helen was a year or more older than him but very pleased to have been taken round the floor by the bright boy from Cruckban. He was doing the right thing, fraternising with the right class. His parents would have approved.

It was an evening of delight for both of them; they were having a fun time with their many friends. Peter had several dancing partners and was happier for it to be that way; there would be no tales carried about him on this occasion. He deliberately avoided Maggie Dunne, who he noticed was enjoying the attention of a young man from Ballintober. They were exclusive partners throughout the night. She looked stunningly beautiful and was keen to be seen with this man, who was a few years her senior and socially more accomplished.

The journey home was almost as entertaining as the dance itself. It was a subdued affair until they got a safe distance away from the policing eye of Fr Gillen, who had the moral responsibility of foiling sinful desire. He had a major problem with the

American sailors that were based in Derry and were frequent visitors to Ballintober. From the altar, he would denounce their moral behaviour in the popular phrase of the time: "They were overpaid, overfed, oversexed and over here." There were as many as ten others cycling with the McGinn boys on their way back to Dooras and district, but Maggie was not one of them. Occasionally they would spot a courting couple engaging in what was then called "the game of ditching". This was sure to provoke a barrage of unbridled comment, loud enough to disturb the stillness of the sleeping valley. However, it was all good fun, something to be joyfully experienced and not castrated by the lance of respectability. To attempt to stem the flow of nature is but a diversion of the natural order of things. The consequences of so doing should never be wished upon a people nor should youthful energy be a cause for alarm. Society with its natural propensity to preserve can always maintain an acceptable level of behaviour.

On that particular issue, there were at least some signs of change taking hold in the McGinn household. Tom and Ciss were aware of the late hour the pair got back from the dance, but no questions were asked. The next morning they enquired how much the boys had enjoyed themselves and of course whom they were with. It was also implied that the only reason they had attended the dance was the special and parochial nature of the event. Peter was later to learn from Hess that he was not trusted to go on his own. That was the reason for bringing brother John from the college. This comment was intended to dent his manly confidence, a confidence that was perceived to be a looming challenge to the old fellow's cosiness. With the November hiring fair almost upon them, Peter had more than a hint that he was about to take over the reins as ploughman. His father was favourably disposed towards the idea of expansion, which his son had been advocating ever since his return from apprenticeship, and it was now about to happen.

Tom would have to break the news to faithful Dinny, which was no joy for either him or his wife, nor was their son by any means the gloating type. Long years of togetherness had to count for something more than the cold market relationship. For these reasons, Peter's ambitious plans could well turn out to be the rescue for all of them. Tom submitted the proposal a few days before the hiring fair; it was a proposal in so far as it was not a termination of employment. He was straight and to the point, Peter was taking over as ploughman and subsequently assuming greater authority. The plan for expansion was his and his alone; it meant there would still be enough work for all of them. The two men were alone in the stable; Dinny listened attentively and asked a few questions. His immediate reaction seemed to indicate that he was going to move on and offer his expertise to another farmer, but he later agreed to think about it for a day or two.

There was a cold silence around the place for the next couple of days, and the delicate subject was never alluded to during that period. On the morning of the hiring fair, as the men sat at the table after breakfast, Peter was invited back to join them in serious deliberation. Hess was anxious to know exactly what kind of role was intended for him under the new management. For the first time in his life, the young man found himself in a position of some authority and was sensitively aware of it. With deference to his father and indeed to the questioner, he gave a broad outline of what was envisaged as well as how it might work. To everyone's amazement, a new hiring contract was cordially entered into and Hess was once again on his way to the Halliday fair.

The new partnership of Tom McGinn and Son made its way to Strabane later in the day. Their mission was to see Francy McMenamin the horse dealer about buying a suitable third horse. They would be trading in the pony and trap for a medium-sized animal that was adaptable to both the cart and a larger version of the family conveyance. They found a suitable animal and arranged for the dealer to come to Cruckban to take Blossom away.

A few days later Kitty and her mother stood heartbroken as they watched Blossom and all her belongings being driven down the road by a hated man called Jimmy McGurk, who had brought the mighty replacement. Now everything was in place for the smooth transfer of responsibility from the old to the young. A period of adjustment was allowed for, but soon things began moving to a different rhythm. At sixteen Peter was the main man and proud of it. He was out in the fields with his well-groomed steeds each day from dawn chorus until winter darkness descended. With the extra land they had rented, he needed to be ready in time for the spring sowing and he knew that his performance was being monitored by a number of interests.

By the New Year, Peter knew he was well on his way towards achieving a set target. Tom and Ciss were proud of their son but were careful not to sing his praises too loudly in the presence of their demoted servant. Dinny seemed happy enough in his secondary role, as it still offered him the best prospect of comfort and security. In parliament, he told his comrades that Tom McGinn was making do with a lesser man.

The new ploughman's absorption in his work was so complete that he rarely thought any more about losing the affection of Maggie Dunne. He was, however, interested enough to notice that the young man from Ballintober was a frequent caller to the vicinity of her abode. This he knew to be without her mother's knowledge or consent. Perhaps some caring neighbour would be good enough to inform her about what her daughter was up to. That winter he contented himself simply by doing his work thoroughly and well, then relaxing with his books until bedtime. His love of reading remained as keen as ever and was turning him into a well-informed and observant young man. With his work and management now fit to speak for itself, he knew it was only a matter of time before he would be assertive enough to come and go as he pleased. The power of assertiveness, he knew, would be more than a match for his parents' restrictiveness. Their smothering control was ending.

Not once did he encounter any problems from his predecessor. Each did their own thing and stayed well out of each other's way. On Saturday evenings, Hess meticulously groomed the new horse for massgoing the next morning, and it was indeed an attractive sight on the road. Peter had long since ceased to travel by that mode, and he was beginning to notice that as a means of transport it was on the wane. Many of the bigger farmers had purchased motorcars and it would not be all that long before the others followed suit. However, he was not complaining — biking with his friends was always fun and made Sunday pleasantly cheerful. He could talk about his work with the best of them from the world of horsemanship and was always willing to do so. With a weekly allowance of six shillings, he was able to go with the others to Aggie's shop for cigarettes and the Sunday newspaper, which was considered a luxury item for the McGinns of Cruckban.

Everything was going smoothly in Peter's plan for expansion. All the seeds were sown into the well-cultivated ground, and the results were eagerly anticipated. This would be the acid test of the new programme as well as the merits of its executor. First, they had to welcome summer and all that it might bring by way of sport and craic. Soon Henry's would have to be readied for the first batch of Canadians and all the fuss that went with their arrival. The football tournament would soon re-commence and perhaps with brother John back at home Peter would be able to get out and about with more freedom. Hess was now doing the daily run to the creamery with the fast-trotting horse and a rubber-wheeled cart. He was earning additional income for his employer by transporting milk for neighbouring farmers as well. There seemed little doubt that this hill farm was now functioning better than ever before and this was only the beginning.

This period saw the beginning of moves towards a different kind of rural Ireland. Big changes were happening in farming practice, and there was a slow move towards mechanization. It would take a few extra years for these changes to hit Cruckban. In the meantime, Peter had to make a success of what he had. Proven success was the only thing that might nudge Tom and Ciss towards change. The shift of authority from father to son is always fraught with unease, and it requires time, space and tentative delicacy. These were qualities the aspirant possessed in plenty. Time was on his side and he was happy with the way things were.

One morning in May, Peter accompanied Kitty as far as Henry's cottage on her way to school, as some tidying up had to be done there before the visitors arrived. His ownership of this place was no longer something he thought much about; it was only a small part of his overall ambition. At the same time, he liked to go there and admire its transformed appearance. It was a place he could feel at ease. On his way back he was much surprised to see Maggie Dunne standing at the door of her house and looking in his direction. Before he had time to think or react to the uncomfortable situation, she had retreated swiftly back inside. Why, he wondered, was she not at work? It probably had something to do with her ailing father. It felt so strange that he should be passing that spot and her not running to meet him. They had well and truly grown apart. What a pity that feelings of the heart should bring a beautiful friendship to its terminus point.

chapter seventeen

That summer John was back at home after finishing his Leaving Certificate examination. He was a relieved young man and glad to be finished with this particular institution. He also competed unsuccessfully in the bishop's examination for admission to Maynooth Seminary. This was a deep disappointment for his parents, especially his good mother. The fire of hope had been rekindled in her during that final year with him showing renewed signs of interest in the priesthood.

Now the priority was for him to find worthwhile employment, preferably in the locality. Tom, for some reason or other, developed an obsession about the National University; this had something to do with his admiration for his scholarly friend John Gallagher, but he quickly recovered after hearing about the cost. Now more than ever Peter valued his acquired status. What he had seemed to be secure and free of controversy or competition. This made him feel for the brother to whom he was very close and whom he valued as a friend. It was his hope that the summer would bring renewed inspiration and refreshment to all of them.

In most ways, it was a good summer. The weather was mixed but the crops looked good. On a couple of occasions, the football had to be postponed for reasons of inclemency. As for the visitors, well, they did not come to Ireland for the weather, it was to see their friends and enjoy the hospitality. Hospitality the McGinns were more than happy to afford the people who were bringing colour to their lives. This without doubt was of benefit to everyone, and there were less restrictions being placed on the boys. They were now regular visitors to the village, even on the evenings when there was no game to be played. Slowly but surely the two boys from the hill were becoming socially integrated and able to savour the wholeness that this freedom bestowed upon them.

Again, they were very much into the Dooras football tournament, as indeed were all the people of the entire district. It was an interest inspired in no small way by the blessing bestowed upon it by Fr Gillen. On one occasion, he graced the proceedings with his presence, as he had been on a pastoral visit somewhere further up the road. He was very impressed and pleased at what he saw and wished the organisers much success for the remainder of the tournament. A few people were curious as to where he had been, but by the time they had all assembled at Aggie's for the after-match refreshments, it had been established he was visiting the Dunne home. This was a sure indication that something was the matter there; most likely poor Sammy had suffered another relapse. Peter listened for a while without commenting, and then got to thinking about seeing Maggie that morning a while back. It also seemed strange that never once did she appear at any of the games they had played so far. He knew more than most about Sammy Dunne's disability and depression; he could never remember a time when this man was otherwise. Again, his thoughts turned to Maggie. She would now be the captive to all of it, as this was the busy time for her mother at the creamery.

Beyond thinking about them there was little Peter could do for his impoverished neighbours. For him these people were out of bounds. Nothing more was heard about this over the following days, not even in the village where all the happenings in the district were sure to get an airing.

It was towards the end of June and John was helping Peter with the spraying of the potatoes in the middle field next to Henry's. At eighteen, John was becoming more uneasy about his future and he mentioned his anxieties to Peter as the two trod heavily through the thick foliage of the potato crop. His apprehensiveness about his future caused him to have grave doubts about the so-called advantage he had been given. He wanted so much to do what was pleasing to his parents; the sacrifices that were made on his behalf required nothing less from him. There were aspects of the priestly life that appealed to him — he could see it as the highest of callings, conferring high status and even power. At the same time, how could he be sure of having what people called the "true vocation"? After all, the bishop must have had doubts about his suitability.

Peter felt ill equipped to give council to his agonising brother. He was not lacking in empathy or sympathy, but he saw it as a torturous dilemma requiring more inspired intervention. Both agreed it best not to over-invest their time with this one and to shift focus away to things of a livelier nature. They were determined to make the best of these summer days that had them together for this little while. Whatever the future had in store for John it was unlikely to accommodate his closeness to his brother. However, gone were the days when their every movement and outside contact required parental approval. The message was slowly sinking in that these were young men whose tastes and values could no longer be dictated. However painful this may seem, it is nothing more than the natural progression that inhabits the family and society. Nevertheless, every phenomenon has its effects; the McGinn boys would be no different, for better or worse, their earlier impoundment would resonate in some way, perhaps in some form of rejection or rebellion later in life.

"That's another job well done," said Peter. "It should keep the blight away from this fine crop of pinks." They looked around the beautiful countryside in an effort to assess how the crops in general were looking, or how they were in relation to their own. Both concluded that theirs were as good if not better than anything within their view. So engrossed were the pair that they almost failed to notice Sammy Dunne walking down the lane that led from the wooded area above his house and him carrying a large bundle of firewood. They were very pleased to see him out and about. Obviously, it was not the case that he had taken ill again; it seemed that everything was well and the two women were at work.

chapter eighteen

It was early morning on the first Monday of August when the narrow-gauge train pulled out from Ballintober railway station. Packed full of young people from all over the parish and other areas as well, it was taking them all to Bundoran for the bank holiday excursion. In this, the Dooras and Ballintober contingent were as one. All rivalry set aside, they would partake of all the fun and games together. Peter had saved enough from his weekly allowance to enable him to sample most of what was on offer. After paying his train fare John was hoping to have ten shillings left for spending, but his brother was in a generous mood and would see to it that he did not run short. The crowded carriages were noisy from an over supply of youthful energy; nothing would be allowed to get in the way of this fun-bent party.

By foot, the entire party made its way from Bundoran station to the sandy beach. The day was bright and sunny, and there was laughter all about. Peter walked with some lads from the football team, while John found himself walking with a girl called Dolores Higgins from the other side of the village on the Ballintober road. She was about sixteen years old and had just sat her Intermediate Certificate examination. He soon found she was keen to be in his company. This he did not mind in the least, as she was pretty and this was his day for living.

The day passed quickly and the fun was mighty. The fact that they were all doing these things together made it all the merrier. Cheap snacks were availed of at lunchtime — there were plenty of seaside cafés available with menus that suited their pockets. In the afternoon, it was a tour of the crowded pubs. Most of these extended to the back yards where tables and chairs were provided, with lively music coming through. Most of the young ones were drinking minerals but enjoyed the atmosphere just the same.

Peter and his friend Barry McCrory found themselves two seats inside and near where the musicians were playing. Barry, now in his early twenties, was drinking stout and in a lively mood, and they were poised to stay there for a while. John was with the main group that sat or stood out in the yard and Dolores sat next to him; they were enjoying themselves to the full.

"Let me sample the black stuff," said Peter to his friend, and then lifting the bottle that was almost empty he downed it in a shot. "A bit bitter, but not at all bad," was his immediate judgment, and then setting his soft drink to one side he stepped over to the bar and ordered two bottles of stout.

After Peter had consumed the second bottle, Barry advised that it being his first experience with the 'Substance Arthur' it might be advisable to leave it at that. In any case, they had spent almost two hours there and it was a beautiful day outside. "How about us going for a dip, Peter?" They went out to find that John and Dolores had already left with the others; they too were answering the call of the breaking waves. Out in the open Peter's steps were light. He felt a better man than ever before, now would be his time to meet the Bull Herron. "Peter, my friend, we take this stuff to make us feel good, at least we think it does and aren't we entitled to our illusion."

Behind the rocks, the men got into their football togs. Some of the girls had brought swimsuits with them, and everyone would get their turn in the water. Few of the Ballintober excursionists were able to swim. The two McGinns were able to manage a few breaststrokes they had managed to acquire in the deep lint dam at the bottom of Henry's hallow field. For that reason, none of them ventured too far out or away from each other, not even Peter, whose valour had just been augmented.

John was a little keen to impress his friends and began to wade further out towards the deep. When he got to a reasonable depth that was considered suitable for swimming, he turned around to face the shore. To his amazement there was little Dolores Higgins standing just a few paces away from him. He called on her not to come any further — he was going to swim back to the shore and said for her to wade in behind him. Swimming comfortably, he felt sure that the group was admiring his skill in the water; he was doing better than he ever imagined he could.

His showing off came to a sudden end when he heard

Dolores scream for help. Realising that something was wrong he stopped to look back and discovered that he was out of his depth. The frightened onlookers were in a state of panic; some were coming fast to their aid. Then a strong lifeguard caught John and pushed him out to Barry McCrory, who was wading in fast in front of Peter. A second guard was retrieving Dolores, who had already gone under. A much-relieved John McGinn walked out of the water between his brother and friend, while the two lifeguards were carrying Dolores a short distance behind. It was only when the process of resuscitation was being applied that the real horror of what had happened began to strike. It was learned that Dolores had ingested a dangerous amount of salt water, and they were unable to revive her. Very soon, the doctor and ambulance were on the scene and Dolores was on her way to Sligo Hospital. John was taken to a nearby tearoom where he was given a cup of tea and seated in a warm comfortable place.

The many people who had gathered started moving away, ruefully concluding that nothing more could be done and the day was still young. Not so the Dooras parish group who were standing fearfully numb and not knowing what to do in the face of impending tragedy. The joyfulness of this holiday outing had turned into gloom and darkness, all in a matter of seconds. John McGinn was by far the most deeply traumatised. He had the sympathy and deep concern of everyone in the group and many others as well. Peter stayed close by him, knowing that he was suffering greatly and fearful about what might be happening to Dolores. There was also an inkling of guilt beginning to weigh upon John's mind. He regressed to a foetal posture and said he wished he had stayed at home.

While this was taking place, the doctor who had travelled with the patient in the ambulance informed the driver that it was all over. Dolores Higgins was the latest fatality of the cruel sea. It was a strong undercurrent that had swept under her and John. The fact that he had managed to swim the few extra yards was the saving of his precious life.

The Garda Sergeant arrived at the tearoom to deliver the tragic news. He took Barry McCrory aside and told him that he wished to take a statement from one or perhaps two of the people who were there. Barry informed the sergeant that he was witness to all that had taken place and would willingly sign a statement. He mentioned that John was the one nearest to Dolores when she drowned, but he was now in a very distressed state and should be spared the ordeal of talking it through. The good guardian of the law was most compliant; he would hear Barry's account and talk to Peter as well. The man was most sympathetic towards all of them.

Their distress was heightened even further by having to wait another two hours for their train to leave Bundoran. What a way to end a day that was supposed to have been one of fun and laughter. The tragic news reached the stricken family via Fr Gillen who had been contacted from the hospital; it would not be a happy homecoming for the excursion party.

The shadow of gloom and poignancy hung over the entire community for a time after, but the business of sustenance must be attended to; life always moves us on. Andy and Sarah Higgins had two other daughters and a son to live and work for; they would have to continue on their earthly mission. Nothing less was expected from them. With fortitude and a simple faith that allowed them to accept what had happened, soon their daily routine returned to nearly what it once had been.

The days and weeks that followed the tragedy were dark and bleak ones for poor John. He seemed to have lost interest in all that was happening around him, but worst of all was his reluctance to talk about what had happened. His state of mind was a cause for concern. In spite of John's misgivings, the Higgins family attributed no blame to him in relation to the loss of their lovely daughter. In kindness, they said so to him when he called to their grieving home with his parents and brother. Their sensitivity and deep concern for this tormented young man was laudable and moving. They understood what all this was doing to him and wanted to be part of his healing and recovery.

The period that followed was fraught with anxiety about John and his disturbed state, and everyone acted in a way that was thoughtful towards him. None more so than Aunt Rose, who was still staying at Henry's after the others had gone back.

John continued to do a little work in the fields but there was no compulsion on him to do so, and what he did was by choice. In spite of much coaxing from Peter and friends, he missed a couple of vital games in the tournament; he had simply lost the will to enjoy it any more. In the midst of it all he got word that he had passed his Leaving Certificate exams, obtaining reasonably good grades. Not in the mood for celebrating his rite of passage, he did nonetheless think about its implications and where it might lead him. The fact that he still hadn't ruled out the religious life was not lost on his mother. At the same time, she made no attempt at swaying him in that direction. Others including Fr Gillen had warned against this kind of intervention.

Tom and Ciss, along with Aunt Rose, seldom missed an opportunity to discuss John's situation, but were always careful to do so in his absence. They all recognised that this was a critical time for him. It was during one of these engagements that Rose suggested that John might benefit from coming with her to Canada for a while. She also informed them that there was a large seminary in her parish. It was run by the order of Dominicans, many of whom she was friendly with.

Perhaps this, more than any other factor, had to do with the idea being entertained. After all, she would be around for another three weeks, so they would all have time to consider this option. Only if John genuinely wanted to, would she consider introducing him to any member of the priestly order. There would be other avenues open to him out there.

In the circumstances, John was open to the suggestion of going to Canada and became interested right away. From then on, he pursued his elderly aunt relentlessly, making daily visits to her and sometimes more. Finally, Tom transported Aunt Rose and John to the post office where Mary the postmistress of Dooras connected Rose with her daughter Bett in Montreal with an overseas trunk call to inform her that she was bringing John back to Montreal with her. By this time, the entire focus was on John McGinn and his immediate future. Aunt Rose's offer and its subsequent parental acceptance were indeed timely; it was what brought John out of terrible darkness.

The remainder of John's time in Cruckban was taken up mainly by preparation for his leaving. There would be passport and emigration procedures needing attention. These were clearly things he could not do on his own; it would be much safer to have them done under the Boss's supervision. In many ways, it was so reminiscent of what went on six years earlier when all things ceased in the milieu of going to boarding school. Equally, the same was the final parting, the only difference being the hackney car and the sweet lady who hired it. The departure of Rose was always a weepy occasion for Ciss and Kitty, only this time their tears were from a deeper heart as they watched John gather his things. In sorrow, Peter tried to be like his father and control his emotions in a manly fashion. By whatever way, John was in the car with his minder as the heartbroken four were left in sadness to observe his departure to the new world.

Two days later a telegram arrived to say that all had arrived safely and that a letter would follow in due course. The home atmosphere was not all that affected by John's absence, as the family had gotten accustomed to this situation over the years of his schooling. It was nearly three weeks before John's first letter reached Cruckban, and it was lengthy and detailed. He was very happy staying with Aunt Rose, and he praised the kindly attention he was receiving. Paul had found him a position in the office of a transport company, where the work was demanding but interesting. A separate note was enclosed for Peter. In it, John enquired about almost everything around the home and district. How was their team progressing in the competition and who had taken his place at the centre of the field? He also wanted to know how the Higgins family was doing. His thoughts were still very much with them and Dolores. He would have liked to write to them, but it would be hard for him to find the right words.

All the letters that followed were indicative of reasonable contentment, and it was understandable that he continued to be interested in what was happening at home. For that reason, Peter's replies were very important to him. They were graphically descriptive of everything local, even things that were not considered important at home. They told of how the harvesting was progressing and that the crops were better than ever before, so a substantial return was assured. Peter was now going to Ballintober on Saturday nights with his friends. He had finally confronted the old pair about this, leaving them with little choice but to concede. This, he informed John, was but the beginning. His contribution to the home enterprise had to be acknowledged, and he was his own man at last.

Man to a point, but not fully. This point was brought home to him when Kitty arrived home from school still crying from the trauma of being belted with that leather strap. The marks were visible on the backs of her little legs, and it had obviously been a painful and frightening ordeal for the child. Tom and Ciss were deeply upset and showed an anger that should have spurred them into action. Tom gave the usual line with force and seeming conviction; the question was, how much? From experience, Peter knew full well how this would all come to nothing. Bull Herron was the law and enjoyed the protection of a mighty authoritative shield.

As expected, wiser counsel did prevail. Ciss and the Boss reasoned that this being Kitty's last year, it might be better to exercise restraint. Up until then they had managed to maintain a sense of dignified responsibility in relation to the school authority, and their reputation might best be served by letting it remain that way.

This attitude of supposed reason was more than Peter could take. He went to bed early that night and thought deeply about the situation. He had arranged to take the two heavy horses to be shod at Gallagher's Forge the next morning, and it occurred to him that Bull always passed there at around half past eight on his way to work. Lying alone in that loft, he could feel the force of his anger take hold. This had as much to do with his own troubled memories as it had to do with what happened to his sister. After a restless night, Peter was out and about long before the others. He was on his way to the forge much earlier than usual. He was greeted cordially by the Gallagher brothers and commended for being out so early; it was only twenty past eight. These men of brawn got quickly to work; the hearth was aglow from the breeze of the bellows as the sparks of the melting iron fell from the anvil like the fragments of a shooting star under each hammer blow.

While this was happening, Peter stood outside the door of the forge, holding the two leads in one hand while maintaining a steady lookout towards the road. It was almost half past eight, so he knew the Master would soon be approaching. After tying the two leads to an iron spike that protruded from the sidewall, he moved out towards the road. This was his moment, the big challenge. The lone cyclist on the road was nearly two hundred yards away from where the challenger stood. He was pedalling fast as usual and mindful of the road in front of him. With as much of a smile as he was capable of offering, he greeted,

"Good morning Peter." He got no reply; just a straight and stern look instead. The dour look of the old Bull returned, it was as frightening as ever and it worked. Poor Peter froze to the ground; neither limb nor tongue seemed capable of serving his intentions. This is how it was for those vital seconds, and when the moment passed, the Bull was safely out of sight. With a heavy heart and feeling less than adequate, he went back to his horses and the company of the farriers. The answer was plain and simple: Peter the man was still afraid of this tyrannical creature. The object of fear is indeed a potent force and always difficult to overcome.

Not all of this was related to John in Peter's letters; he preferred to strike a happier note for the benefit of his brother so far away from home. It was that sense of distance that began to disturb the family a little. Yes, they knew what it was like with him being away from a young age, but this time he might just be gone for good. Less than six weeks after John's departure, a melancholic atmosphere began to pervade the household. The praying was intensified, mostly for his safety and future intentions. Peter was beginning to grow a little tired of hearing his brother's virtues being extolled monotonously several times each day.

However, others were observing his virtues as well, as it became known the morning Fr Gillen arrived at the house. He had just received a letter along with a questionnaire from the Superior of the order in Montreal concerning none other than John McGinn. Needless to say, this was the catalyst of revival. It heralded yet another flurry of amusing escapades. John had at last made the momentous decision and, as before, it took on a life of its own.

chapter nineteen

It was called an Indian summer — the warm October sunshine was unbelievable, and the dust was rising from the reel of the potato digger in the middle field. The crop of Kerr pinks was yielding heavy. Peter was so proud of it; this was what he had predicted in the springtime. There was a look of excessive satisfaction on the faces of his parents; they had so much to be thankful for. It seemed almost assured that the bank deposit would increase substantially with the sale of the farm produce and their hopes for the future of their eldest seemed assured.

Difficult though it was, they did refrain from divulging anything about John's sacred calling to anyone outside the family. Indeed the question was asked more than once by the potato gatherers but the answer was always guarded: "John is doing very well in Canada." This was as far as they ever allowed themselves to go on this subject. It was even withheld from Hess, who must surely have suspected that strange things were going on.

Strange happenings of another kind also caught Peter's attention. It had not escaped the attention of the villagers that Maggie Dunne had stopped going to work in the factory. It was also noticed that the young man from Ballintober had not been seen on the road for some time. From these observations, there could be only one conclusion drawn, and it was not a joyful one. Aggie McCrory, through her friendship with Mrs Dunne, would have been first to know the awful truth, but she was too much a lady to pass such a story on. Through other channels and by deduction, the news did break and got its first airing in parliament.

Ciss and Tom McGinn expressed feelings of deep sorrow for the unfortunate family on the night that Dinny brought the morbid story to them. It was told in the presence of Peter and they talked as if he had not been there, perhaps deliberately so, or were they attempting to talk to him through each other? "This should be a lesson for all young men, to beware of the dangers that lurk in this wicked world." They did not elaborate as to where this wickedness resided but did refer to the value of good parenting, and where it was lacking the consequences were seldom good.

It was a discussion Peter had no wish to be part of. Quietly he left the company and headed up the stepladder to the loft. The impact of what he had just heard was bewildering and disconcerting, and he felt deeply for his former friend and sweetheart. From the little he knew about these kinds of things he could only conclude that it was the wickedness of the world that had impinged upon her goodness. Nothing unvirtuous should ascribe to Maggie Dunne or her poor parents. However, in this his thinking was at odds with the rest of society. There was little or no tolerance for them that offended the tenet of respectability. From thence, she would be looked upon as a fallen woman, and she would have to pay the price. Not so, the bright young man from the bigger village. It was soon discovered that he had left the country, but to where, no one knew. Knowing that what he had done to one who was little more than a child was going to attract the attention of the law, he quickly made off.

All this now explained to him why Maggie had not been seen out since early summer and why she had been at home that morning when she had avoided him. He thought about how she was going to contend with what lay before her and his own discomfort if ever he should meet her again. It was his past involvement with her that caused him to think in this way, after all he knew her better than most, even though it was nearly two years since the time of their parting. His feelings of pity then changed to anger and resentment. He cursed the infatuation that drew him towards her in the first place, and more so the circumstances of his own situation, with its origins in an outdated kinship to class and poverty.

His anger intensified when he considered the slick guy from Ballintober, whom he had bitterly resented from the first time he saw him with Maggie. Yes, the world was indeed a wicked place and its evils are fed from many sources. It was always convenient to apportion guilt away from the powerful; society cannot afford to disturb this mighty collective. That was how it had to be for this helpless young girl and her people; she was the author of her own misfortune.

Apart from Maggie's pathetic plight, there was the added

problem of increased poverty for Sally Dunne to contend with. She was so fortunate in having a friend like Aggie McCrory, but there is only so much that a friend could do in a case like this. It had to be remembered that this was an age when almost everyone existed on scarce resources, and, of course, there was the moral question of how right it was to be over-engaged with a situation of the kind. Sally knew full well how limited her options were and that time was running out for her daughter. Soon she would have to decide what was possible or practical. To keep Maggie at home for her confinement, or have her sent to that dreaded home she herself had known less than sixteen years earlier. It was the only form of social assistance available to the poor and destitute and it was worse than being back at school. If in her power, Sally would try and save her child from such a painful and humiliating ordeal.

The service of the district nurse was free of charge, and if needed, Dr Martin's generosity could be relied upon. Sammy Dunne knew he had to be strong; his concerns were for a wife who was totally sapped of energy and for a daughter who had been his vital life support for so long. He would go along with whatever Sally thought was possible. There should be no moral objection to Maggie remaining at home in her plentiful state, even for the birth itself, as there were no other siblings in the house with her. It was considered most improper to have children or young teenagers exposed to this phenomenon of nature.

Sammy's depression always manifested itself in self-blaming for his sinful wrongdoing to Sally. He had left her at a time when she needed him most, the early stages of her pregnancy with Maggie. Sally had been an orphan child brought up by an aging grandmother in a neighbouring parish. She came to work in Glenleigh Creamery shortly after the old woman had passed on, and she met the popular Sammy Dunne soon afterwards.

Having surrendered herself to the merciless enclosure of the institutional home, her stay there was long and agonising. It was said to be at the insistence of Aggie McCrory that Sammy eventually signed the necessary claiming document that would deliver Sally and her year-old child from custody. They got married a short time later and were as happy as circumstances would allow them to be. In his sickly state these haunting memories revisited him relentlessly, only this time it was more sombre. History was repeating itself and it was his only child who would be paying the price for his selfish and sinful past. Aware of his own dependency and inability to help, he prayed for the strength not to be an added burden.

In the weeks that followed, he played a helpful role to Maggie, right up until her time was due. Every day he kept busy collecting much-needed firewood. He was kind and supportive in everything he said or did. It was a case of him going that extra mile to be helpful, and at times, this was by no means easy. Nevertheless, there was benefit in this for both of them and it helped hardworking Sally as well. It was reassuring for her to know that they were still good friends and helpful to each other.

Shortly before her sixteenth birthday, Maggie Dunne gave birth to twin boys. It all happened in the outshot room of the little shanty. She had a severe time but the nurse was expert and managed on her own with Sally's assistance. Everyone was pleased to see it over, and that all three had survived with every sign of them being well and strong. Little Maggie was now a mother. Her childhood had been taken from her, and hard times lay ahead for all of them. The next day the babies were taken to Ballintober chapel for baptism and given the names James and Brian. There was no celebrating their arrival; they were simply looked upon as the product of lustful irresponsibility, which respectable people could never condone.

It was an event that aroused considerable local interest, and was talked about for a while. People were generally sympathetic and helpful in some practical ways, perhaps in a spirit of loving the sinner but not the sin. Very soon, other happenings would overshadow the plight of these uninteresting folks, and they would be left alone. At home, it suited Peter McGinn that the subject was never mentioned in his presence. Only once did Ciss remind him of his good fortune at being free of these people and the seriousness of being caught up with the wrong company. This was the ethos he had been brought up with; it was the only one he knew. Well-intended though it may have been, it did discomfort him more than a little. At the same time, he was happier then than ever before, as he was now doing what he loved best and was free at last to go as he pleased. This was his future and it wasn't to be squandered through a stubborn adherence to an opinion he still could not be sure about. The only thing he could be reasonably sure about was the unlikelihood of him ever again being with Maggie Dunne. Even in an atmosphere where feelings still existed, the situation was that it would be out of the question for him.

In the course of time, their paths did cross again, but it was really awkward and uncomfortable for both of them. It was a Saturday evening in early spring and not yet dark. Peter was cycling in the direction of the village while Maggie was on her way back from Aggie's shop. She was pale and drab, nothing at all like the lively Maggie he once held in his arms during those days of happy innocence. Her nervous smile to him was obviously one of deep embarrassment; his awareness of this caused him unease as well. His heartbeat was rapid as he pondered what to do. Should he stop and ask how she and her babies were doing? No, that he would never do. On the other hand, just smile "hello" and keep going? The latter was the easy option and the encounter was over before he knew it.

As he proceeded on towards the village where he would meet his friend Barry McCrory, he got to thinking about how it was for Maggie. In no way could she be happy in her role as mother to two fatherless children. The imposition she was to her suffering parents must have been troubling her greatly, but there was nothing she could do to make it any easier. Again, he thought about his own involvement with her, and wondered if in some way it could have contributed to her misfortune.

Misfortune it surely was and nothing less. Here he was totally free and heading for town with his pal. Barry and himself were on a similar mission. Peter had found a new girlfriend and Barry was going steady. This was neither the time nor the place to be thinking about the fairness of things, but it was plain to see that the advantage was stacked heavily in favour of the male of the species. The short walk to Aggie's shop was as far as poor Maggie could ever hope to travel. No weekends or happy outings for her to look forward to. However, her situation was not unique. Throughout the land on that same Saturday evening, many young men were out celebrating the very freedom that they had thoughtlessly denied to others like Maggie Dunne. Like most disturbing thoughts that melt away under the influence of things more appealing, Peter's gave way on his meeting with Barry. An interesting evening lay ahead for both of them.

chapter twenty

Mickey the postman placed the letter on the kitchen table. "It's one for the young fellow," he said to Ciss, who was wetting the tea. She knew at a glance it was not from Canada. Long gone were the days when either she or the Boss would have opened a letter addressed to Peter. At the same time, she was in the grip of anxious curiosity about its origins. No sooner had wee Mickey gone out the door than she summoned Tom from the yard. On inspection, he was able to tell her that it had been posted in Newtowncunningham two days earlier. They would just have to wait until Peter returned from the May fair of Raphoe. If in the right mood, he might ease their anxieties by telling them who it was from and what it had to say. However, regardless of mood he would first peruse it carefully lest it should contain anything of a personal nature.

When Peter returned, the strong scent he brought with him that comes from freshly consumed Guinness did not appear to bother them. For some reason or other, this was an acceptable form of recreation. "There came a letter for you this morning," was how Ciss greeted her son. "Yes, I know," Peter replied. By strange coincidence, he had met up with his old friend and cousin Paddy Farrell at the fair. They had a lot to chat about and notes to compare in relation to their mutual interest. Like their elders, this could best be done over a drink or two. In the midst of it all Paddy talked about his plans to get married the following October and wanted Peter to be his best man. He also explained that he had sent Peter a letter that contained all the information he was now relating in person. Without hesitation, it was Peter's pleasure to accept the honour his cousin was affording him. This would be yet another experience for the boy from Cruckban.

A few days later saw the arrival of another letter. It was from John in Canada to his parents. He would not be coming home for the summer holidays; his old job with the transport company was open to him again for the summer months. They were a little surprised that the letter contained no mention of the seminary or the priests who ran it. Without being over-concerned, they both concluded that the place probably did close down for the duration of the summer. It was also good to know that he was safely back with Aunt Rose and earning money as well. She would not be with the first contingent of Canadian visitors, who would be arriving at Henry's in mid-July. For whatever reason, Rose had decided to wait a little longer, perhaps until late August. Her coming was of greater interest to Tom and Ciss, as her assessment of their son's progress would be informed and honest.

After Sunday dinner, Ciss took off on a cycle run to Strabane, as she had not seen her friend Olive Devine for some time, and it was a beautiful day to be out. There was absolutely no doubt about her liking for this special family relation. It was a friendship she had worked hard to keep alive ever since they had first met in the Gallaghers' house in Dublin. Spending an evening together had a niceness about it; it was the sort of thing that close friends usually did and they had much to talk about as well. Apart from all of that, Ciss had another reason for going there on this occasion. Of late, she had begun to notice that Peter was going out more often, always on a Wednesday night as well as the usual weekend outing. He was meticulous about how he dressed, and to his mother this could only mean one thing. Oddly enough, it was wee Kitty who supplied the details of what her brother was up to. It was common knowledge around the village that young McGinn was courting a girl named Margaret Devine from Strabane. Kitty and her schoolfriends were of an age to be interested in such things. Armed with this information, vigilant Ciss was on her way to find out the rest of the story.

After cycling the six miles to Strabane Ciss was made welcome and Olive and herself settled down for a chat in the living room. Most things relating to the fortunes of both families got an airing in the course of the evening. On the subject of John, Ciss kept faith with the policy of saying nothing beyond what was safe, though she had no problem whatever in talking about Peter, saying he was a good worker and very enthusiastic.

"Enthusiastic in other ways as well," Ciss went on as she related what knowledge she had acquired to her half-interested cousin. Olive informed her that there were many families living locally who shared their surname and all of them were decent people. She would certainly keep her ears and eyes open and gladly pass on whatever she found out. Unknown to Olive her daughter, who happened to be listening to the conversation, was friendly with a younger sister of the girl in question. Needless to say, news then got out about Ciss' investigation, and Margaret heard that Peter's mother had been checking her out.

When Margaret mentioned this to Peter the following Wednesday, he was embarrassed beyond words and felt deeply inadequate in her presence. Truthfully, he knew absolutely nothing about what his busy mother had been up to, or indeed, what she was trying to achieve. However, in his heart he knew what it was all about. The episode with Maggie Dunne was still lurking in his mother's mind.

What kind of woman is my mother? Peter thought to himself as he cycled home alone much earlier than usual that night. It was a most uncomfortable situation for him to be in, and nothing like what his precious date was intended to be. He even lacked the will to suggest another meeting with Margaret for the weekend. It was best to leave things for a little while at least. Now the question was, how to deal with his dear mother. The last thing he wanted was to offend her, but after what she had done to him, he was going to confront her in some way. He knew the story would be told and re-told around Strabane by those young ones, even by their parents. Worse still, it could even make its way back to the village. At home, nothing was said about the incident over the following days. Peter decided it was best to wait until the weekend when it would be his time for going out again. This weekend was going to be sacrificed for the sake of making one important point to his meddling mother.

He knew that his staying in was going to create an itching curiosity around the place, and most likely to invite the kind of comment that allowed him to say what he wanted to. It would be his opportunity to tell them why he was not going out — he was being turned into the joke of the parish through the actions of his own mother.

On Saturday night after teatime, Peter made no attempt to get ready for town. Holding a clean and carefully ironed shirt in her hands Ciss asked what time he was leaving and remarked that he was later than usual. He kept his composure thoroughly as he delivered the well-rehearsed reproach. His reaction alarmed her a little, and she seemed deeply wounded and bewildered. She was rendered speechless for a change. What he had said went deeper than intended.

Without commenting, she left the kitchen and went back to her laundering in the sitting room. Peter took a book and went up to his room. The house seemed quieter than usual after the unhappy exchange had ended. The Boss had gone to town and Kitty was doing something by herself outside. To herself, Ciss was amazed at how fast the true purpose of her visit to Olive had reached her son's ears. At the same time, she was attaching no blame to her friend for mishandling the information she had given her. Too late, she realised that what she had done was ill conceived and counter-productive. It was a distress she was going to have to bear alone. On no account could she share it, not even with her husband, who knew nothing about her meddling. She also knew that Peter was hardly likely to say anything more about it to anyone else. The relationship between this mother and her son would eventually be restored to what it once was. It was to nobody's advantage that it should remain otherwise.

Restoring his relationship with Margaret Devine was not to be for Peter. It took a few weeks for him to get out and about again and going back there was certainly not part of his plans. He was much relieved that the story had not gathered sufficient momentum so as to be an obstacle to him rejoining the group. Again enjoying the company of his friends, the pictures on Saturday nights and dancing in the old school hall on Sunday, he was careful not to engage in any steady courtship. Before long, he acquired a taste for the casual encounter. From this, he began to earn a reputation as a bit of a ladies' man and he found life to be quite exciting once again. The dispute with his mother soon faded into the forgotten.

For Ciss the process of healing was aided greatly by the arrival of her annual visitors, and interesting days lay ahead. It was an interesting time for Kitty as well; she had finally come to the end of her schooling. The decision was made for her to be kept at home to help her mother with the housework. With more intensive and profitable farming comes a corresponding demand on the housewife. For a start, a greater number of casual workers have to be employed over a longer season. The increase to the livestock herd would in no small way add to the farmyard chores. Kitty was very compliant with her parents' decision, as she fully concurred with what they were proposing. Financially the McGinns were now better able to send their daughter to a prestigious boarding school than ever before, but this was never considered. It was obvious that Kitty did not want this; she was a child who liked to be with her family and home environment. A big factor in this was undoubtedly her personal experience of the education system.

Cousin Bett questioned this decision at length on the evening Tom and Ciss went to visit her and Paul at Henry's cottage. "The fact that a child is not overly bright should never be a reason for not affording her the opportunity." The poor woman was not sufficiently informed of the Irish farming value system that prevailed at the time. It was a system or culture that placed little value on the contribution of women in society — it was a value only considered in relation to its service to man. Ciss was not impressed by Bett's latest pronouncement, but, in the interest of their friendship, she did not argue with her. To her there was nothing ignoble about the farmer's daughter working and learning the farming trade at home with her own family. There is no greater asset to the industry or the community than to become a competent farmer's wife. Of course, all this was far beyond the comprehension of a fancy lady from a large and foreign city. However, apart from the imposition of uninvited opinion, the visit went well and all of them had an enjoyable time.

They arrived back to be met by a tearful Kitty, and Peter almost as bad. Dinny was at the fire heating the stirabout pot; he had just brought the sad news of old Ned McDevitt's death. Unknown to all of them Ned had been taken to the infirmary the night before. His deterioration was rapid and he had passed away late that afternoon. Deep sorrow gripped the McGinn home that night. Their thoughts then turned to Bella and how lonely she was going to be. "I think we should go down there," Tom suggested to Ciss. They both knew that the old woman would be glad of their company. Before they arrived at the cottage, Ned's remains had already been brought there to be waked, so quite a number of others had gathered in. The generosity of the neighbours was evident in the amount of homebaked bread and sweet cake the ladies handed round throughout the entire night. It was a sit up until morning with the same expected for the following night, only the numbers would be much greater.

So highly respected were the elderly couple that the entire McGinn enterprise came to a halt, and only the essentials were attended to. Peter made himself available to help in whatever way he could. Jimmy Peen McDevitt was very appreciative of this, as he had many things to attend to at the time. The two stopped for a drink in Cathers' pub on their way back from business relating to the funeral. Peen was concerned about his mother and how she was now going to manage on her own. He confided in Peter the news that he and Mary Ward were thinking about tying the marital knot and moving to Scotland. All this they had been planning during happier times when none of this was envisaged. Leaving her lonely and heartbroken, to pine away the little time she had left, was more than he could contemplate right then.

It was a well-attended and respectable wake and funeral; many tears were shed at the graveside for a decent old gentleman. That night Peter sat down and wrote a lengthy letter to his brother in Canada. John would be very disturbed on hearing the sad news about the one they all thought would never die, and who had left them with a wealth of happy memories.

After a few weeks had passed and no signs of a reply to his letter, Peter wondered was something the matter. His parents too were showing signs of anxiety about this unusual delay. Then it suddenly dawned on all of them that Aunt Rose would be arriving in less than a week's time. "That's what it is," laughed Ciss, "she will be bringing the letters and all the other news as well."

Aunt Rose brought more than news with her that fine August day; John was first to step out of the Hackney car that brought them to Cruckban. The expression of shock that showed on his parents' faces made it appear that he was less than welcome. At least that was how it appeared to John, so what was on his mind that caused him to think this way? Looking pale and thin, not quite the John that had left them eleven months earlier, his parents bade him welcome, he was at home again.

Peter and Kitty were aglow with delight as the three of them walked down the path towards the front door. Their parents and Aunt Rose were still in the yard. John just told them he had changed his mind about not coming home and was now glad that he had done so. However, it looked as if there was more to be told, and no doubt, time would reveal everything.

Rose asked to talk to Tom and Ciss alone, and Tom put a match to the pre-set fire in the parlour. The three young ones were happy to remain in the kitchen. The returned Canadian would have a lot to tell about the bigger scene, and perhaps a present or two as well. After an hour or more had passed, Ciss came up to make the tea and bade Kitty to see about the boys. She went back carrying a special tray in her hands. There were signs coming from her that the bottle had been opened, but it did not disguise the concerned look on her face. Only John himself knew what was being discussed in the parlour, and he would reveal nothing until that meeting had ended. When his mother returned, she invited him to join them for a chat. Rose began, "I have just been talking to your parents about you not being happy with the Dominicans and that you've suffered a lot from homesickness ever since you left home."

Very emotionally, John began relating his thoughts and feelings about life, how and where he saw his place in it, certainly not in the priesthood. However, the six months he had spent in the seminary were not wasted. In his opinion, it was a real education that had enabled him to see things more clearly. Again, with emotion, he thanked his parents for all they had given him and said how much he wanted to do what was right for them. Having listened at length to Rose, both parents were graciously accepting. Ciss broke into tears as her son talked nervously and directly to both of them. He then went on to tell them about his good fortune in meeting a wonderful priest professor while he was with the order. This was Fr George Purcell, a first-class academic with strong Irish roots; both of his parents came from County Galway.

It was this man more than anything else that took the young novice through a most stressful time and on to making a mature decision. Rose endorsed all that he said about Fr Purcell; she had known him for some time and found him to be everything one could desire in a man of the cloth. She went on to say that he was planning to move to England on research study and might be coming to visit her at Henry's cottage for a few days in September. He would be anxious to meet John's family, and would share his thoughts with all of them in relation to John's decision. She was certain they would derive enormous benefit from his informed wisdom.

Ten days later Fr Purcell arrived and was introduced to the McGinns by Aunt Rose. He was a tall heavy-set man with thick-rimmed glasses, whose dark wavy hair was just showing a little grey at the sides. He spent a long afternoon with the family, most of it with John and his parents, but he made time for the others as well. With great sensitivity and consideration for their feelings, he took Tom and Ciss McGinn through the hellish struggle of uncertainty that besets the mind of the reluctant seminarian. He reminded them that they had a good and dutiful son who needed their unconditional support in whatever he chose to do. In his informed opinion, John was still living the traumatic effects of that terrible drowning tragedy at the time he had decided to try the seminary. Fr Purcell fully understood the ambitious desire of a parent to have a son take holy orders. Indeed, it is most admirable that they should endeavour to foster and encourage in that direction. However, beyond that little else can safely be done. This encounter turned out to be most beneficial to all concerned. John went in pursuit of a steady job, thus putting to final rest any lingering notions about the higher calling, and Fr Purcell became an additional family friend.

For now, the future of each of the McGinn children seemed set on their chosen courses, and the uncertainty of those teenage years eased for Peter and John, as well as for their parents. Peter had decided it was easier to steer clear of romantic entanglements, and he was content to concentrate on improving the running of the farm. The results he was achieving were without doubt making his commitment very worthwhile. Everything was on course for a more settled kind of living.

chapter twenty-one

The weather was unusually mild for mid-January, and Peter was cross ploughing the hallow field for spuds. The ground was dry and turning over delightfully as the crows and gulls scavenged for the reveals of the freshly awoken earth. Over the past three years, Peter had put all his energies into the farm, and he had become an expert ploughman, with a special bond between himself and his two horses, Bob and Billy.

His reputation as a progressive farmer was widely recognised throughout the neighbourhood and beyond. However, with all his success he had not yet managed to take control of matters financial. Tom McGinn still held the purse strings and showed no signs of letting go. This was becoming an obstacle to Peter's plans to mechanise and develop. The Boss was reluctant to move away from a system that was working so well. Tom's contention was that they were making very good money under the present arrangement and there was a sizable deposit in the bank to prove it.

Nevertheless, the younger man could see that the days of horse labour were rapidly ending. In this, he had the support of brother John, who now held a clerical post with the Donegal County Council. They could both see that their method of working was antiquated and would be as good as gone in three years' time. However, it would probably take that long for Cruckban to see the light.

It was Peter's intention to plough the entire Blue Rock Farm this year, so he would be there every day for the next couple of weeks. There was a quiet peacefulness about these fields that he liked profoundly, and they invoked certain romantic memories for him as well.

Holding the plough handles and the reins while calling the horsespeak "hoo" and "hee", Peter was momentarily distracted by the sight of two timid little faces peering over the fence at him. They were captivated by this unique dialogue between the ploughman and his horses, but seemed afraid to venture beyond their own confines.

Full well he knew that these were the sons of Maggie Dunne. It was a kindly smile he gave them, but he moved on without saying a word. They were vigilant and persistent little observers, and many times he crossed that field to find them always watching. As his work took him farther away from their view, he noticed how fast they were at finding another position from where they could observe the operation. It was then that he first spoke to them the words “Hello boys”. They did not reply to his greeting but looked at each other instead. How quickly time passes, he thought to himself. These boys were now coming close to four years old. He knew that Maggie was back working in the factory and had been for the past three years. This lifted a heavy burden off her mother’s shoulders, with the extra money making a big difference to their living standard. To Peter they looked healthy and energetic, not at all like their late Uncle Jimmy.

As the day progressed, he could see that they were showing little signs of diminishing interest in what he was doing. When he and his horses came back after dinner, there were the two, waiting anxiously for his return. By the end of the second day, they were talking freely through the hedge and asking Peter questions about his work. More especially about Bob and Billy and how they came to have people names. In the two weeks that followed, Peter seldom walked the furrow alone, but he enjoyed the innocence of their questioning comments. For two lonely children this man and his splendid paraphernalia meant everything that was good about life. On the day that the last furrow of the Blue Rock Farm was turned over, the three friends said goodbye with a promise to meet again in the spring. Peter would move on to other manly tasks and things of interest, but for little James and Brian it was back to what it was before.

However, the before was by no means bad for them. With the women of the house both working, there was always about enough by way of food and clothing. The long-suffering Sammy Dunne was still their daytime minder and forever their dependable friend. He was well able to converse with them on the subject of horsemanship and how much of it he had done in his day. He told them many tales about the bigger fields on the Captain’s farm, each of them as big as the entire Blue Rock

Holding. That was not to make little of their friend Peter, whom he recognised to be one of the best workmen in the district and far beyond. He also said how lucky they were that it was young McGinn they had instead of Dinny the servant man. On no account would that cantankerous crank allow a pair of scruffy boys anywhere near where he was working. This gave them some idea of what the man Hess was like long before they ever set eyes upon him.

They were not identical twins; James was bigger and a little stronger than Brian was. It was difficult to say whom they most resembled, Maggie or the absentee father. That was not important, however, to children of their kind, children who would have to learn and never forget their place in the class arena. But these two were loved and cherished by the three who were their worthy guardians and nothing could be more important than that. They were the ultimate in innocence, not in the least contaminated by the forces of avarice that shaped and controlled this stratified world. Yet it was a world just waiting to impinge upon their carefree living, and there would be people to see to it that they were brought up in a proper manner.

However, they had not been told about that future. Sammy liked talking about happier things to his boys. On fair weather days, all three of them would go out collecting firewood in the wooded area behind their house. It was not an adventure that would afford them much contact with the outside world other than the occasional appearance of Biddy The Rum.

In all the years that had passed since the birth of her boys not once did Maggie converse with her childhood friend Peter. He had little choice but to put all thoughts about her out of his mind and that was best achieved by doing what he had now learned to enjoy, playing the field as the ladies' man. At the same time, he could not but notice that she was once again a strikingly beautiful young woman. She too was hearing about the things he was getting up to in the world that once was hers and which had ended before it began. Through his friendship with the little ones Peter was beginning to know more about the family and how things were for all of them.

James and Brian lived for nothing beyond the day when Peter would be back doing the routine jobs of tending the crops. So involved they became that each of them claimed ownership of Bob and Billy. It was a secret they shared with Peter and all three of their parents. Peter wondered about his liking for these twins — was it their childish innocence or had it something to do with his lingering affection for their mother? However, right then the "why" mattered little, he was able to see that it was good for them and he felt the better for that. He even introduced them to Aunt Rose and her friend Hannah, who had accompanied her from Canada that summer. Both of these old ladies were abounding in kindness towards little children.

Through that source, Ciss got to hear about the boys, of their almost constant presence with Peter in the fields and the occasional little party in the cottage as well. The menfolk were already aware of this since the time they had all been there for the spring sowing. Tom did not consider it an important enough issue to be bothering his hardworking wife with. There was nothing very unusual about young boys making a nuisance of themselves around where workmen are busy. Ciss too would have understood this and for that reason had nothing to say, certainly not to her son. Through her own generous nature, she could see that there was good in all of this, but with that particular family, there still seemed to be a problem. It was a problem Peter was well aware of, making him careful not to encourage the boys to ever think about coming to Cruckban. Their presence there would be a source of discomfort.

Both Maggie and her mother kept warning the boys not to be getting in this man's way and suggested that they may not even be wanted on the McGinn property. However, there is no place in the minds of little children for reasoning out a strange legacy of suspicion and mistrust that they knew nothing of. Getting in the way or not being wanted was not a concept that ever entered their childish minds. Nor indeed should it, as far as Peter or the ladies at Henry's were concerned. At times, when she was alone with her boys, Maggie would ask them about Peter and if he ever mentioned her name to them. On this, their response was never explicit, as they always had more important things to talk about. However, Maggie had her memories, which were still important to her. They were of happier times that now seemed remote and irretrievable.

This was not to say that she had turned her back on the outside world completely. With the encouragement of her parents, she was beginning to think about the occasional outing with her workmates. After all these years, it was going to be a difficult re-emerging for her. However, with the encouraging support of a few true friends she would get there and hopefully be a wiser woman. She became a regular attendee at the Sunday night dance in the old school hall and quickly regained her popularity.

It was there that Peter began to re-acquaint himself with her. As a neighbour and out of courtesy, he would give her the occasional duty dance, and they would talk to each other as if things had not changed that much since their early days. She apologised for the boys and hoped they were not too much of an annoyance to him. Dismissing the suggestion with a laugh, he switched the conversation to things of a more general nature. This would bring them to the end of the dance and the courteous "thank you" at the time of parting. That was as far as Peter could allow himself to get involved with this beautiful but fallen woman.

chapter twenty-two

Almost two years had now passed and Cruckban as well as its Boss were still very much in the dark. Even though the 1950s brought big changes to the area, with the inception of rural electrification and the introduction of tractors on many farms, an impatient Peter was back ploughing the Blue Rock Farm with the two tired old steeds. No longer could he share the enthusiasm of his young friends, whose belief in the old way had not diminished in the least.

They had now reached schoolgoing age. He began to think about this and even mentioned it to them. It was a subject neither of them liked to hear talked about, so they had obviously heard something about what went on there. He thought of the joy he and his work was bringing to their simple existence and how this tough regimentation would be taking much of it away from them. But then, they had to be brought up in a proper manner and who was going to challenge that dictate?

A dictate of another kind was being issued in the form of an ultimatum from son to father. This was going to be his last year for working this out-of-date method. Peter was now twenty-three and he had no hesitation in saying that he was the main contributor to the sizeable accumulation of wealth now enjoyed by the family. He bluntly stated that in the autumn some of that money was going to be invested in a new tractor along with the necessary implements that went with it. The confrontation was over in a couple of minutes; it was greeted with silence, which suited the challenger's purpose. He knew that his mission had been accomplished and was happy to continue working out the remainder of this passing era of drudgery. With that important piece of business now out of the way Peter got to thinking about his little friends and how they would feel about losing their precious Bob and Billy. However, the changeover would not be happening for at least another nine months, so he thought it best not to say anything to them about it until nearer the time.

It was most unusual that a young man with drive and ambition should ever bother himself about the fantasies of two six-year-old boys. Nevertheless, that was Peter McGinn, who had a strong liking for them and was becoming more and more interested in their welfare. He noticed Fr Gillen talking at length to their mother outside the door of the old school hall before the start of the Sunday night hop. Even though the war was long over and forgotten, this poor priest still had to police the proceedings, as the American sailors continued to infiltrate the scene there. His talk with Maggie was most likely about her father, but it could also have been about getting the twins started at school. There would be no let-up on the pressure coming from that quarter until the order was obeyed.

Knowing what lay in store for the boys, Peter would not be in a hurry to disturb their happiness with news of another kind. Work continued in the usual way until all the crops were sown yet again. It was a routine activity never again to be repeated on the McGinn farm. Its executant was not going to lament its passing, but at the same time, it was something he once had a passion for and enjoyed for a time. However, time moves us on to new challenges and hopefully greater prosperity for those who face up to them.

As a measure of the changing tide, which was still exclusive to the owner class, some farmers were availing of the spring respite to attend the agricultural spring show in Dublin. This was a spectacular event where young men like Peter McGinn and his cousin Paddy Farrell would get fed with ideas that their elders would curse as elaborate, destructive and unnecessary. Peter had a special reason to be there on this occasion and Paddy had been there before. They would spend most of their two days viewing the machinery stands and talking with the exhibitors from the various trading companies. There was a host of side attractions, which the two found interesting and entertaining.

Most of the exhibits both new and old were replicated in miniature and were for sale. As Peter moved around viewing the vast display, he spotted two miniature horses, one black and the other chestnut brown. Made from leather like material and attired in working harness they bore a remarkable resemblance to his very own Bob and Billy. No medals for guessing whom he had in mind as he put his purchases carefully into his overcoat pocket. For James and Brian these would represent the very best of life's varying milieu. He began to imagine their excited engrossment with these tiny artefacts and for that reason felt good within himself.

Apart from a visit to the Abbey Theatre on the night before their departure from the city, they spent most of their time in the vicinity of the show grounds. There was a carnival-like atmosphere throughout; it was an assembly of true countrymen with a comradeship that made them feel very special. In a peculiar way, Peter could feel an affinity with the character Christy Mahon in the Abbey's production of Synge's drama, *The Playboy of the Western World.* While not going quite so far as to use the loy on his old man, he nevertheless felt the elements of the rebel surge within him and at times hard to quell. He was in need of some kind of forum whereby he could challenge the assertions that espoused restrictive authoritarianism in the name of respectability. However, this was a time of happiness and friendship, far removed from either bitterness or rancour, and he would go home much the better for it.

Coming home this time was different from what he was used to. All traces of the child Peter had given way to a man who was seeing the bigger picture. The post-war era heralded many changes and saw a sizeable increase in creamery milk production. In fact, old Dinny with his horse-drawn float was not able to accommodate all of the new suppliers that were getting in on the act. Peter saw an opportunity there that was well worth exploring and he acted immediately. He would hitch up one of the other horses and do a special collection himself. So, for the remainder of that summer Hess and himself gladly took all the milk on offer to Glenleigh Creamery, and the extra money made it worth his while.

All this made him a very busy young man, and it meant longer working days on the farm. None of this bothered him much, as he knew that the system was going to change forever in the autumn. He presented the Dunne twins with their gift horses from the spring show; it was a gesture that brought an unbelievable smile to two pitiful little faces.

The last week in August was a busy time for Peter with the commencement of the harvest and by Sunday evening, Peter was in need of a relaxing drink in Cathers' before the weekly dance. He went with his friend Barry McCrory who was still seeing his Strabane girlfriend but now with more serious intent.

The dance hall was crowded when they arrived, and he spotted Maggie Dunne chatting to a friend. He approached her and asked her to dance. As they danced a foxtrot through the crowded floor, Maggie thanked him for his thoughtfulness towards her boys. She was a little upset that the school holidays were now at an end. The boys had already made their appearance there for a couple of days before the closure. Now she was able to sense their deep unhappiness about going back there again — things were obviously no better than in her own and Peter's day.

While dancing with Maggie Peter became aware that the effects of the few drinks he'd had might have become obvious to her. She accepted his apology with an assurance that she was more than happy to be dancing with him. Then she looked into his eyes with an alluring smile. Their conversation continued for a time after the music had stopped, but soon again, they were dancing closely and very attentive of each other. By the time the last dance was played, the two had spent most of the night together, and now it was time to cycle home out the Dooras road.

Like that summer's evening many years ago when they first kissed outside Tom and Bella's cottage, Peter and Maggie were again alone on the final part of their journey home. When they came to the place of parting at the bottom of the Cruckban road, Peter hesitated on saying goodnight. Instead, he put his hand on her shoulder and continued with her for the rest of the way. The encounter was brief, honourable and sweet, a sensuous delight for both of them. They parted company close to the little house where Sally Dunne sat waiting for her daughter's return; there was no talk about another meeting.

Reality informed Peter that it would not be in his best interest to go again down that road of involvement. His past experience taught him what the likely consequences of so doing would mean for him and his future. In any case, he was not all that anxious about getting seriously involved with any girl, not even with one who was more acceptable. As for poor Maggie, she would in time learn that what had happened was nothing more than another of Peter's weekend escapades. For a while, she thought about him and why it was on the night he had a few drinks taken he paid her more attention than usual. Wondering what was going to happen, she was back at the dance the following Sunday night, but only to learn that there would be no repeat of what took place the week before.

It being harvest time, Peter had other things to be thinking about than the parochial dance. An hour or two in Cathers' pub would be more restful and less problematic. The problem of his uncomfortable attachment to Maggie Dunne was set to keep it that way from there on. The old school hall was removed completely from his weekend schedule, and he became out of touch as to what was happening there.

In Sally Dunne, there was a kind and gentle mother, vexed for her daughter's unhappiness about being the victim of rejection. To all of them it appeared that this young fellow selfishly preyed on the one who was vulnerable. Now it seemed he was deliberately avoiding her, obviously not wanting to be seen with her in public. But that is how things were at the time; the heavy cross of guilt and shame rested on the shoulders of the single mother. Maggie was old enough to know the culture and value system of the time. Taking her mother's advice she decided to put it all behind her and get out and about once again.

It was out of this development that she met a handsome young man who pursued her with unrelenting persistence. There was one major impediment, however; he wore the uniform of the American Navy. His name was Roy, and he had a mother of English parentage. In spite of the many pronouncements from the pulpit, he accepted and respected Maggie for herself as much as for her simple beauty. This gave her a renewed feeling of well-being as well as belief in herself. However, it also affected her thinking in relation to her own area and people in a very negative way. From where she was coming this was understandable, life had not been overly kind to her, and except for the few, society had been loath to comfort her.

Sally wished for nothing more than that her child would be happy, but on this occasion she could not concur. It was the first time she had ever rowed with her troubled daughter. She warned that on no account should Maggie bring this man to the neighbourhood. He would be spending the next six weeks at the Derry base and that was much too long for comfort. Sally's greatest fear was that Fr Gillen would be calling to lay down the law to her and her sickly husband. Without doubt, he would be one of the first to hear about such an unholy carry on in the midst of his community. There were many tears shed on both sides in that little home all through this stressful time. This had the effect of making Maggie determined and resentful not only towards her mother but towards the entire set-up that was impaling her. What she had found she believed to be her deliverance, but how could she ever contemplate such a move?

Through the good offices of Hess, word reached the McGinn residence about the foolish behaviour of one who should have learned her lesson. It was surprising news for Peter, who had not been circulating much of late. Whilst Maggie was rejecting her environment, a similar mindset was beginning to take hold in him as well. He looked to a day, not too far off, when he would be man enough to go to her in openness without having regard for the trepidations of others. However, news of this development put paid to his wishful thinking, and lovely Maggie was dancing to a different tune.

chapter twenty-three

Peen and Mary McDevitt had just returned from Scotland where they had both been working since the beginning of summer. They were back to stay with old Bella for the winter. Going there and back on a seasonal basis was the kind of life the two had gotten used to since their marriage a few years earlier. Being willing workers they were most welcome with the McGinns for the potato gathering. It was early October but the work was made difficult because of unsettled weather. Peter was anxious to get the King Edwards dug and ready for the first shipment.

The potato merchant's brother, Bernard McDonald, who was also an extensive grower, delivered the sacks for packing the potatoes on a brand new David Brown tractor. It was a most attractive machine to look at, red in colour with twin seats cushioned in dark leather. This was the one that had appealed most to Peter when he visited the machinery stand at the Dublin spring show, but unfortunately, he was not now going to be the first in the area to own one.

Preparing the ten tons of King Edwards for inspection and export got under way, and Peen joined the two McGinn men and Hess for the operation. The potatoes were carted from the field to the barn loft above the cow byre and stable. Working under roof made the final task of grading the spuds much more comfortable. All of them were protected from the heavy rain that was too frequently falling on the land. For obvious reasons the Boss and his son were in high spirits, as the return from what they were doing looked promising indeed. Hess had a slight advantage over his employers in being able to engage with Peen in talk about Scotland and the districts where the Irish most frequented. Harmony and coordination was very much in evidence from the way the work was progressing and by noon on Saturday, most of the sacks were full and ready for inspection. Peen asked to be let off after dinner as he and Mary had a few errands to do in town.

Work continued in the barn until after three o'clock, when

the Boss had to prepare for his weekly outing to Ballintober. Ciss and Kitty had gone off earlier to do some shopping for the October Station Mass that was due to take place in their home in little more than a week's time. It being a Saturday evening, John was at home and he was charged with responsibility for making the evening tea for Peter, Dinny and himself. Having an empty house gave the boys the chance to put into effect a plan they and Peen had been hatching for some time. With a little engineering expertise they were about to exploit poor Hess's fixation with war. After tea, the boys went out again, leaving Hess alone to wait for the BBC news on the wireless. As they passed the sitting room window Peter gave John a cigarette and took one for himself. Striking a couple of matches, they both lit up and moved on towards the barn where a couple of sacks remained to be weighed and stitched.

Before their smoke was finished, there came an almighty screech from the front door of the house. All that could be deciphered from it was "the fucking war has started boys". Looking down they could see Hess prancing like a hefted ewe with the old cap in his hand. He was spitting sparks of excitement that over a hundred Russian fighter jets had been bombing London since early evening. Several mighty ones were dropped on the houses of parliament at Westminster; he thought that one of them might have been "atonic". The man on the wireless went on to report that the Russian leader Marshall Stalin was calling on England and America as well as their allies to surrender forthwith or face total elimination. As the news was being relayed, the man reported that the headquarters of the BBC had been hit hard and more strikes were imminent. Dinny said that the crash was so loud he thought the wireless had exploded or that the house had collapsed, "then the hoorin' thing went dead".

The young McGinns did not appear to be sharing his zeal, nor did they attempt to go back in with him to see if the airways had been restored. No joy for him on that front, however, the old box was still dead and looked as if it would remain so for the rest of the night. Hess reappeared wearing an overcoat; his bony cheeks were flushed red and he was talking to himself. He headed for parliament a self-assured man, in the knowledge that his predictions had finally happened. To think that the Russians had flattened Westminster and knocked the BBC totally out of action. "Ah, but sure I always said it, this will be the greatest of all the wars."

His first call was to Aggie's shop for his pipe tobacco; she was alone behind the counter and listened without much interest or understanding of what he was going on about. It was a different story, however, when he got to the parliament. There his illustrious coteries were fully in tune with him. They were able to verify his story by way of content and timing; the radio there was also out of commission. Nevertheless, they had heard enough to generate a lively discussion for the rest of the night. Yes, it was all now happening and Dinny was to be proven the one of vision who never failed to warn his fellow man. Back in Cruckban Peen and his fellow conspirators were getting the old wireless restored to function — they had to have this done before the others got back from town. All three of them arrived together, the two ladies waited in town for the Boss; they needed his company for travelling home in the dark. It puzzled them as to why Peen was with the boys so late on a Saturday night. Well, he had a few snares set on the hill and was back to listen for rabbit squeaks. The kettle was hanging from the crook and singing loudly over the turf flames, and Kitty filled the teapot. Their chat was light-hearted but not a word was spoken about the war or Dinny's agitated state. Picking up what looked like a sack of hunting gear the visitor then thanked them and said goodnight. Just like in the old days, the entire McGinn family were now together and alone listening to the ten o'clock news from Radio Eireann.

Tom and Ciss were at a loss as to what their man Dinny was talking about, or could it be that he was starting to dote. They had not been told about Peen's clever practical joke, which he had affected through acquiring some engineering know-how. It was something he had picked up in Glasgow and purposefully brought it back with Hess obviously on his mind. With a carefully prepared and well-rehearsed script, he was ready to work on the mechanics as soon as Peter and John confirmed that the house was empty. Ciss' parlour became the studio, with two concealed wires connecting to the speaker of the wireless up in the kitchen. Authenticating a BBC accent was all that remained to be done and Peen the artist was certainly good at that. The lighting of matches outside the sitting room window was his cue to go on air. It was the Hawk McArt he engaged to be his accomplice in parliament; he would brief the others as to how they should behave when their risen colleague entered the chamber.

Peter and John eventually let their parents and Kitty in on the secret of the bogus war report. Dinny grew rather disgruntled with the apathy of the people, an apathy that was permeating even parliament itself. He wondered why it was that people were so cool about such an important happening, or why Fr Gillen made no mention of it, or at least asked for prayers on that account.

At the Station Mass in the house the following week Dinny tried to give the matter a little speak only to be greeted with the strangest of silence. It was his belief that Churchill and the Yanks had all the radio stations blanked out until they had managed to cut a deal with Stalin. "Most likely it meant the handing back of West Germany, but the truth will eventually come out, they cannot black out the truth forever and once again I will be right." As for the people attending the Station Mass, most of them had heard the story but none dared ruin his grand illusion.

After Mass, the tea ritual got under way. Mary McDevitt and a couple of other women got to helping Ciss and Kitty prepare and serve it. The priest's breakfast was served in the parlour. He would be seated there along with the Boss and both were waiting to savour the delights of what Mrs McGinn was sure to be serving. This allowed the others to engage in talk of a less pious nature and hopefully far removed from the subject of war. Soon the talk turned to the latest bit of scandal in the parish, as it was something fresh on their minds. Maggie Dunne had left home without any word as to where she was going, just a few days earlier. It was widely believed that she had gone with the American sailor who had been seen a lot in the area over recent times. Their concerns and sympathies were for Sally and how she was going to cope with all that was now being thrust upon her.

What a selfish and thoughtless act, to walk out on a mother who struggled so hard to keep the family together and alive. She was now in a much worse plight, with a husband still alive against all the odds and two six-year-olds that hardly ever went to school. In recent years, things had not been all that bad for the Dunne family. They had been earning enough to survive and bring up the boys in a reasonably happy atmosphere. However, for poor Sally the story was always the same — there would surely be something to pull her back to the misery that fate seemed so willing to allot her.

Peter listened to this flow of conversation with a degree of unease. It was not the kind of thing he felt comfortable about engaging in. Nevertheless, thinking the unsaid words that were more sympathetically disposed towards Maggie, he wondered what had gone wrong and how it finally came to this.

In tears of distress, Sally was asking the same questions of her friend Aggie over a cup of tea in the kitchen behind the shop. She talked about how bad things had become between her and her daughter in recent times. Maggie's defiant behaviour had been a constant source of tension and rowing between them, and it was having a bad effect on Sammy as well. She was absolutely sure that Maggie was with Roy the sailor and most likely across the water. Now all she could hope for was that contact be made, just to say she was well and would be coming back to them soon. In her kindness, Aggie tried to be the comforter, saying that no blame could be attached to a woman that God and the world knew to be goodness itself. She was confident the Good Lord would in time make all things right for Sally and her family.

A week later hope came in the form of a letter with a Liverpool postmark. It was short and without a contact address. Maggie was sorry it had to be this way but she wanted to make a life with Roy, hopefully in England. They were staying with his grandmother and looking for a place of their own, and when they had settled somewhere, she would likely be back for James and Brian. She would be forever grateful to a good and loving mother for all she had given her as well as Daddy and the boys, and it was breaking her heart to see it end in this way. Instead of bringing her hope, this letter did nothing but confirm what Sally already knew and to pose a question about the children's future.

The gloominess of the situation was not being helped by the continuous rainy weather. The McGinns were fortunate in having the potatoes dug and secured before it worsened. After a night of heavy rainfall Peter went down to Henry's to check that the burn was flowing safely past the cottage. The volume of muddy water was ferocious but the holiday home stood secure.

In Wellington boots, he walked back along the laneway, picking his steps through the muddy pools that reflected a watery sunshine. He stopped and listened to what he knew to be the sound of children's voices, and, listening more intently, he detected an element of alarm in their exchanges. Climbing over the fence that separated his land from the area surrounding the Dunne abode, he moved closer to where the commotion was coming from. Brian, the smaller of the Dunne twins, was running frantically from the direction of the wood and towards the main road. Peter called, "Is anything wrong?" The boy turned and began running back up the hill, saying that Peter McGinn was coming to help.

Peter was on the scene immediately, behind the much out of breath Brian. There he found Sammy Dunne lying face downwards in a pool of water that was formed by the overflow of the nearby stream. James was almost immersed from trying to hold the lifeless head out of the water while his brother was seeking help. Peter did not hold much hope for the feeble Sammy as he struggled to move him to a drier spot and say words of comfort into his ear. Before raising the alarm, he sent the boys to fetch some coats or blankets to keep the patient warm.

Sally was brought by car, and she arrived just before the ambulance came to take her husband to the hospital, where he was pronounced dead on arrival.

To meet the requirements of the law an inquest had to be held to establish the circumstances of the unfortunate man's death. It was a formality executed expeditiously and with sensitivity. With Sally gone to work at an earlier hour, Sammy and the boys had breakfast together at a later time. His condition had deteriorated considerably since Maggie's sudden departure and for that reason, the twins were being kept from school to be company for him. There was nothing unusual about him going out for a time after breakfast, but his failure to return brought some alarm to the little ones. They had become accustomed to his ways and patterns of behaviour, and they were also aware that he was always in danger of falling. However, their enduring memories would be of a kind and fatherly figure who was always there to talk with them, a friend they had lost.

Brave Sally was in mourning, but as always, she had reason to show strength and resilience. Not being able to contact the daughter who for so long had been her strength, added to her self-accusing grief. She worried about the effect the news was going to have on her dear child when it would eventually get to her. There seems always to be a haunting of regretful guilt that besets the grieving. For Sally this should be minimal, but what of poor Maggie? Nothing less than the committed love and affection of a willing partner would take her through, and hopefully she had found just that.

Apart from her daytime friend Aggie, Sally had no one but the children to keep her company through her dark days of grief. What company they proved to be, giving her every reason to be strong and hope for a better future. She knew that going back to school would best serve their future, but that was something they certainly did not want to do. The old reliable weapon of fear had established itself firmly within them and it was going to be their downfall in a much bigger way.

Every morning Sally prepared them faithfully for the journey before she went to work, getting them dressed and ready. A few pieces of bread in their schoolbags was as much as she could manage for their lunch. Her own early start did not allow her to see them off in the mornings; she just trusted they would do as she said. Soon it was brought to her attention that they were not obeying her wishes. Only twice had they been seen in class during the previous two weeks.

It was the Hawk McArt who was most ready and willing to bring her that kind of news, and he began calling to her house quite often. Having more time on his hands than most, he offered to come and get the two schemers on their way each morning. It was added pain for this suffering saint to see her two beloved so unhappy and afraid, but there was little she could do but agree to the offer. Better they endure the harshness of this arrangement than to incur the wrath of them that had the power to make it more severe for all of them.

Before the McArt method was put into operation, Sally had an unexpected visit from an aging Fr Gillen. His message was terse and forthright: "Better get these boys to school before more severe methods are adopted." He walked with the boys as far as his own place and warned them to go straight on and join the others further down the road.

Everything seemed to go according to plan, well, for a couple of days at least. By the middle of the week, the cunning pair was taking advantage of the demographic change that had taken place. No longer were there schoolgoing children coming down the Cruckban road, which meant the twins would be on their own until they reached the village. Instead of joining the others, they took to the fields and soon made their way back to an empty house where they could play at will with their Bob and Billy horses.

During this time, Hess was becoming restlessly curious over the amount of attention the widow woman was receiving from a certain doubtful individual. There was no reason in the world why this poor woman should rely exclusively on Hawk McArt. Therefore, he decided to spruce himself up a bit and pay her a friendly visit on his way to parliament. It would be to enquire if she needed help of any kind, and to say that his goodness was there for the asking.

When Sally answered his knock on the door, he wasted little time in pushing his way past her into the kitchen, suspecting she might not be alone. On this occasion she was, except for the two boys, so now Dinny could say his piece. She thanked him with gratefulness for the kind offer, but in the meantime, she was able to manage on her own. He then restated his willingness to be her support and would gladly call at any time if help were needed. "Seek only the assistance of those who are genuine," he advised, "because there are more than a few around here who are anything but."

The Hawk was able to hear every word spoken as he stood outside the door; he happened to be nearby at the time Hess was approaching the door. He concealed himself for a while so as to allow things develop, as he knew there would surely be something worth hearing. After getting an earful, he abandoned any thought of visiting and headed back to the house of parliament instead.

He was clever at concealing his anger and sought to sublimate it in a sly way when facing his rival later in the night. It was a safe bet that the subject of the widow Dunne would come up during the deliberations in parliament. Not an unsympathetic word was spoken about the woman who within a matter of weeks had lost her daughter to a sailor and then the tragic death of her man in the strangest of circumstances. Hess went on to say that he was in regular contact with her and pleased to say she was coping remarkably well. He was certain to be the first she would call upon if things were otherwise. "Indeed," said the Hawk, "apart from the boys not going to school, she is indeed coping well. Mind you, she is lucky to have me in the mornings to get the two rascals on their way. Aye, lucky isn't the word for it", he continued. "Do you people know that she is getting free advice about who to seek assistance from? Ah yes, only those who are genuine, and there are more than a few around who are anything but."

At that, Hess pulled the pipe out of his gob and spit carelessly towards the fire. "What the fuck are you on about or where the fuck did you hear all this?" With a smirk on his face the Hawk said, "I heard it over the wireless on the same station as you got the war report yon Saturday evening."

This was the straw that broke the camel's back. Hess reached for the tongs and sprung to his feet, and with all the force of his being, he fired them across the kitchen towards McArt. Well off target, the missile went straight through the window and landed near the road where a few villagers were standing. Then the door was flung open and out stepped wee Dinny in a warlike manner. Retrieving the tongs, he shouted in to the others, "Send that pig's arse out till I bend these things over his fucking skull. Come out you dirty cunt till I get a whack at you." The door was then closed and bolted from inside and the only response he got was through the broken window. It was a sore retort and delivered by the Hawk telling the risen Hess to get up the road to Biddy The Rum.

Before the night was through the entire village knew that the two had been quarrelling over the recently widowed Sally Dunne. This was a terrible affront to a decent and innocent woman. Surrounded by trouble and grief, such thoughts were far from her mind. But idle and thoughtless minds know not when to pause or consider the consequences of their actions. This woman's reputation had a right to be guarded against any kind of posturing on the part of others. She possessed a faith in the goodness and sincerity of all people, undoubtedly too much so. In spite of what the Hawk was telling her, the boys were still not going to school and the worst thing of all was about to happen.

Shortly after this incident, as Sally was working hard in the butter packaging section of Glenleigh Creamery, she was summoned outside where someone wanted to talk to her. Recognising the Ford Prefect to be the one driven by the parish priest, her heart almost came to a stop. Again, he was forthright but slightly apologetic. The Garda Sergeant and himself had been to her house and there found the two who had been consistently absent from school. Regretfully they had no option but to have them committed into care — it was certainly done for their own good. The orphanage was near to the Derry border and very well run by a reputable order of nuns, and the boys were already on their way there.

Sally's screaming was heard quite a distance away, her weeping and trembling was like never before. "My poor wee boys that never harmed anyone, what am I going to do without them, and God, what have I ever done to deserve all this, please God look on me this day with some pity." Then turning to the priest, she asked what she could do to get her children back. "When you are in a position to do what is right for them, which means sending them to school as well as giving good example yourself." The latter had to be a reference to her two gentlemen callers and perhaps their quarrelsome exhibition in the village. The car then drove away leaving Sally in shambles, too traumatised to feel ashamed but for the first time really alone.

chapter twenty-four

All hands came out to see the shining red tractor being unloaded from the lorry. Except for the fitted all-weather cab, it was exactly the same as the one Bernard McDonald brought to the potato field a month or so earlier. The cab made it suitable for transporting the women to church or even to town. The tractor was given the name Red Davie, and Ciss said what a pity to spoil its beauty in the muddy fields of a tillage farm. It was an exciting day that signalled the demise of the old and trusted ways that had fought and lost the gallant fight.

Now it was time to part company with two faithful old friends. Bob and Billy had sadly outlived their usefulness. The fast-trotting half-blood and the rubber-wheeled cart were being retained with Dinny still in charge. It was small comfort to Peter that he no longer had to worry about explaining these things to his young friends; their sorry plight was bothering him a lot more.

His first errand was to McDonald's produce store for another consignment of potato bags, but equally important was showing off his new tractor. He was keen to talk to Bernard and seek his advice about the purchase of implements. When all the business had been transacted, Bernard switched the focus to another topic, one that for him was all consuming. He was endeavouring to re-establish the Ballintober GAA Club, which had gone out of existence five years earlier, with a view to having a team participate in the county junior championship. He was arranging a meeting for the following Tuesday night in the old school hall. A good turnout was hoped for. Fr Gillen and Master Herron would both be attending. They were very keen that this would succeed. He said the venture would very much depend on the amount of interest and energy the likes of Peter and his brother John was prepared to put into it.

There was no excuse for them not attending this interesting gathering — they now had the pleasure of travelling in plushy comfort whatever the weather. The turnout was indeed very good. It was an all-male assembly and the organisers were delighted with the full parish hall. Fr Gillen welcomed everyone to the meeting and agreed to accept the post of Honorary President. It fell on him to take proposals for the election of the officer board. With the large attendance and much enthusiasm in evidence, it should not have taken long to execute this piece of business. Herron became club Chairman and very surprisingly young John McGinn was chosen as Vice-Chairman. It was in finding a suitable Secretary that some problems began to emerge; no one was willing to take on that role. In order to get over the impasse the chair moved to elect the trustworthy Bernard McDonald as custodian of rather limited finances, but soon it was back to the post of Rúnaí.

Several names were proposed but all declined on the same grounds: lack of faith in their own competency. Out of exasperation, the priest handed over the business of the meeting to the Master, who he thought might exert some pressure on a few of the young men present. It was an erroneous assumption to think that this move would have a positive effect on the past pupils of Ballintober School. All it achieved was a greater degree of resistance from all of them. Again Fr Gillen interjected by appealing to their sense of pride and faith in themselves. "You young men should be ashamed to admit illiteracy or incompetence. Surely not all of you are devoid of a sense of pride and self-worth?"

There is nothing in the field of human interaction to generate lively debate like the making of a provocative comment. It was Peter McGinn who grasped the nettle. He conceded that the priest's assertion was a correct one, but there had to be a reason for it. "Surely it is an indictment of our society and its institutions that young people should be at such a disadvantage." The comment might well have been ignored had it not received the "here here" accolade from a sizable number of the participants. From the chair, Herron's expression was reminiscent of bygone days. What was said cut like a stinging lance. Although lacking the energy of his former self, Fr Gillen felt the need to call a halt to this kind of impertinence. He reminded everyone that the business of the meeting was to provide a facility for the benefit of our youth. There could be no tolerance of those who would use it to blame others for their own inadequacies. Then turning to the Master he said, "Such insolence should not be tolerated by the Chair." Before the Bull had time to call order, Peter came back to say that he was not the one to divert from the business of the meeting. "With due respect, I do take issue with words such as ashamed, and inadequacy, not to mention self-worth. In my opinion, the shame of it lies in other quarters." Looking the Chair straight in the eye, he finished, "We were taught only the ways of fear through violence and brutality, but we are going to change it, that I promise."

This gave him the final word. It was perhaps the first time such a challenge had been mounted and it gave rise to considerable thought. However, it was Bernard McDonald with his deep concern for getting the project up and running who took the heat out of the exchanges. He made what seemed a sensible suggestion and one that might work. In his opinion, it was a waste of talent to have John McGinn holding a rather meaningless job and with John's permission, he would propose him to be Secretary. It was the final resolution to what should have been a simple procedure but for other reasons turned out to be a bone of contention.

In spite of his indiscretion, Peter was elected to the committee, which consisted of five others in addition to the officers. Success is an elusive quality but at least the Ballintober GAA club was formed, albeit with some personality discordances, and Peter McGinn had finally lanced a festering boil.

Nevertheless, his behaviour did not win the approval of the entire parish, and for a while, it was the subject of considerable comment, though not all of it was damning. For some it was an encouraging sign that people were beginning to think for themselves, and respect was something that had to be earned. A lot of Peter's insubordination was triggered off by the presence of the one who had abused him as a child, but recent happenings in the neighbourhood had had a fuelling effect as well.

Peter prepared himself thoroughly for the inevitable reproach from Fr Gillen and hoped it would be somewhere other than at home with his parents. Putting an effort into avoiding this, he deliberately began letting himself be seen around the places frequented by the priest. One such place would be Ned's corner on the forenoon of next Tuesday; it was Fr Gillen's time for calling to Bella McDevitt on his pastoral visitation of the sick and elderly.

When Peter arrived at Bella's cottage, Peen met him outside and wished him the best of luck with his new tractor. He marvelled that inside the cab it looked as cosy as a motorcar. Peen was staying out of the house until after the priest attended his mother; Mary Ward had everything ready and was awaiting his arrival. Although fully aware of this, Peter pretended otherwise and acted like one who just happened to be on the road. His scheming did work, for soon he found himself alone on the road and he could hear Fr Gillen's Ford Prefect approaching. Fr Gillen pulled up alongside Peter and rolled down his window. He wanted to know more about what was going on inside this young man's head. Therefore, the rebuke took the form of a series of profoundly penetrating questions that eluded Peter's comprehension. Quite nervous at first, Peter then took a deep breath and endeavoured to compose himself. Nervously he began to speak: "Father, these are questions I know little or nothing about and perhaps this is how things are supposed to be. However, at the same time I am not going to allow myself to be totally disarmed by intellectual superiority. Such a tendency amongst our people has served only to blind us of our own potential and keeps us shy of opportunity."

This brought about a more reasonable kind of dialogue, which suited the purpose of this unique encounter. But the priest persisted. "Do you understand the offensive nature of your comments, comments that were untrue and unfair to Master Herron, a man to whom the parish should be forever grateful?"

Peter reminded him that he did not name any person that night but felt no need to apologise for what he had said. "The number present who felt incapable of doing the simple secretarial work of a junior GAA club tells me exactly how grateful we should be. These are by and large intelligent young people, lacking only in the confidence that has been hammered out of them as children. How dare anyone say we are inadequate or suggest that we should be ashamed of what life has deprived us of. As our parish priest, I think it most unlikely that you will ever encounter serious wrongdoing from any of us. But that does not mean we are totally lacking in discernment as to what is right and what is wrong."

After receiving an unexpected compliment for the way he had spoken his piece, Peter was reminded that at his age he was neither experienced nor mature enough to be making such comments. As to how his good parents would view his recalcitrance he calmly stated that he only spoke for himself. "It was never my intention to be offensive or disrespectful but I cannot not help having opinions about the cruel things that have happened and were still happening in our midst." On that he would not allow himself be drawn any further. However, his hearer, being a clever and perceptive man, knew that this had to be a reference to the sad story of the Dunne twins. Still, it was a subject neither of them was allowed to share.

In the end, Fr Gillen started up the engine and released his captive with a chilling word of advice. "Channel your energies in a more positive direction. Form these communistic opinions if you may, but please keep them to yourself. You are treading a dangerous path." The communistic tag was one sometimes used by priests for anyone who dared to express opinions that were considered unsuitable for their purposes. It was a tag that was difficult to shake once acquired, and it was one that would have been particularly repugnant to Peter's parents. However, Peter was no communist, at least not in the sense that the term was understood at the time. At least these exchanges took place in private and were unlikely to ever get into the public domain.

chapter twenty-five

Not so private was the contest that took place the following Sunday in McDonald's field. It was a trial match between Ballintober and Dooras for the purpose of selecting the best fifteen to represent the parish. The still fit and sturdy Master was both a player and the one in charge of the side from the bigger town. His counterpart for the Dooras men was their popular and agile captain Connie from Glenfad, also a strong robust defender. There was considerable rivalry between the two sides but not so much as to go to war — all of them were fighting for a place on the parish team.

The first fifteen minutes were seriously tough. John McGinn's speed was causing problems for the opposition, having taken three consecutive points in that period. He was well on his way to adding yet another when he was stopped by none other than the Bull Herron. It was a dogged challenge, the kind the Bull had long been noted for, a knockout blow to the rib cage with his shoulder. John had to be taken off the field and his departure was a serious loss to the men from Dooras. The opposition took full advantage and soon took control of the game by clocking up a number of scores. Connie signalled Peter to move in from the wing to the centre where his brother had been. With dogged determination Peter went for every ball that came anywhere near his end of the field and gained possession most times. Before the half-time whistle, he found the net and brought his team within a point of being level. In the second half, he pointed twice but it was never enough to take the lead, and the other side kept the upper hand.

With little more than ten minutes of play left John returned to the centre forward position, allowing his brother back out to the wing. It was a move that almost worked and could have saved the day had Peter not reacted the way he did. Collecting a long delivery from defence, he soloed along the wing to within striking range. As he steadied to shoot, he could see the Bull Herron speeding out to meet him. Instead of kicking for goal, he waited to face the attack. With a charge that could have done justice to his bovine namesake, Herron leaped to impact forcefully against the lighter body. The agile Peter neatly stepped aside and threw a clenched fist into the face of his assailant. It was a mighty blow, one that had been a long time in reserve, and it took the wind from the paltry pedagogue, who lay beneath him in a winded state. Peter promptly got his marching orders but walked proudly off the pitch to the exact spot where the miserable misbegotten had been taken.

Physically recovered but very humiliated, with blood dripping from a nasty cut to his swollen cheekbone, the Master was surely going to have an uglier than usual Monday morning face. Holding a handkerchief over his injury while looking at Peter through his seeing eye, he promised revenge by having him expelled from all future participation. Peter just smiled and told him it would have all been worthwhile. "Herron, we know you to be thick, cruel and insensitive, but were you so stupid as to think I would never grow up?" Then pointing towards Ballintober bridge he said: "There was the scene of our last encounter; on that occasion you were the victor. As for my future with the club I can only say that as a member of the committee, just like you are, my fate shall never be your call."

It was a turbulent end to a week that saw a country lad face the powers that be and bring a bully to his knees; it would be fondly remembered as the week of payback. Many of his former schoolfriends from both villages praised Peter openly for having the guts to do what others would have liked to do. All were united with a promise that the parish team would never take the field without him. He thought about not attending the next club meeting on Tuesday night, but when the time came, he decided otherwise. To stay away would have been seen as an admission of fault, or worse still a sign of cowardice.

Not a word was spoken at the meeting to indicate displeasure towards the fast wing forward from Cruckban. Perhaps this was because neither the Master nor Fr Gillen were in attendance. Of course, it was the custom that the priest only makes rare appearances of solidarity at these gatherings. As for the Chairman's absence, it could only be due to extenuating circumstances, but who would hazard a guess as to what these might be?

Time was the eventual healer. The Ballintober Club of

Gaels got itself well established, with the Dooras end subscribing six members to the junior championship team. The McGinn brothers were included and always gave of their best for club and parish. Peter's relationship with the Bull was workable but nothing more than that.

chapter twenty-six

Christmas preparation was the last thing on Sally's mind, as the season of goodwill held little promise for her. Five weeks had now passed since her boys had been taken from her, and the pain and loneliness was unrelenting. Every Sunday she cycled the fifteen miles each way to be with them for the one-hour weekly visit. Each time was the same, with the two boys pleading for her to take them home and her promising it would not be much longer. This repetitive routine became so disturbing that she considered staying away from the place altogether.

Having exhausted every avenue open to her in the hope of finding someone who might help her secure their release, she almost capitulated to doom. Her biggest regret was not quitting her job and existing on the few shillings of widow's pension. That was again her offer for getting the twins back, but the people she was appealing to never considered it seriously.

Being on her own and working full time meant that a weekly contribution to the orphanage was expected from Sally towards the children's upkeep. To that, she would have had no serious objection if only she could be certain it was helping to create an environment in which her loved ones could be happy. However, their unhappiness was quickly wearing her down, and she looked physically unwell. Observing this, Aggie and Dan McCrory came to her rescue and each Sunday evening took her to that gloomy and depressing place.

The arrangement worked well for a few weeks into the New Year. Then the management of the bakery informed Dan that the van must be used only for delivering company products. His instructions were that on completion of his delivery round on Saturday afternoon the vehicle was to be left on the premises. It was common knowledge amongst the other drivers that this came about through the scheming of the spinster lady who liked to be called Miss O'Connell. She was the office clerk who had assumed powers that were never given to her. Ballintober bakery was but a branch operation of a much larger concern in Derry City from where it was controlled and financed. Her power lay in the fact that she was an informer who operated a hotline between Ballintober and the Derry headquarters. It was an arrangement that suited the faceless people who owned the operation because their only concern was the making of profit. The bakery was a valuable asset to the local economy, employing both men and women. Most of the deliverymen were like Dan, driving the company van and being paid a weekly wage plus a small commission on sales. There were a few others who provided their own transport and worked on straight commission only.

It was Miss O'Connell's job to keep a record of all dispatches going out as well as returns coming in. Each agent knew exactly what to expect by way of commission each week but was only paid on the official figures that this inarticulate lady produced. The local manager happened to be a quiet, decent sort of man who lacked assertiveness and needed to be on good terms with everyone around him. For that reason, this witchlike creature with a vindictiveness to match took advantage of his weakness. She liked to be giving out the orders and boasted loudly how much the men were afraid of her. She was often openly abusive towards the workers, especially those whom she did not like.

She had a deep dislike for Dan McCrory ever since the time he had successfully challenged her calculation of his bonus. Now it was her time for revenge and she executed it with gloating glee. For Dan and his wife it was a slight disadvantage but something they were well able to live with. Nevertheless, it robbed them of a facility that enabled them to do the kind of mercy acts they were noted for. Their main concern was in not being able to help the destitute widow to see her children. It was their kindness and goodness that had brought Sally through the darkest of days and saved her sanity. Now it was all being jeopardised through the actions of one sick and warped individual.

By the following weekend, the countryside was covered white from a heavy snowfall. While it would have been possible to make the journey by motor there was no way that Sally could have cycled that distance. It was a sad and distressing Sunday for her, perhaps one of the worst she had ever experienced. She could feel every pain of disappointment that was tormenting the two little souls wondering what was keeping her.

The days that followed were uneasy ones for all of them and by Friday evening, the weather seemed as bad as ever with no signs of improvement. Work on the land was at a standstill, Peter and Dinny took to hedge cutting down on the Blue Rock Farm. Looking in the direction of the desolate abode, Hess remarked how bad things were for the widow Dunne. He was beginning to lose sympathy for her, as time and again she would refuse his offer to help. It seemed his goodness was being lost on this woman. He lacked the understanding to judge that in the circumstances poor Sally had a moral reputation to protect. Her primary concerns were little James and Brian, but also her own self-respect. So protective was she of her reputation that never once did she visit the twins in the company of Dan McCrory without his wife being with them. "Who is the gentleman with you?" was the sort of question the sisters were likely to ask. Neither did she forget the advice given to her by Fr Gillen on the day her boys were lifted, advice on the importance of giving good example. Peter did not take much heed of what Hess was saying, but at the same time, it did get him thinking about his two little friends, whom he had not seen in a long time.

Knowing them as he did, they could not but be unhappy in confinement. From his own experience of how children were treated, he feared the worst for Maggie's boys. He thought about Maggie too and his past involvement with her, but more so about the terrible thing she had done to them that needed and loved her. Did she know about all that had happened to her family since that day when she had thoughtlessly walked out and left them?

As the day progressed, his concern deepened. He would have liked to go to Sally and enquire about the boys and perhaps give her something to take to them. After all, he and they had been a big part of each other's lives for over two years and she would surely have known that. However, he feared that his past involvement with Maggie might make him a less than welcome caller. He would have been seen as a big part of her problem on more than one occasion.

Dinny left before quitting time to commence the farmyard jobbing, while Peter went over to Henry's to set a couple of fires. With the heavy frost came a danger of damage being done to the inside water system of the unoccupied house. It was close to dark when he was walking back past the little house with a dim light coming through the window. "What should I do?" he thought, as he came nearer. "Why should I be afraid of doing what I know to be right?"

It was a surprised look Sally gave the young man on her doorstep, but also one of questioning. Addressing her as Mrs Dunne, Peter stated his reason for calling — it could only be about James and Brian, as he could not have talked comfortably to the woman about her daughter.

Without uttering a word, she heard him through while keeping her hand to the half-opened door. With a nervous smile, she thanked him for caring enough to call. On no account would she take his money, even though she did appreciate how good he had always been to the children. "While I don't have very much, money is by no means my biggest worry right now. Even if I was to accept your offer, there is no way I could get it to them." She told Peter the pitiful story about the previous Sunday, and she knew the outlook for the one to come was even worse. She was in a state of painful distress about the two of them not being able to understand why she was not coming to get them. "God help them, every Sunday that I call they think is going to be their day for getting home. Each time it's the same heartbreak for all of us, I am always the one that lets them down." Her greatest concern was how they were after last Sunday's bitter disappointment. There would be no one there to reassure or comfort them. They had to go to bed with a feeling of being abandoned, and no reason or excuse would be offered them. All week she prayed for them and more so that the Good Lord would send the thaw.

The thaw was not about to happen, of that Peter was certain, but he could not say so to this suffering woman who needed help from somewhere. "Mrs Dunne, if you will allow me, I can take you there on Sunday afternoon on the tractor, it's as comfortable as a motor car." Sally had already seen him take his mother and sister to Sunday Mass and it certainly did look comfortable. Again, she refused on the grounds that it would not be proper for her to impose on other people's goodness all the time. However, in truth it had more to do with her modesty and thoughts about how others might see it.

Assuring her that it was something he wanted to do and that they could get there with comfort in about forty-five minutes, she agreed with an emotional thank you.

chapter twenty-seven

"Out for a drive" was as much as Peter was prepared to give away as he rose from Sunday dinner and donned the heavy overcoat. Not a question was asked or a word spoken as he went out the door, leaving a curious lot behind at the table. All they could do was listen to the sound of the machine humming down the road.

Sally was ready and waiting and he told her to bring an extra coat or rug for warmth. What a relief, she thought, that the cold was keeping the villagers indoors this day — she was getting away unnoticed. Apart from thanking him once again, few words passed between them on the cold journey. As they neared their destination, she advised him not to come too near to the main gates. It would be better if he stayed a distance and let her walk the rest of the way. The visitation period was one hour and she was sorry for keeping him on such a cold day.

In less than half an hour, she re-emerged out of the gateway and started walking towards him. However, before she even got close he could see that something was the matter. Stepping down off the cab, he helped her back on to the passenger seat, but was afraid to ask what was bothering her. With difficulty, she told him that Brian had been taken to Letterkenny District Hospital the previous day, and James was in such a state she had to leave him in hysterics with one of the sisters. The nun was sympathetic enough but unable to tell her much about what had happened to Brian. It had something to do with his breathing. Immediately Peter's mind went back to wee Jimmy Dunne all those years ago. He was also pretty certain that the same thoughts were troubling the mind of his passenger.

Starting the engine he looked at her and said, "Right, we go to the hospital then," and with that they were on the road to Letterkenny. The journey was long. It took them up through the Lagan Valley and past some of the places Peter had known when he worked and lived with his relations in that area. Night had fallen by the time they reached the entrance to the old grey building that housed little Brian Dunne. This time it was different; both of them were going in to see the patient and no one was going to question them.

The public ward with its double row of beds contained a mix of male patients and was not the most becoming of sights. Brian sat up on a small cage-like bed; he did not appear to be very ill and was well able to show his delight at seeing his visitors. Seeing Peter completely overwhelmed him, and he had a host of questions to ask about what was happening in the fields and with the horses, especially his own Billy horse.

With tact, Peter told him about the red tractor but said nothing about the demise of their precious Bob and Billy horses. Sally left the two alone and went to get some information from the medical staff. She returned later and did not appear to be over-concerned about what she was told; she was very relieved to hear that from the X-rays there was no sign of tuberculosis. Brian was suffering from a heart deficiency but at his age, there was a strong likelihood he would grow out of it. On hearing this, Peter got up to leave the boy and his mother alone together for the rest of the visiting time. He told Sally to stay for as long as she could and not to worry about delaying him; he would be outside and ready whatever time she wanted to go home.

After saying his goodbye to Brian, Peter came out feeling in need of a drink. As he walked down the poorly lit street in search of licensed premises, he noticed a softening of the frosty air — it looked like the thaw was setting in. Being amongst strangers, the scene was not all that inviting, not at all like the Sunday night craic he was used to in Cathers'. Nevertheless, what he was doing was preciously more fulfilling than the routine banter of a local pub and it pleased him immensely. He knew that his being away from home for so long would be the cause of much curious speculation back in Cruckban. Although it no longer bothered him all that much, he would rather they knew nothing about where he had been.

Walking back with a slight breeze behind him, he knew the thaw was real and active. He said so to Sally as she came out of the shop beside the hospital gate where their transport was parked. Then with reasonable reassurance about Brian's condition, they commenced the long drive home.

As Peter's new tractor rumbled up through the dark village of Dooras no one knew who it was carrying other than the driver. This was a relief to Sally, although she had more pressing concerns on her mind right then. Apart from the noise of the engine, it had been a silent journey home, as neither was in a mood for conversation. Much later than either of them had anticipated Red Davie came to a halt, almost on Sally's doorstep. Again she apologised for delaying him all that length of time; she felt bad about ruining his Sunday night outing. It also bothered her that he had to endure the cold without having anything to eat while she herself had been given a cup of tea by one of the nurses. With timidity and uncertainty, she asked if he would like to come in for a drink. She remembered about the half bottle of whiskey that had not been opened; someone had brought it to her late husband before he died.

Very quickly, the fire was burning bright from the dried firewood that was piled and ready beside the hearth, and soon the kettle that hung from the crook began to whistle. The mug of strong hot punch was indeed delicious, and Peter savoured it as Sally worked quietly at making the tea. With his help, she began to talk about the terribleness of her situation, which offered no apparent way out. "I will never be able to get the sight of wee James out of my mind, after seeing him in that state today and me walking away from him." Strange though it seemed, she was happier about Brian, at least he was experiencing a kindness that was pleasantly new. At no time were the circumstances of them being taken into care ever alluded to.

Peter would have liked to ask about Maggie, and whether she had knowledge about all that had taken place in recent times. However, he was not the one to be asking about Maggie, and with an empty stomach, the strong drink was going to his head faster than it should. Peter was feeling a bit hazy, but the mug of fresh tea along with a portion of the sweet bread that Sally had bought in Letterkenny quickly restored his alertness. Not enough though to inspire any ideas that might bring a glimmer of hope at the end of a harrowing day. He was deeply sorry, but his sorrow was of no benefit. He wished for nothing more than to be of help to this poor woman and her children. "No one but yourself Mrs Dunne could be more upset about James and Brian than I am this night."

Sally lamented, "I don't understand why my prayers are

not being answered, why is God not helping me? I've never done anything to offend him or my neighbour. But I am not going to give up on his mercy and goodness, and hopefully soon he will hear my prayers.

With these exchanges Peter got up to leave while expressing the hope that things would be better when they next met.

Stopping his tractor to light a cigarette a short distance out the lane, from the lighted match he noticed a shining object on the seat beside him. It was a set of white rosary beads of imitation pearl. It was obvious that Sally had been praying them in invocation while they were travelling back. Picking them up he stepped off and ran back to the door, which he knocked upon gently. A totally different woman to the one whose hospitality he had just received stood there before him. With heavy black hair hanging loosely about her shoulders, she held a white cloth to her face to hide a flood of tears. Not knowing what to do in a situation that was totally new to him, Peter hesitated. Without saying a word, he handed her the beads. There was heaviness in his heart as he re-entered the house; she looked fragile and embarrassed. Then without hesitation, he put his two arms around her and drew her tightly to his body. Her entire being was trembling as he enclosed her warmly. With a gradual easing of tension, she rested her head against his chest and before long, they were kissing passionately.

chapter twenty-eight

It was Tuesday before the thaw was enough to allow the ploughmen back on to the land. The recommencement had greater significance for the McGinns, and all of them came out to watch the new operation as Peter opened the first back on the potato ground. By his standards, it was a late start but with the speedier method in place, he would soon catch up. Hess warned of a future danger. With the weight of these machines and their large wheels acting as rollers, the good land would eventually harden like a concrete floor. It would take time for this wise message to get through to the people. The wealth of wisdom is indeed hard to acquire. However, as for here and now, the others were pleased to let the future correct its past. As darkness descended, Peter had turned over most of the barn field — it was a vindication of the progressive way.

Others too were progressing in their field of endeavour. No sooner had Peter stepped off Red Davie that evening than John came to say he had been offered the post of Staff Officer. Not only would this mean higher remuneration and status, but it would also set him on the road to higher prospects as well. The proud parents were justifiably elated; Tom put it all down to the value of a first class education. As for Ciss, well there was nothing to beat good breeding and respectability: "Mix with the right people and you will be noticed where it counts." A wise sentiment no doubt, even in relation to modest achievement. After all, John had not been conferred with a PhD. Nevertheless, it was a time to be grateful, everything was going well, and at least they could safely say that the family had turned out well and it was an achievement to be proud of.

True to his promise, Peter made his way down the fields to pay Sally a visit. Mentally he questioned his own judgment about re-engaging with what had always been problematic. Could it be that he was born to be the black sheep? Was what happened on Sunday night real, or was it just an emotional reaction to extreme adversity? Whatever it was, he was not for allowing it to pass into the forgotten without confronting what made it happen. Immediately he could sense Sally's discomfort at him being back at her door. She hoped he had come to enquire about Brian and for no other reason. Word had come from the hospital to the phone in the creamery office to say the boy was well enough to be discharged and was now back in the orphanage. This, she said, would be some comfort to James, even though both of them were pining there. In Sally's situation, there was little joy to be derived out of any kind of message.

These exchanges all took place on the doorstep — it appeared Sally was not for allowing Peter past the threshold. She said it was best that way, because what had taken place the other night was a terrible mistake for both of them. "On no account must we ever allow the likes of this to happen again, and I trust you appreciate the reason why." Peter agreed that in the circumstances, she had a right to feel that way, "but of all the people in this world, how could anyone doubt your character? What we did was harmless and good. I regret none of it and I hope you don't either." By this time, he had moved inside and there were tears in Sally's eyes. The door then shut behind them, and all was good for another time.

Not so sweet were things between them when he came to see her the night after. On no account was he to cross the threshold or ever come near her home again. It was out around the village that young McGinn was slipping down the fields in the dark of night and spending illicit time with the widow Dunne. Sally's friend Aggie, who had a genuine concern for her wellbeing, gave this information to Sally in good faith. None other than Biddy The Rum had carried the story to her shop. How it got out in the first place was a bit of a mystery, but someone must have watched Peter go there and then perhaps waited to count the time. Some virtuous vigilante or moral crusader was out about their civic duty.

Sally was frightened by it all and angrily put the blame on Peter's persistence. "Out of desperation I accepted your help last Sunday, and now what a price I will have to pay." He could well understand her feeling the way she did and made no attempt to minimise her plight. It was obviously a serious setback to her crusade for her children's return. However, he did try to reason with her that what had taken place between them had been good for both of them and he would never want to change it.

"How can you say it was good for me when it's going to be the cause of me not getting my weans back. Had your concern for them been as you pretend, then you should have known to stay away from me. Not for the first time you have brought me grief, just like you did to my daughter Maggie. It was her leaving that caused Sammy to die of a broken heart, and I once had to bear the brunt of your mother's tongue because of you."

This was the first time Maggie's name had ever been mentioned in all their dealings since he first approached her a week earlier and it hit him hurtfully hard. Looking at her with wounded dismay Peter turned away from Sally and the door that closed behind him. Careful not to be seen coming out the lane he walked back the fields and on to the Dooras road. He was going to the village for cigarettes and to hear if anyone had anything to say. Why, he wondered, had he such a talent for getting involved with the wrong kind of women? If that kind of gossip was out and around the village, then Sally was correct in thinking that her worthiness for guardianship was questionable indeed. But his own complicity in her ignominy was something he could not rest easily with.

In the village, things were much the same for him as usual. He received no strange looks or smart comments from anyone, and him after putting extra effort into being seen by as many as possible. This seemed odd in view of what he had just been told by a very worried and frightened Sally. Stranger still, there was never a mention of it in his own home, and Hess's silence was more than baffling.

As it happened, it was Dan McCrory's quickness to act that had put paid to the spicy story. At Aggie's behest, he went straight to see Biddy The Rum. Sternly he told her that what she had reported in the shop was totally untrue and that young McGinn would make an example of whomever should repeat it. Furthermore, the Captain, who owned the house Biddy was living in, had a high regard for Mrs Dunne. "Biddy, I would not like to see you left without a roof over your head, and that is exactly what could happen, so beware." That was how a damaging tale got stifled even before it got out and Sally got back to trusting that someone might again hear her cry for help.

The next morning, as Peter busied himself preparing for the start of his milk collection round, Kitty came out to the shed to tell him that two men had arrived in a lorry to deliver the new trailer for the tractor. The driver and his young helper were trying to unload the trailer by themselves. Kitty said that something had gone wrong because the young one came into the house very frightened and in pain. It had upset her and her mother to hear the bigger fellow being abusive towards the young lad. He had been using the foulest of language on the teenager as they attempted to unload the trailer from the lorry.

Peter came to the kitchen where Ciss was bathing the youth's foot with tepid water. He could not have been more than sixteen, big for his age but still with the softness of a child. With the pain subsided he was able to tell a little about what had happened. His boss had ordered him to lift the end of the trailer so it could be unloaded from the lorry, but the drawbar of the large trailer was much too heavy for him to hold up by himself and when pushed forward it fell on his foot.

Peter then went out and found the lorry backed up against a high brow at the back of the yard. The trailer was indeed large, occupying almost all of the lorry floor space — it needed to be big and sturdy for the purpose he had in mind: it had the capacity to carry the entire milk supply of ten townlands. From behind the lorry appeared a burly looking fellow of bulldog appearance. He managed a smile and said hello. Peter had little trouble recognising him as Norman the bully of earlier acquaintance and obviously not in the least mellowed. Norman made no reply when questioned about his behaviour towards the boy. Peter told him that such conduct would not be tolerated on the premises. "In the circumstances I cannot take delivery of this thing, so do not attempt to take it off the lorry. I will be in touch with the supplier about this incident. Are you still deriving pleasure out of making life miserable for them that are little more than children? I do hope you value your own position, for make no mistake about it, you won't have a job when I have finished with you."

This put a worried look on Norman's face, and he apologised for what had happened, putting it down to the fact that he was busy and under pressure. By this time, the two women and the boy came out to look on and listen. Ciss appealed for them to get on with what they were doing and let the matter rest, the boy was all right, a bit shocked but the injury did not appear too serious. Peter then turned to the boy and asked his name. "Denis," he replied.

"Well Denis, I think you should let the doctor see your foot, because it could give you trouble later in life." He also advised him to consult with his parents about taking whatever action may be necessary. "I also feel they should know that you are not safe in this man's company. We know what happened and are prepared to stand with you on this one."

Again, the big fellow stated his regret, saying he never meant any harm to young Denis. He hoped they could all understand his position: "Always busy, right now I should be back at the garage for another delivery. The last thing I need is for a customer to report me for wrongdoing; it would be serious for me to have to bring this trailer back and much worse if you were to report why."

The last thing Peter wanted to do was to bring about any person's downfall, but this time the demon of bad memories were pushing him to the limit. "If I did not know you and what you are capable of, your pleading might just work. I have not forgotten what you did to me when I was just like Denis, but don't worry; I will settle that score with you later. You bully and violate the weak, not because you are busy or stressed out, but because you are a coward with a sick mentality. At the same time, what have I to gain from beating the shit out of an amadan like you?"

Even with the arrival of Tom and Hess to the scene, Peter stood firm — at least that was the impression he gave. He talked quietly to his father before announcing that he was going to the post office to make a phone call. This added a greater weight of worry to an already anxious Norman, who was now trying to converse with his helper in pretence joviality.

After his son's departure, Tom took control of the situation and a much-subdued Norman got quickly to work on taking the trailer off the lorry. From a distance, Peter watched the operation in the afterglow of triumph; he had laid to rest yet another demon from the hell home of bullying.

chapter twenty-nine

Winter not yet over, the creamery was still only receiving milk two days per week. It was one such day and Red Davie with trailer attached occupied a spot outside the manager's office. After delivering the milk churns, Peter climbed back up into the tractor. On the driver's seat lay a brown business type envelope. Peter thought it strange of Sam the manager to be doing such a thing; he always delivered the monthly cheque or any other kind of letter personally by hand. The only thing written on it was the name Peter, so he knew it was something of a more personal nature. Before getting back to Cruckban, he stopped to see what it contained. It certainly had nothing to do with creamery business, just a written note on plain writing paper.

Dear Peter,

Do not be over surprised at me writing to you, but the truth is I cannot continue without finding a way to relieve my troubled mind. For reasons that you already know, I had to take a firm stand the other night and I am afraid that is how it has to be. At the same time, it was most unfair of me to doubt your sincerity and not to appreciate your kindness. A kindness I should have accepted as genuinely sincere and the cause of my fondness for you. For that very reason, I was foolishly more to blame than you were. Peter, please understand that it was my tormented mind that caused me to say those hurtful things for which I now beg your forgiveness. As for James and Brian, sorry, but no change there, still very unhappy and I am praying hard for the miracle of their return, I would like you to do so as well. Again Peter, please accept that I am truly sorry and I hope you find the happiness you deserve.

Sally.

It was not a love letter but it contained enough to stir the emotions of its recipient. Peter put it carefully into his coat pocket; it was going to be perused for meaning more than a few times that day. He was pleased she thought about him in the way she did and her sentiments touched him deeply. Now more than ever he wanted to be with her and to talk things through. But her written message was clear: "That is how it has to be." For him the little house was out of bounds. Yet Peter was moved like never before and beseeched the Lord for fruitful thought. "Oh, that some power might inspire me with wisdom to find a means of delivering those two children to the woman I love."

Whatever about inspiration he knocked gently on her door shortly after dark. He was nervous and somewhat afraid.

"I told you not to come here," were the words that greeted him. His reply was immediate and perhaps inspired.

"Sally, I have found a way for you to get James and Brian back and I think it's a way you cannot refuse. Sally, what if you and I were to be married and become a family? This could well be the miracle for which you have been praying and I have been hoping."

It was a hasty proposal and quite startling for Sally and it left her mute and visibly weak. Gaining some composure she asked was he trying to make fun of her, but quickly retracted by saying, "Sorry Peter, I should not have said that to you."

Standing in the middle of the floor, he watched her quivering motion as she tried to compose her thoughts. "Being as I am, Peter, my feelings for you are stronger than I think it right for me to say. But there are too many reasons why we cannot seriously consider what you are suggesting, and most of these have to be out of consideration for you." Again, she gazed at him in a manner that revealed deep affection. "I am the mother of a girl not much younger than you are. Apart from it not looking right, my feeling is it could never be right. Have you thought about the effect this could have on your parents and what it might mean for your own future? I do not doubt that your mother is a good woman but I have a strong feeling she dislikes me more than just a little. Never have I ceased to dream of a day when my boys will be back with me, but to have you as well would be my wildest dream fulfilled. But wild it is, reality and common sense tells me a different story."

"My dear Sally, your dream can become our reality if only

you will allow me make it so. Whatever about our birth dates, you and I love each other and that is why I want to be with you. Us being together is both good and right, so it surely looks that way as well."

Sally then cited the problem of approaching Fr Gillen, whose blessing such a union would require.

Peter reassured her that Fr Gillen wouldn't present a problem. "I have settled a few old scores of late and one of them involved the good man himself, so I don't expect many obstacles to be coming from that quarter. Our wanting to be married has to be honoured and respected by every facet of society, especially our holy church. Come, we are going to see the priest this very night."

It was a smallish room off the hallway near the front door, which served both as parish office and pastoral counselling room. Sally had been there many times before to seek the merciful help and prayers of her parish priest. Fr Gillen made a good attempt at not looking overly surprised when Peter told him the nature of his business with Sally. In an unthreatening and indeed non-judgemental way, he questioned them both about their certainty as well as the implications of what they were committing themselves to. Peter was sure and explicit about his intentions towards Sally; he said that for the present it would have to be strictly a secret between the three of them. He was under no illusion as to how this development was going to impact upon the cosy citadel that was his family home. Though it was going to be confrontational and problematic, he was determined to deal with his parents in his own way and in his own time, and they were not to hear about this from any other source.

"That, I can tell you Father, will be happening very soon, as it is our intention to be married as soon as you can possibly arrange it."

Fr Gillen said that there were no impediments either civil or canon to them getting married. At the same time, it was going to take a few days, perhaps a week for the required documentation to be drawn up and legally sanctioned. From his own experience, he was fairly certain that everything would be in place by the middle of the following week.

There was one problem, however. He was going to be

away from the parish most of that week and would not be back until Friday evening. As for the following week, it so happened that he had no less than two other marriages on Monday morning. Tuesday being the day before the Lenten season begins, he would again be out of the parish until the afternoon. In time-honoured tradition, Saturday was not considered the most popular day for the nuptial feast, but it was either that or wait until after Easter.

"Saturday week it will be then," Peter proclaimed as he looked to his timid betrothed. She was still in a state of confusion, finding it hard to believe that all this was now happening. It was only when Sally got back home that she felt ready to talk things through with the man she was now set to marry. She was worried about the many things to be done in preparation, and so little time to do them. But her greatest worry had to be for Peter, who she was pretty sure would lose his inheritance. In this, her sense of guilt was profound and he could see it was causing her to fret. Taking her in his arms, he lovingly reassured her that her worries were at last coming to an end. "I am capable of providing adequately for all of us, and remember I am still the owner of the Blue Rock Farm. My immediate concern is about facing my parents with news that will be anything but pleasing for them. It will not be a joy for me either, but I owe it to them to be truthfully honest and tell them that no thing or person can make me change my mind."

This showdown would need to happen not later than the coming weekend. It was important that this be done before the news got into the public domain, as they wanted to be seen together as a couple before their wedding day. Peter was not looking forward to it, as he knew it could create a family rift that might never heal.

It all took place the following Friday after dinner. Old Dinny had gone to the barn field to fetch a cartload of turnips for feeding to the livestock. Kitty had gone to the village for some household provisions. Peter felt it was a good time to break the news to his parents, and he did so in a forthright and simple manner. The reaction was as he expected — Tom sat in shocked silence with his head in his hands and Ciss screamed at him and implored the holy family, each by name. Why was he turning his back on his family and rejecting their values of decency and respectability? Every blemish of his entire existence was revisited, from the sleepless nights of his delicate infancy to the daily ordeal of getting him to school. Then there was that carry-on with the Dunne lassie who ran off with a sailor. "But getting yourself involved with her mother who should be in mourning for her dead husband. Is that not enough to tell you the kind of woman she is, not to mention those two orphan children?" Peter sat and listened, making no attempt to respond. Then Tom came in with a comment that rekindled in his son early feelings of inadequacy. "In view of your disloyalty and selfishness, I have to question the value of an individual such as you in any family."

"I know what you mean, Dad," Peter replied. "I remember you saying that when I was a child and you putting it in even blunter language. But the problem is, I was born, it all took place without my knowledge or consent, and I cannot now be responsible for that mistake."

Again, it was Ciss' turn. "I never trusted that woman for as long as I've had known her, but it amazes me to think she could stoop so low as this. "Son, you don't have the intelligence either of your father or your brother, but at least try and be like them. You have been taken in by a clever lady who once had her eye on your dying uncle and his property."

Peter reminded them that none of this was going to change the way he felt about Sally Dunne.

Tom, still cogitating the thrust of what his recalcitrant son had delivered, was now endeavouring to adapt a more benign approach. "Peter, nothing in the world means more to your mother and me than our family. My main concern is about you and your future wellbeing. Thanks to you, we can now look upon ourselves as being well off and equal to the best in the farming community. But we cannot allow it to be squandered on a set-up like that!"

Then, through pitiful tears, Ciss sobbed, "It's all going to be yours one day, please don't throw it away on this disgraceful nonsense and make yourself the laughing stock of the country-side."

Peter was not in a mood to readily concur with his mother's sentiments. "What is disgraceful about being plagued by sickness and poverty, or who claims the right to laugh? I am pleased to be leaving you so comfortably well off and the best of luck to whoever would take my place. But right now nothing is more important than the woman I want to be with."

At this, Tom, the wild man, quietly quit the scene, leaving his wife Ciss with the hopeless task of redeeming their son. She again alluded to the values of respectability and family name. Did he think about what this would do to his brother and sister, both of whom were highly thought of and who mixed only with the right people?

Peter had one question to put to his mother; it was one that had bothered him ever since he could remember. "Mother, could you tell me once and for all, what is it about this woman that you so much dislike?"

Ciss denied any suggestion that she had ever disliked her neighbour, but she had to be suspicious of Sally's attention to Uncle Henry.

"But mother, from what I can recall you were never much fond of Uncle Henry either. I don't think he would ever have been with us had it not been for the Blue Rock."

"Son, there are a few things that I think you should know before you visit this shame upon us. Henry was not always the good old man that you knew him to be. The truth is I have always been afraid of him ever since I was a child staying with my grandmother. I had the terrible experience of being left alone with him once when Granny had gone to the shop."

That was as far as she was able to go by way of regression; she would have needed skilful help to carry it through. There was obviously a lot more hidden deep inside, but here the conditions were not conducive to the offloading of emotional baggage. But in the strangest of ways, Peter may have helped her for the first time to touch this deeply buried sore. He was not the one to give her counsel, but at least the lance may have gotten close to pricking the boil. By now, he had lost the desire to probe further into her secret past, yet he knew there was something more she had to say.

"Did that woman never tell you that her dead husband was your Uncle Henry's son? Did she not tell you that the Blue Rock Farm should be hers and that she is going to have it by whatever means? I think you ought to be smart enough to see her game, or are you such a dud as to let her succeed?"

Peter had had enough. He had said his piece and learned a few surprising things as well. Before he took leave of his heart-broken mother, he expressed his sorrow about causing her such distress. "But you must accept I will be leaving here within the week."

Out in the yard he repeated the same sentiment to his father, but added that he expected some form of payment for his years of hard and dedicated work. Tom agreed that something would have to be worked out, and said he would talk to John and Ciss that evening. This was a strong indication to Peter that Tom now hoped brother John would play a future role in the affairs of Cruckban. Peter was out and he knew it.

He went back to work with mixed emotions, certain of his feelings for Sally, yet upset for a dear mother who could not help being what circumstances had made her. Thinking of how soon he would be leaving home for good, he was better able to remember the good things of his childhood formation. He could not see his old deceased uncle in a light other than the one for which he remembered him most. Then he got to thinking about the day death had came upon Henry on the roadside and him with a sizable amount of money in his pocket. He remembered that Peen McDevitt was the one who found him and the last to share words with him in consciousness. Peter decided to pay Peen a visit to find out if the old man had revealed anything in his last moments.

Peen was willingly compliant and related the distant event to Peter as accurately as he could remember it. He could vividly recall the few muffled words that the old man had tried to relate. "But of these words I was only able to decipher the name of Sammy Dunne, which he repeated more than once." To Peter, this was more than enough; Henry was trying to make amends before his final exodus. He was taking the cash to the son he had failed so blatantly and for so long.

Peter thanked his good friend for the information supplied but gave no reason as to why he wanted it. On his way to see Sally he thought about how that money had been commandeered by his frugal parents and now formed a good part of his own two hundred pound bank deposit. However well his parents had intended it, Peter could no longer see this money as being solely his own.

As Peter sat by the fire that evening in Sally's simple living room, he felt himself beginning to relax. It would be a night for talking, at least for as long as their romantic affections allowed them to be practical. Sally was a little surprised at Peter not knowing about the bloodline that connected him to her late husband. "But it was in blood only, totally without any kind of affinity or sense of kinship. But in fairness he did help out at the time wee Jimmy died."

At this, Peter began relating the moving story of what he was certain Henry had in mind as his dying wish. "Half of what money I possess rightfully belongs to you and you will be needing it between now and next Saturday."

It was only after firm persistence that Sally abandoned her pride and agreed to accept what was undoubtedly hers. So with two hundred pounds between them they were both joyfully happy to be setting up home together.

But true love never runs smoothly, as Peter and Sally were to discover the next evening when they returned to Sally's house after doing their business in the Hibernian Bank. It was the Monday after the big showdown and it had been their first outing together in public. For both of them it was an important stage in their becoming a couple.

Sally was first to go into the house and to her astonishment daughter Maggie was inside waiting for her. Hearing voices inside, Peter followed to find the two with their arms around each other and them in a flood of tears. Composing himself somewhat before greeting his childhood sweetheart, he then complimented her on how well she was looking. Her response was muted and told of a soul that was heavily laden with torturous grief. The tragic tale of what had happened to her dear dad as well as the twins had been brought to her by a young man from Ballintober who had recently moved to a place near where she lived in London. Roy, her partner, had tried his best to console her, but they decided it might be better if she went back to face her mother.

Peter too thought it better that the two be left alone for a period of talking and healing each other's hurts. As he moved to leave them, Sally asked him to come back again as soon as he could. He had reached the secure zone from the battle line of contention with his enraged parents, and now it looked as if the same was about to begin between Sally and her daughter.

However difficult it was going to be, there was no way Sally could avoid telling Maggie about her romantic involvement with Peter McGinn. When he returned a few hours later, the two were sitting silently by the fireside and he could sense an air of tension. Maggie broke the silence as she spoke harshly to Peter. Outlandish and disgusting was how she described his relationship with her mother. "I happen to know you well enough not to have faith in your intentions, and Mother, I think you should have known better than to involve yourself with that family."

Through tear-filled eyes, Sally looked back to where Peter was still standing. He moved up to her and placed both his hands upon her shoulders. His supporting presence made her feel more at ease, and she responded by brushing her fingers gently over his. The women had grown tired of what had obviously gone on between them while he was away. It had been a painful and exhausting couple of hours for both of them, and neither of them had the will to continue further.

Maggie stood up and went to the little room off the kitchen where her bed was always ready and waiting for her. Peter and Sally were now talking in whispers to each other. The mother daughter encounter had been tough and hurtful; it invoked the memories of a dead husband and father as well as the plight of two orphan children. Sally was glad of its ending and hoped that tomorrow might bring a change of heart.

It was Tuesday of the week and Maggie was first out of bed. Like so often before she lit the fire and cooked breakfast for her resting mother. She sat on the side of the bed as they talked about things other than the bone of contention that had so marred their reunion the evening before. She would have to go back to Roy the very next evening because he was leaving on Friday for another six weeks at sea, and she needed to be with him for a time before his departure. Sally refrained from making any kind of moral judgment as to how her daughter was living her life. All the signs were that Maggie was happy with the young man who had taken her away.

Maggie said she planned to visit the cemetery before she left to pray at the grave of her two loved ones. Then she would see Fr Gillen about getting the boys out of that orphanage.

Although she was still not ready to taken them with her, she was determined to assert her rights. She then confided in her mother that she would also be seeing Fr Gillen about her own marriage papers, as she planned to marry Roy in early summer.

Sally was feeling really good after their morning chat but wondered why it was that the name Peter McGinn never once got mentioned. Was Maggie still opposed to this marriage? Time was running short, and they would only be together for one more time later that evening.

There were positive signs of a more cordial atmosphere that night, and Peter could feel its presence as he sat down with the two of them in the small kitchen. They smiled hello to each other as if the previous night had never happened. What, he wondered, was Maggie's new game plan? But the goodness increased when Sally announced that Maggie was getting married in the summer. Peter congratulated her warmly and wished her nothing less than all the happiness that married life can bring. Then, like a pious penitent emerging from the absolving grace of a benevolent confessor, Maggie put her arms around him. "Peter, I want you and my good mother to be happy too and I have no doubt that you will be. After watching the two of you last night I began to realise how wrong I was, but I know everything is going to be alright from now on."

She handed Peter an envelope that contained a letter from her parish priest; it was for Fr Gillen, who was away from the parish for a couple of days. "Peter, I am entrusting you with the business of getting my marriage papers and sending them over to me." She was sorry to be leaving them again so soon and not to be there for their special day; hopefully they would be able to attend hers.

The conversation turned to the future, and at Maggie and Peter's insistence, Sally agreed not to go back to work. It was time she said goodbye to Glenleigh creamery. She would be sorry leaving the place that had sustained her and her family, where she had earned the means to be the selfless carer that she was.

The next morning Sally accompanied Maggie on the mid-morning train from Strabane to Derry where they would spend the day together and visit the boys, who would unfortunately have to remain in captivity for some time to come. Then they would say their goodbyes and go their separate ways, each with a lighter heart.

chapter thirty

It was during eight o'clock morning mass on Saturday that Fr Gillen gave the blessing to the union of Peter McGinn and Sally Dunne. Aggie McCrory and her son Barry, in the presence of not more than ten other daily Massgoers, witnessed the marriage. With frowns of amazement, these pious observers came to wish every kind of blessing to the new Mr and Mrs McGinn. The bride looked serene and beautiful in the outfit Maggie had helped her to choose in Derry. Peter was happy and proud that she was now his wife.

Their mission now accomplished, the party of four came back for a special breakfast that Dan McCrory was in the process of preparing. He would later take the happy couple to Porthall train station, as it was further down the line and part of his Saturday delivery route. Sally was again taking the midmorning train to Derry, this time with a new husband by her side. Maggie had booked them a room in a sedate little hotel situated on the high Rosemount area of the city; it was their wedding present from her and Roy.

Busy as usual was the maiden city on a Saturday afternoon but they enjoyed their leisurely stroll around the shops and other places of interest. In the evening, they went to the cinema, where they found a double seat in the balcony and snuggled up against each other. They were savouring the preciousness of finally being a married couple.

The hotel and its staff were warm and welcoming. With their modest belongings, the honeymoon couple were ushered to a luxury room that was theirs for the night. They found a quiet corner of the lounge for a relaxing drink before dinner. As they settled into the soft, richly upholstered couch and admired the watercolour above the ornate fireplace, a much darker reality intruded upon their sense of wellbeing. There was nothing splendid or grand about the large place that housed their darlings James and Brian. Then taking Peter's hand Sally whispered, "We must not let our sorrows take control of this special time that is ours and truly deserved. Let's live this to the full; I still cannot believe that all this is happening, it is simply wonderful and please God the children will soon be with us."

They ate in the dining room, where the neatly dressed waitresses were attentive and the food was excellent. After dinner they returned to the lounge where a lively music session was about to commence. It was a gathering of friendly people who were talkative and wished them many happy days.

Sally awakened to the brightness of an early spring morning and found herself alone in bed. Peter was standing at the bay window looking out. "Peter, are you all right love?" was her call to him. "Yes Sally, I am all right ... Sally, I am happier than ever before and able to see how good and wonderful life can be. Come and watch with me." She stood in front of him and leaned back against his warm body. With one arm around her, he pointed out the window towards the magnificence of what was before them. The trees and bushes were alive with the melody of birdsong and on the still waters of the Foyle rested a motionless misty cloud that the dawn seemed afraid to disturb. It was like being on the threshold of a fairyland, with all the wonder of God's bountiful bestowal. It was a special moment for both of them, and in the fullness of sweet afterglow, they watched the sunrise over the sleeping city.

Sunday Mass in St Eugene's cathedral was formal and ceremonial compared to what they were accustomed to at home. From there they hired a city taxi to take them back home as both of them had now the means to afford such a thing. But first, they had to make a detour out to see the two suffering weans, to bring them gifts and perhaps a more hopeful promise. The sister who admitted them remarked to Sally how early it was for Sunday visiting, it was dinnertime for everyone including the children. It was also noticed how well she was looking and dressed so attractively. Then, as expected, she inquired, "Who is this young man you have brought with you?" With an air of confidence so unlike the broken woman they had gotten to know, Sally looked to Peter with a smile and said, "This young man is my husband."

Whether or not it was advisable, Peter decided to use his newly acquired status in the form of assertiveness. To Sally's astonishment he declared that they had come early for the purpose of taking their children home, where they belonged.

This, the good sister said, was not possible as it was not in her power to release them. But she was dealing with a man who was not easily deterred and who asked to see a higher authority. They were left alone in the main corridor for close on thirty minutes, by which time the taxi driver came to advise that additional delays must not be at his expense. That, they assured him would not be a problem, the business they were about could not be measured in terms of cost. Finally, they were brought to see the Reverend Mother. She sat at a large table facing the door where the interviewees had entered. The dark habit she was wearing exuded authority, and she wore an expression that indicated that she was not fully happy with this turn of events. She began by congratulating them on their marriage but had to point out to Peter the facts of the situation. "You being married to the children's grandmother does not confer rights of guardianship to you, young man. They cannot be handed back in the absence of a court order."

Peter asked that they be shown a copy of the order that had them committed in the first place, "...that is if such a document has ever existed."

The reverend mother gave him a long look and then replied, "Again I must remind you that you have no right to make such demands of me."

His reply was immediate and direct: "This woman whom you rightly call their grandmother is only known to them as 'Mammy' and has been the best they could possibly have had. Surely, this gives her the rights that I am seeking on her behalf, so we won't be leaving without answers."

Growing a bit agitated the nun conceded that she did not know much about the legality of these things, but if they cared to wait, she would contact someone who did.

Again, they were left alone but this time not for too long. She came back and informed them that she had spoken to the one who had sent the boys to her in the first place — "your own parish priest. He is not in possession of any document relating to the Dunne children, nor would he be opposing their return to the lawful custody of Mrs Dunne."

"Mrs Dunne..." Peter joked to Sally, who was still unclear as to the significance of what had just been said to her. The aging priest's faux pas was a further sign of his diminishing vigour and perhaps he was losing the zest for confrontation.

Finally, it was time to see the boys. Although Sally had already told the boys that she was for marrying Peter and that he would be coming to live with them, they could not believe it was him they were actually seeing. Little time was spent collecting their few belongings and soon all four of them were walking down the corridor towards the exit door. A younger and quite pleasant sister of the community came to say goodbye to the two she called "her little friends". With tears in her eyes she hugged them warmly before moving swiftly out of sight; she had all the signs of being possessed of goodness and compassion. It was the sister who first admitted them that was seeing them off from the premises, and she had little to say beyond telling the boys to be good.

With all of them seated in the taxi for home, Sally noticed uneasiness about both of them and asked what the matter was. They said their Bob and Billy horses had been taken from them as punishment a few weeks earlier. The sister who saw them out was not one they dared to vex by asking to have them back, not even on their day of departure. They had learned through experience to tread gently there. Without saying a word, Peter stepped out again and ran back towards the door. Before he got there, the door opened. "What is now the matter?" the sister asked him. "Very little," he replied, "but the entire world to a lonely orphan. I want you to get me the rest of their belongings." "Oh yes, I know what you are talking about, they are down here in the dining room. You see, in a place like this there are certain rules to be observed." Peter accompanied her to a cold and uninviting room where a lady wearing a white apron was clearing a long wooden table at which the children had been fed. He retrieved the objects from a high shelf where they had been for the previous six weeks. Like their owners, they, too, looked sickly forlorn, they were out of habitat and given back to their inanimate state.

The twins were not totally without sorrow when leaving. They could see at a side window three other little faces observing their final departure. "That's Kevin, Mickey and Anna," James told the others as they drove off towards the gates and freedom. "They will not be getting home, because nobody ever comes to see them," was Brian's comment on a scene that would etch forever on the minds of those who witnessed it. Peter and

Sally gave thought to the good fortune of their own situation but with a heightened consciousness of what it was like for the forgotten. Surely there had to be another and better way, or was finding it beyond the capacity of smug society still at ease with its own inadequacies.

That Sunday saw the coming into being of a new family that no earthly power could deny. The little home became a haven of joy as all four of them celebrated their blessings in modest style. James and Brian were moving fast at repossessing every nook and chinkish den. It is only when such things are lost can the value of their worth be appreciated; that is surely true of every age. But in observing the vigour of their play, Peter began to notice that Brian was less up to it than his brother, and this was something he and Sally would have to be seeing about.

Just as darkness began to fall their togetherness was disturbed by the sound of an engine that was by now familiar to Peter's ears. He could see Sally's apprehension as they both watched John and Kitty getting down off the tractor and the two boys running to admire the handsome machine. They spoke pleasantly to the children and looked surprised at them being there. Kitty was first to enter; she was carrying a neatly wrapped package, which she gave to Sally saying it contained wedding gifts from John and herself. She then congratulated them both with warm embraces that were received with emotional gratitude. John was still outside with the boys contending as best he could with the weight of their questioning about the what, why and how of this amazing apparatus. He was relieved to escape into the house and do as his sister had done by way of courtesy to his brother and new sister-in-law.

With John now in charge of operations in Cruckban there was an awkward uneasiness about his manner. He was sorry that things had to be as they were; it was certainly not what he wanted. Kitty was confident that Mum and Dad would, in time, come round to their natural fondness and everything would be as it was before. Peter too believed that his parents would eventually soften their stance and that he and Sally would be ready to welcome them with equal fondness. As for things being as they were before, his mind was clear and definite. Never again would he till the rocky slopes of Cruckban. Nor would he ever dispute these arrangements with a brother and sister who had been and hopefully would continue to be his closest friends.

For that reason, he was claiming the tractor as well as its equipment. He had already informed his parents about this on that day of sore reproach. "That has already been taken care of," said John. "It was only on that condition I agreed to get involved. The machinery is rightfully yours and I am delivering it all to you this very day. With the benefit of a first class education, I have good prospects for further advancement in the County House. So the farming method will have to change once again." He then outlined a plan that would eliminate tillage and the renting of land completely. The entire enterprise would be confined to Cruckban and would be less labour-intensive. Milk and livestock was what he had in mind. This was going to make his mornings and evenings rather busy, but Dinny and the Boss should be well able for a much-reduced daily routine.

Peter thought about his parents. Their status would again reduce to the level of the whinbush farmer. But he had high hopes for the success of his creamery milk run, which would soon become an everyday routine. He intended making full use of the fifteen acres bequeathed to him by Uncle Henry. There was, however, something else on the holding that he wanted and needed. He told John and Kitty that he planned to take possession of Henry's cottage, but he knew that to do this at the expense of the Canadian relations would not go down well with his mother. After all, there was nothing she valued more than to have such popular and high-class people pay her attention. Kitty looked at John with an amused smile. They were both amazed that their brother had failed to notice how much that relationship had cooled off over the past year or so. According to Kitty, it all began a couple of years earlier when Ciss invited her other friend Olive Devine and her husband Robert for Sunday dinner. Her mother had planned it for the specific purpose of introducing her special friends to each other. It was a quiet friendly affair with John and Peter gone to a football match. From the outset, Bett focused her full attention exclusively on the Divines; something or other attracted her to them. Perhaps it was that the two women with their professional training shared a common academic background. But it was also significant that both families were in possession of considerable means, a fact that became obvious early in their exchanges. It was also the first year of the eight since they had started coming to Donegal that Aunt Rose was not with them. Like her friend Hannah, she had aged noticeably over that lengthy period, and it was unlikely they would ever be coming back.

The friendship between Bett and the Devines developed at a rapid pace with poor Ciss finding herself very much on the margins. With the passage of time and Aunt Rose no longer in the picture, contact with Cruckban became less and less. Instead, a strong line of communication had opened up between Montreal and Strabane, with greetings and gifts galore. Many things were planned and enacted, unknown to Tom and Ciss McGinn. Things had just moved on. This no doubt was deeply destructive of Ciss' sense of pride and self-worth. She in her goodness had facilitated the coming together of the two sets of friends she was so proud to be talking about. The feeling of rejection hurt her deeply on realising she had now lost both of them. It was a case of people outliving their usefulness; the peasant folk of a hilly farm were not sufficiently stimulating to compete against the lofty Devines and their associates. In this competitive market, poor Ciss was simply outbid by cousin Olive.

After hearing, all this Peter vowed to Sally that before the week was out they would be in possession of their very own home. John would make the long-distance phone call to Canada the next day, and he would inform them of the new development. Both he and Kitty were fairly certain that their mother would not be in the least perturbed at the termination of this once exciting arrangement.

Bett was more interested in the circumstances of Peter's marriage than she was in the subject matter of John's message. On that issue, it was Paul who spoke, and he asked John to convey his sincere gratitude to all for their goodness over the past eight years. He wished to send sincere good wishes to Peter and his new wife and said they were welcome not only to the cottage but also to all that was in it as well. Bett came back on the line to endorse her husband's sentiments, but there were a few valuable items she would like them to pack safely for collection. These consisted of a Royal Albert dinner service and tea set; there were also a few pieces of Waterford crystal that would look rich on the display cabinet of Olive and Robert's holiday home in Portnoo. It was a spacious and attractive dwelling where she and Paul had spent two wonderful weeks last summer.

From this, John was able to conclude that these people would suffer no pain over the loss of the Irish country cottage. Within a couple of days, Henry's had become the family home to Peter McGinn, his wife and two happy children.

On Monday morning, Peter drove the boys back to Ballintober for the recommencement of their formal schooling. After accompanying them right to the classroom, he signalled Miss Maguire that he wished to speak to her. He told her he hoped she had the humanity to understand what and where these delicate souls were coming from. "For that reason I will be keeping a close watch on how you are treating them and I will not tolerate what I know you are capable of." Like a flash, she turned back inside and opened the partition door into the Master's room. She called Herron to her aid.

"Mr McGinn here has brought the Dunne boys back to me and is now attempting to lecture me on how to conduct my class. As Master and Principal, I think he should know that this is your responsibility not his."

The Bull looked like being in a situation he would much rather not have been, but he had little choice other than to support his assistant. As he moved to do so, Peter intercepted with insolent brevity. "Herron, you are a failure, just like the lady beside you, but do not over-rely on your position here."

With that, Peter left them to ponder his parting promise: "I will be watching both of you."

That was the last time for these protagonists to engage each other in any form of combat; their swords were finally put to rest. It was a welcome development and hopefully things would improve considerably for all of the children.

Having regained their childhood James and Brian looked forward to Saturdays, with so much going on to engage their interest. The old plough horses Bob and Billy had faded from their memories and even their toy replicas were consigned to redundancy and were adorning the window ledge in their small bedroom. Now it was Red Davie that commanded most of their attention. The milk collection run was a special adventure that had them up extra early on Saturday mornings. It gave them a feeling of importance to be travelling with Peter from farm to farm as their many young friends jealously admired them along the way.

The first monthly cheque from the creamery far exceeded Peter's expectations. It being only the start of the season the signs were that Peter was on to quite a lucrative business. Sally was so proud of the home she could at last call her own; she thanked God for all their blessings and prayed that all misfortune was at last behind them. It was a wish shared by everyone who knew her and what she had been through. The upturn in her fortunes was sudden and delightfully real; it seemed that nothing could possibly harm her again.

Chapter Thirty-One

Easter week brought the finest of weather to prepare the ground for the spring sowing. The dust that rose from the ruffling harrows clouded most of the tillage fields. All the fertile area of Peter's patch was being readied for a crop of oats and the boys were thriving amidst the action. They walked behind him pace for pace as he fiddled out the golden grains that spread fan-shaped before landing on to the welcoming seedbed. A tiring day it was for all of them, sowing the seed and harrowing it in, and the work went on till rather late. Sally played a supporting role; she fed the three workers savoury fare and laughed with them in unison. Feeling good about their day's work, they retired to a well-earned rest and Sally prayed for a good result.

They were all early to bed as the morning round was very much on their eager minds. The little fellows said 'goodnight' and settled into the little bed that was hardly big enough for the two. At the same time it was big enough to occupy most all of the floor space of the little room. It was the perfect end to a fruitful day; there was little better that life could give.

Morning call came early, as Peter had to be on the road. Out there, those creamery cans were being filled and readied for his morning collection. Just as Peter got out of bed, James entered the room with an uneasy look about him. He called on both of them to come and see what was the matter with Brian, who was not responding to the wakening call for the new day. In mighty haste, Peter went to the bedside with fearful heaviness in his heart. Sally screamed and begged him to say that Brian was all right. He searched in vain for the pulse of life, and then, taking her hand and bringing James closer to both of them, they braced each other for grief's ghoulish return. No one said it, "Brian is dead", but to the three who loved him, he had simply drifted away to a better place. He chose the peaceful stillness of the night that followed his happiest day.

Peter ran to the Captain's yard where young Leslie was in the cow byre tending the machine that was doing the milking.

From there the relevant people were contacted by phone and Leslie relieved Peter of all responsibility to his customers over the next three days. Dr Martin was soon on the scene and with characteristic compassion, he focused his attention on Sally and James. He asked them to remain in the kitchen while he examined the body in the company of Peter. As the doctor proceeded, Peter noticed an object locked tightly in Brian's tiny hands. On closer examination, he could see it was the little Billy horse that had given him so much pleasure for part of his short life. This brought on a renewed flow of emotion to the already heartbroken. It had to have been in the dark of night that he left his bed to claim his only worldly possession. Was he awake or in sleep at the time, was he alive or did the angels conspire with him in this final earthly act?

Brian's celestial smile gave comfort to the grief-stricken. After a few days Sally's resilience returned, aided no doubt by her strong faith, like when she lost her first son Jimmy Dunne. But what about poor Maggie who had gone with Roy to meet his parents in America? What a cruel message awaited her return to London. For Peter it was a strange and confusing time. It was something he was not prepared for, and the reality of the final parting perplexed him. However, he and Sally had to be for each other what no one else could ever be. In so being, they were making it possible for James to be again the happy child he deserved to be. They consoled themselves in the belief that Brian was happier than ever before and that was how God wanted it to be. "Everything is going to be good again, Brian is with Jimmy and Sammy, they are watching over us and praying for us."

Praying indeed they must have been, for within a matter of weeks came a strange new development. An engineer from the County Council came to their door seeking a lease to quarry the Blue Rock for road building and maintenance. The Blue Rock Quarry became a prominent works operation and remained so for many succeeding years. It provided a steady and substantial income for Peter McGinn and his family. In the wake of such tragedy, things began to take off in a more auspicious kind of way.

On the eighth day of December, Sally gave birth to a healthy and beautiful baby daughter who brought the name Mary with her. Mary was a blessing in every way, bringing renewed life to Tom and Ciss, two aging souls, now congealing in listless lassitude. She was their first grandchild and won their hearts in a way that rendered all past difficulties into oblivion. This was the way that Peter wanted things to be with his parents. Sally played her part and succeeded in establishing a close friendship with her husband's parents.

Peter was content to let all arrangements remain as they were, and financially he was in a sounder position than ever before. John too was succeeding both in his job and in the running of a much-reduced farming operation. He purchased a second-hand car, which was of enormous benefit not only to him but to his parents and sister as well. It was used to transport baby Mary to Ballintober to receive the first sacrament of the church with Kitty and John as godparents.

chapter thirty-two

Never in the forty years that succeeded Brian's untimely death did Peter and Sally McGinn experience anything but success in their many endeavours. The creamery milk run with Red Davie was particularly successful and developed at a phenomenal rate. It was from this humble beginning that B. R. Freight with its fleet of container trucks came into being. The now disused Blue Rock Quarry from which the company got its name is the main depot where all business is transacted. To the roar of the Celtic Tiger, business is booming under the competent management of James Dunne.

In a changing world, there are little visible signs of the old order and what it used to be like, but its memory has stood the test of time. Nearly half a century later Peter was very aware of this as he walked down the old Cruckban road one morning, after staying the night with John in the old family home. He could not see even a trace of the weeping track that was such a painful part of his childhood days. But in the distance, he could see that old grey school building, now derelict, and still oozing a stench of evil. Its story has been told and will continue to be told in a more enlightened age. He was able to count on his fingers the number of his contemporaries still living in the parish. Many of them will find occasion to summon to mind those dark days of lost childhood. Most of them are like him and John, sons of the land and nearing the end of their working lives. Alas, for many it was the old story of lives sadly wasted, going from one deprivation to another. Leaving home ill equipped to face a challenging world, not even fit to write a simple letter home to reassure a heartbroken mother. Cruckban could well be described as the last remaining relic of that age as it has changed very little since.

Peter often stops in to pass the time with his brother John, who lives there alone with his cattle, sheep and chickens. He had been faithful to the old people right to the end, including Hess, who outlived both Tom and Ciss McGinn. He spent the last seven months of his eighty-two year life span in Lifford hospital. The McGinn brothers and their sister Kitty McDonald were the only family he ever had. They waked him in Cruckban, just as they did for both of their parents. For them it was also an emotional parting as they laid old Dinny to rest in Ballintober graveyard, marking the end of a memorable era. He died without seeing the war he had been waiting for.

John was over-generous to Peter's and Kitty's children. Kitty's son, young Kevin McDonald, is the one he most relies on for the busy times. He likes to pay the occasional visit to the office where he worked for so many years. Former colleagues fill him in on happenings that are no longer relevant to him. Still, it had been the life he was proud of; it had given him rank and prestige far beyond what was affordable to a meagre hill farmer. This was the consolation prize that sustained him throughout, he lived and perhaps will die under the illusion that he was privileged and educated.

Henry's cottage has long been demolished to make way for its splendid replacement, but it always remained a happy place. It was there that Sally and Peter so loved to be visited by the lively grandchildren that James and Mary had both given them. In her happiness, Sally remained remarkably young throughout her life with Peter, but the inevitable onslaught of aging took hold during her final year. She maintained a dignified contentment and serenity right up to the end. "Her life was exemplary by any standard." These were but a few of the moving words spoken by their parish priest and good friend Fr Patrick Kilroy. Her reward was in knowing that she helped in bringing achievement to the ones she loved. But her goodness extended far beyond her own family. She never forgot where she came from and remained in close affinity with the strata of human existence from which she had struggled to survive.

Peter knew that her dying pain was mainly one of sorrow about leaving him to be lonely, but he was consoled in the assurance that she had left him the two special ones that would never be far away. Mary is now one of ten teachers employed in a modern and efficiently run Ballintober School. Her husband happens to be one of the overseas truck drivers for B. R. Freight. It had long been understood that they would one day move into the family home. "Perhaps now is the time," thought a solitary Peter as he made his way back to a lonely house.

the end

Printed in the United Kingdom
by Lightning Source UK Ltd.
134562UK00001B/358-393/P

9 780954 453091